Praise fo

"In *The Cairo Curse*, our favoi _____ *Mistletoe Countess* fame, find mysteries and mayhem aplenty in Egypt. And none of us are surprised because where Grace goes, let's face it, a certain amount of chaos will follow. I adored watching the married romance between Grace and Freddie grow and strengthen as they continue to settle into their life together, but readers who are new to this couple will have no difficulty in following along and will undoubtedly be swept into their story within a few pages. From England to Egypt, from dining in formal attire to crawling through tombs, and from delightful adventures to deadly confrontations, *The Cairo Curse* is the perfect combination of romance, adventure, and suspense all written in Pepper Basham's trademark style. This delightful romp is a must-read for romance, rom-com, and suspense readers alike."

   - Lynn H. Blackburn, bestselling author of *Malicious Intent* and *Targeted*

"With exquisite descriptions, a vibrant heroine, and whispers of danger haunting the tombs of the ancients, Pepper Basham's *The Cairo Curse* will transport readers to exploring the wonders of the pyramids and their mysteries that await."

   - Grace Hitchcock, award-winning author of *My Dear MISS DUPRÉ, Her Darling MR. DAY, and His Delightful LADY DELIA*

"An adventure packed with mystery and humor, Ms. Basham takes readers to Egypt's exotic landscape and serves up an unpredictable and entertaining plot rivaling that of the great Agatha Christie. Move over Detective Poirot, Freddie and Grace have arrived."

   - Natalie Walters, award-winning author of *Lights Out, SNAP Agency,* and *The Harbored Secrets series*

A Freddie & Grace Mystery
(Book 2)

The
CAIRO
CURSE

PEPPER
BASHAM

BARBOUR
PUBLISHING

A Freddie & Grace Mystery
Book 1 - The Mistletoe Countess

The Cairo Curse ©2023 by Pepper Basham

Print ISBN 978-1-63609-472-4

eBook Edition:
Adobe Digital Edition (.epub) 978-1-63609-473-1

All scripture quotations, unless otherwise noted, are taken from the King James Version of the Bible.

This book is a work of fiction. Names, characters, places, and incidents are either products of the author's imagination or used fictitiously. Any similarity to actual people, organizations, and/or events is purely coincidental.

Cover Model Photograph: © Lee Avison / Trevillion Images

Published by Barbour Publishing, Inc., 1810 Barbour Drive, Uhrichsville, Ohio 44683, www.barbourbooks.com

Our mission is to inspire the world with the life-changing message of the Bible.

ecpa Member of the
Evangelical Christian
Publishers Association

Printed in the United States of America.

Dedication

to Benjamin,
my world traveler and story creator.

Acknowledgements

I am thrilled to be able to continue the story of Frederick and Grace Percy and I couldn't make it happen without the wonderful team at Barbour! They've been such encouragers to make a Freddie and Grace Mystery series come to life.

As ever, I feel it's impossible for me to get through a story without some of the best sidekicks in the world – Joy Tiffany and Beth Erin!

I can't list all the people on my Street Team because I'll undoubtedly forget a name or two, but I can't imagine trying to get these stories out into the world without their amazing support as some of the best bookish cheerleaders on the planet! THANK YOU!!!

To my mom and #RamboDad who never fail to support my stories – and Dad never fails to find a way to insert Rambo into each of my books.

I am so thankful for my wonderful family and love that stories have always brought us together. It's so sweet to know my husband and kids celebrate these imaginary friends with me.

And to the greatest Story Creator of them all, who has written my most important story into His Book of Life. May little glimpses of the tale He's writing in my heart make it into each of the books I write.

Chapter One

February 1914, Havensbrook

Gunfire erupted from outside, sending Frederick Percy, Earl of Astley, leaping from his chair. The seat crashed against the floor behind him in time with another shot. *What on earth!* He grabbed the first weapon-like item he could find—his grandfather's cane—and dashed toward the sound, nearly colliding with his butler moving in the same direction.

"Did you hear the gunfire, Brandon?"

The older gentleman's brows rose as high as they could go without becoming part of his snowy hairline. "Indeed, my lord. From the south garden, if I guess correctly, sir."

"My thoughts exactly." Frederick tapped the cane against the floor and took a step in the direction of the garden door. Then stopped, a sudden sense of dread forming a lump in his stomach. His butler's response was much too cavalier for an emergency. "Have you seen Lady Astley of late, Brandon?"

"Not since after breakfast, sir."

"Well, then." Frederick returned to his office for his own pistol and prayed whatever inspired a gunshot near his home would prove more benign than dangerous. After surviving several near-death experiences over the past Christmas season, Frederick was quite finished with drama for a while. Though drama seemed to follow his new bride in spades.

He met the butler back in the hallway.

"Might I offer an insight, sir?"

Frederick pivoted in his approach to the door and turned back to Brandon. "Insight?"

"Yes, sir." The man released a deep sigh which pulled his pristine posture into a slight slump. He then sent Frederick a look which somehow inspired a grimace before Frederick even heard the man's words. "Her ladyship was speaking with Mr. Blake after breakfast, sir."

"Mr. Blake?" Frederick rolled his gaze heavenward, the tension in his jaw uncoiling into a slight annoyance that manifested in an ache over his right eyebrow. He loved his cousin. There was no man Frederick trusted more. But for some reason, the idea of Blake and Grace together followed by the sound of gunfire did not bode well.

For anyone.

"About pistols, my lord."

And the answers emerged, along with an increased throbbing in Frederick's head. "Thank you, Brandon."

Setting a slower pace, he moved toward the south side of his manor house, another shot reverberating nearer. Within a month since Christmas, his American wife had learned how to drive the car and throw knives, two skills she appeared to excel in more than knowing the fashion of the season or how to address the complicated hierarchy of the aristocracy. His lips almost split into a grin as he recalled her stumbling over addressing the Duke of Westonbridge two weeks ago by calling him "Your Honorable Lord" and then in quick correction, "Your Grace, or at least I hope you are since I fumbled your title so atrociously."

Of course the duke had fallen under Grace's spell within five minutes, as everyone else who met her seemed to do since she'd moved to his crumbling Derbyshire estate two months earlier. Well, everyone except the villainess who'd tried to kill them just before Christmas. But that was hopefully a distant story, and their next chapter would be a lovely, peaceful belated honeymoon—he increased his steps at the idea—with a little surprise tagged on for his lovely Lady Astley.

Frederick nodded a good afternoon to the police officer inconspicuously posted near the house so that Frederick's mother could work out her sentence of house arrest in connection with his father and brother's deaths. He released a sigh. No, she was no murderess, unless glares and harsh words counted, but she'd harbored information that could have protected others. The law had been gracious with her due to her age and status, merely revoking her freedoms from leaving Havensbrook, so his mother's life stayed very much as it had since Frederick's father's death; however, the added blemish of "criminal" to her reputation ensured she spent her days away from the public eye.

And if the police officer appeared in no great distress over the gunfire, Frederick knew all too well what must be happening.

Just around the edge of the house, a large garden opened to the south, its walls still well intact, though ivy-grown and tangled. Another shot reverberated through the damp air, followed quickly by laughter and his wife's exuberant exclamation of "I hit it."

Frederick's lips pinched into a frown. Why he ever expected his cousin Blake to mind Frederick's subtle requests was beyond him! The garden gate stood open, welcoming him forward into an even more tangled array of vines and twined greenery, the winter roses, a remnant of the garden's healthier days, sleeping until spring.

He hadn't had the means to make things right with Havensbrook before but, with Grace's wealth and her generous heart, he could now. Another way to make amends for the past, he hoped, though

God had already bestowed on him much more than he deserved.

His cousin stood to the right, hands on the hips of his gray suit jacket, but Frederick's gaze followed Blake's focus to the woman in the center of the garden. Her bright auburn hair was twisted up beneath a deep purple hat that matched her coat, both in contrast to her pale skin. Her laughter echoed toward him, so filled with joy and hope. Two things he'd thought lost forever before he'd met her.

Yes, God had given him much more than he deserved, and sometimes, he wondered if God had given him more than he could manage.

Perhaps keeping a sense of humor truly was his greatest tactic. Grace had certainly helped remind him that he still had one. "It seems I missed the invitation."

His interruption pulled the pair's attention from their shared focus on the pistol Grace held in her gloved hands. Grace's smile flashed with instant welcome. Blake's took a mischievous tilt.

"Oh Frederick, did you see how well I hit the target?" His bride's deep blue eyes brightened as she gestured toward a row of cans set up on the opposite side of the garden. He could only presume she'd hit one. "It only took four attempts so far."

Blake discreetly held up five fingers beneath the elbow of his folded arms.

Frederick paused by her side, glancing down into her upturned countenance. The aggravation at this undisclosed shooting lesson slowly ebbed at the look of sheer pleasure on her face. "Excellent work for a first try, darling."

She nodded toward Blake. "Mr. Blake assured me that you'd take over my lessons once he got them started."

"Did he?" Frederick raised a brow in his cousin's direction.

"It would not be very generous of me to withhold such an honor, Freddie." His gray-green eyes twinkled as he gestured toward the cans. "And there's still plenty of targets on which to practice."

Grace's smile broadened again, and she stepped forward to aim the pistol, her expression turning uncharacteristically somber.

Frederick moved to Blake's side. "What are you doing, man?" His whisper scraped out the words. "Don't you think we've been through enough of late to add pistols to my wife's rather unique set of skills?"

Blake's brows shot northward. "Having both of you nearly killed on several occasions in the past two months is the very reason she should learn." He shrugged a shoulder. "Besides, she'd already planned to set up a lesson with Aunt Lavenia next week. Did you really want Aunt Lavenia teaching her about pistols?"

Frederick stifled a grimace. Aunt Lavenia was the best sort of woman, but heightened passions and her aim did not bode well for anyone, especially the nearby trees or passing pigeons.

The pistol fired again, and another can spun into the air.

"That's two in a row," she shouted, waving the gun without any awareness of its direction. Blake and Freddie dodged the trajectory, and Blake, with his usual diplomacy, slipped up beside Grace.

"Excellent, my lady." He tugged the pistol from her hand. "You have a true knack with pistols." He shot Frederick a wink which only incited additional pain in Frederick's forehead. . .and maybe a lump in his throat. "But one must always take care to point a loaded weapon away from the innocent."

"Oh yes." She nodded, her lips pinching into a frown to match the crease of her brow. "I can see how that would be important, but I have plenty of time to work on my skills before we leave for Italy. By then, with Frederick's help, I should certainly prove my shooting prowess like a regular Annie Oakley."

Frederick sent Blake a look for clarification, but seeing Blake's failed attempts at controlling his grin, Frederick decided he'd rather not ask.

"She is an American sharpshooter, my dear Lord Astley." Grace placed a hand to his arm, clearly aware of his complete ignorance of the name. She was the oddest assortment of acute observation and lack of pretense he'd ever seen. "I saw her once when she performed in Buffalo Bill's Wild West Show. Grandfather took me." Her nose wrinkled with her grin. "Did you know she could shoot a cigar from her husband's lips at thirty paces?"

Grace's gaze dropped to Frederick's lips as if planning a similar test of her own.

"I'd expect a bit more practice on your part before you give it a go, my lady," Blake interjected, barely controlling his laughter from the sound of it. "Though I would like to witness such a performance."

Frederick's glare failed to mar his cousin's unyielding grin.

"Well, I am horrible at faking confidence," Grace continued, tugging at the edge of the gloves and shaking her head as if the admission disappointed her. "So I would like to know exactly what I'm doing should the circumstances ever require me to actually use my pistols seriously."

Frederick deemed necessary a detour from any more talk of Grace and pistols, if for nothing else but his own peace of mind. "You are very adept at faking confidence, if you recall. I've seen you in a ghost hunt."

"Who says I was faking confidence then? I was quite prepared from my extensive fictional research on the matter." Her gaze caught his, and she stepped closer, those glimmering eyes warming his heart. "Besides, I had you with me. And there is no need for faking confidence with my very capable hero nearby."

How he had ever managed to live life before meeting her, he couldn't remember. His attention lowered to her smile. "I must admit, it is one of my favorite places to be."

"Please," Blake cleared his throat and moved back a step. "Do allow me a chance of escape before demonstrations occur."

The laugh in his cousin's voice only spurred Frederick's action as he touched his palm to Grace's cheek and dipped his head to take a lingering taste of her lips. She was no help at discretion, because she wrapped her soft arms around him and continued his delightful plunder of her ready mouth as if she'd started the whole thing. It was fortunate Blake took his leave as soon as possible, because the "demonstrations" continued for quite some time.

"We're leaving in two weeks?" Grace froze, fork in mid-air, her attention shifting from Frederick to Blake and back again. "But I didn't think we were going to Italy until the end of March."

"Actually there's been a change of plans." Frederick attempted to quell his smile from giving away the surprise, but the shock on both Blake and Grace's faces loosed his control.

"Change of plans? Surprises?" Blake raised his glass, reverting to nonchalance. "Unlike you, cousin."

"I've become quite fond of the unexpected as of late." He raised his glass, his gaze slipping to Grace, who still held her fork upraised. She looked positively splendid in blue, even with her bottom lip hanging a bit loose. "I received a letter from Georgia Withersby Archibald, a cousin on my mother's side."

"Georgia?" Blake lowered his glass. "I haven't heard from her since she married. What did Archibald call himself? An adventurer, was it?"

"*Entrepreneur*, I believe was the word."

"Ah, code word for too rich, I believe it is." Blake took another drink.

"Take care, Blake. He married into the family."

"Poor man, and the origin of his riches, as I recall." The statement came with nettles.

"Is the 'poor man' comment related to the married part or

'our family' part?" Grace interjected, her brow pinched and her attention bouncing back and forth between them again.

"Both." Blake winked and turned back to Frederick. "Georgia and her brother, Timothy, are the lone twins in the family, Lady Astley, and have enjoyed quite the insouciant lifestyle from their father's unexpected wealth through the railway. Marrying Sydney Archibald wasn't a necessity, but unfortunately, she found herself overwhelmingly in love with the man."

"Well, I can certainly appreciate such a discovery." Grace finally lowered her fork, her smile slipping wide as she looked at Frederick. "And I wouldn't call it a bit unfortunate."

"It is safe to say, Lady Astley"—Blake leaned back in his chair and turned toward Grace—"that you have chosen much better than our unfortunate cousin."

"Blake." Frederick shot a warning glance across the table, which merely reflected back with a groan. Yes, Frederick had heard the rumors too. Sydney Archibald was generous not only with his own self-praise but also with his amorous behavior, and poor Georgia had suffered the embarrassment of his once-private affairs becoming unashamedly public within a year of their wedding. He'd hoped they'd been unfounded, but the look on Blake's face proved otherwise.

"I get the sense that Mr. Archibald is a cad?"

Frederick barely stifled his grin at Grace's practice in using a word she'd likely heard from Blake, if truth be told. "Let's just say his heart was much more moved by Georgia's bank account than her lovely brown eyes."

"How very unfortunate for her." Her face brightened with its usual hopeful glow. "But, love can grow in time, even to the most unlikely sorts. It's a very common theme in fiction."

"Ah yes," Blake nodded. "The determined bachelor with a will of iron is slowly melted by the warmth of a woman's beauty."

"Not her beauty so much, Mr. Blake, as her disposition." Grace's lips tilted in the playful way that inspired Frederick to all sorts of kissing thoughts. "Though a lovely figure may win the battle, a generous heart, strength of character, and quick mind win the war, so to speak."

"Well said, Lady Astley." Blake shot Frederick a humored grin. "If only the rest of the world lived so determinedly by those rules."

"You tease me, Mr. Blake, but you know I'm right." Her attention turned back to Frederick, and a sudden shadow fell across her features. "So, are we going to see them instead of traveling to Italy?"

"Don't worry, darling, we are still planning to honeymoon in Italy, but since we've had to delay our honeymoon for a few months and since you've had so little opportunity to travel, I thought you'd enjoy an extended trip."

"Oh good heavens, Freddie. You're not thinking about it." Blake sat up straight, lowering both palms to the table. "Can you imagine your dear Lady Astley in the middle of the desert trotting along on some camel?"

"The desert?" Grace's eyes popped wide. "Camel?"

Oh, Frederick could almost see her imagination dashing off. . .with a camel at the run. And that's exactly why he thought of the idea. Grace would love it.

"Georgia's husband has recently joined an archaeological expedition, and when Georgia learned of our marriage, she sent her congratulations along with an open invitation to join them. I thought we could stop there on our way to Italy and then—"

"On an archaeological expedition?" Grace nearly rose from the table. "Do you mean it? I've always wanted to see a camel and a desert and sort out how someone could enjoy spending so much time in the dirt only to locate an ancient dead body or centuries-old broken pottery."

"It all sounds very much like the perfect honeymoon to my mind."

Frederick sent another wasted glare in his cousin's direction.

"And where is this place? What desert?"

"Egypt." He watched the delight bloom on his wife's face. "Land of the pharaohs."

Blake's groan was overshadowed by Grace's laughter.

"Oh Frederick, you know me so well. A real adventure of the most storybook type. Ancient tombs, deserted villages, mummies?" Grace brought her hands together and raced to his side, placing a kiss to his cheek.

"Sounds like the epitome of honeymoon destinations." Blake raised a glass.

Grace giggled and then sighed. "I'm so glad I'm learning to fire pistols."

The swell of pleasure Frederick had felt only moments ago vanished.

"I've read about tomb robbers and rascals of all sorts. And wild dogs." She suddenly gasped. "Oh dear, we only have two weeks to prepare? That can't be enough time. How will we ever be ready in only two weeks?"

"Don't worry, darling." He took the hand she had resting on his shoulder. "I've slowly been making preparations since the invitation arrived, so there shouldn't be much left for you to do except gather your things."

"*Not* much left to do?" She blinked down at him as if he'd lost his mind. "How can you say that?" She pulled away from him and started for the dining-room door. "I must contact Mr. Brooks without delay."

"The bookshop owner?" Frederick stood, turning back to Blake, before taking a few steps in Grace's direction. Was there some other Mr. Brooks to which his wife referred? "Why on earth should you need to contact Mr. Brooks?"

"Why?" She turned at the threshold of the door and stared at him for a long moment as if she didn't believe his question. "I only have two weeks to read everything I possibly can about Egypt." She raised her chin a little and smiled. "However, I'm always up for a good challenge. And"—a dangerous glint lit those eyes—"there will be camels."

She rushed from the room in a flurry of dark lace and light steps.

Blake chuckled. "Do you think she realizes that she will not be able to accost Mr. Brooks until morning?"

"I'd wager she will sort it out before she reaches the top of the stairs in the Great Hall." Frederick took up his glass. "And detour her steps to the library."

"In order to pillage it of any resources on Egypt."

"Or camels, I fear."

Blake's smile burgeoned for an instant and then died down. "Take care, Freddie." He drained his glass and met Frederick's gaze. "Sydney Archibald has a reputation he attempts to keep neatly tucked away from his social circles. One which may offer friends in very low places."

"How is it that you always seem to know things no one else is supposed to know?"

Blake's grin did not reach his eyes. "Perhaps it's because I am not distracted by flaming hair and lengthy demonstrations of the amorous variety so I can keep my attention keen to the smaller interests."

"Hmm. . ." Frederick studied Blake a moment longer. Why did Frederick always feel that Blake hid something? No, nothing ruthless. He knew the man too well, but something else. He breathed out the curiosity and took a sip from his glass. "I would say my distractions are much better than yours."

Blake bent his head in assent, his smile softening, "There are days when I might agree with you."

Frederick studied his cousin a moment longer but didn't press the issue. "We'll accompany a large party of archaeologists and adventurers. Surely that will help keep things tidy and safe."

"I'm not certain the word *tidy* fits the wake of your lovely bride at all, Freddie." Blake shrugged and raised a brow, barely keeping his lips steady. "And of course, why shouldn't you feel safe? Lady Astley will have her pistols."

"I would see you off, but it seems I've been called to London." Blake relaxed in the chair of the sitting room, looking every bit the contented bachelor as always, but Frederick wondered if his cousin didn't harbor a bit of envy at Frederick's good fortune. Even with the shooting practice, driving lessons, energetic chatter, and "American" ways, there was no denying Frederick's life had only improved since Grace entered.

"Business or pleasure?" Frederick raised a hand to pause Blake's response. "Oh wait, I think you only live for pleasure, isn't that right?"

Blake raised a blond brow. "As much as I'm able, but I'm afraid this is a bit more business than I like." His gaze fastened on Frederick, the usual humor leaving his eyes. "Do keep your head up, Freddie. I've done a bit of checking in on Sydney Archibald and his business dealings, and he's not got the best reputation. Neither in choosing reputable businesses nor in making smart business decisions."

"I've heard as much," Frederick sent Blake a grin. "But poor business dealings don't necessarily make him dangerous."

"Perhaps not." Blake stood, keeping his attention fastened on Frederick. "But poor choices tend to gather poor company, and it's the latter than I'm not too keen on."

"You could always join us, you know?"

"Join you on your honeymoon?" The exaggerated eye roll fit more of Blake's usual mood. "As delightful as that sounds, I'm suddenly feeling much more excited about London." He moved to the door, stopping just before he exited. "You're the only cousin I have who is both a good friend and an excellent chap. So take care, won't you?"

Chapter Two

"Ellie is miserable, poor lamb." Grace smiled her thanks to Elliott who drew out her chair for her at the small dining table in their private quarters aboard ship. She'd borrowed the endearment from Aunt Lavenia as well as reading it in a few newer novels and liked the sound of it so much, she decided to keep it in her repertoire.

Frederick didn't seem to mind. He looked up from his place at the table and offered her a tender smile. She wasn't quite sure if she'd ever get used to the way it made her warm all over, but she didn't mind. It was rather pleasant being smiled at in such a beautiful way by such a dashing man.

They'd only been at sea for seven hours, and already Ellie's seasickness had weakened her to such an extent she rarely left her room or the lavatory. Perhaps Grace should have followed her intuition and encouraged Ellie to stay in England. After all, the sweet maid's mother had gotten ill a few days before they'd traveled, with concern of a prolonged illness. Ellie might very well make it to Alexandria and turn right around to England if unwelcome news arrived.

"I'm sorry to hear that." Frederick lowered his glass to the table. "If we'd had more time to make arrangements, I would have searched for another lady's maid to take her place."

"I feel certain she'll be right as rain once she sets her feet on dry ground again." Grace took a sip of her soup and grinned back at her husband. "I know we won't have time to tour Alexandria on our arrival, since we are meeting your cousins in Cairo, but perhaps, on our way out of Egypt, we can take a few days to explore the city. I've read about Antony and Cleopatra and some others, but. . ." She leaned close, lowering her voice and casting a look in Elliot's direction. The valet pinched his lips together and ceremoniously turned his back in order to give privacy. Well, after all they'd been through, Elliott of all people besides Frederick should have learned Grace's clues. She smiled at the sweet acknowledgement before continuing. "But the simple fact it housed one of the largest libraries in the known world does sound incredibly romantic, don't you think?"

"Particularly for a book lover, I should think." Frederick took another sip from his glass.

Grace sighed back in her chair and then immediately corrected her posture, though after a moment's thought she probably didn't need to focus on her posture as much since they were in their private dining room. Her American businessman father had never minded her inconsistent manners, and Frederick rarely pointed them out, even as a British aristocrat, but she knew others' expectations of presenting herself as a proper lady waited in the air like the first chill of winter. And though she'd gotten better over the past few months of practice, she still found the constant reminder of her lack of aristocratic training an unwelcome distraction from more important things like bookish conversations, life-threatening adventures, and the wonderfully romantic gestures of her own handsome hero.

Who cared for posture and place settings at moments like those!

"I hope there's a little less ceremony in places like Cairo." Grace returned to her meal. "I've read from some women travel writers that once you're out among the ruins and the desert, protocol becomes a bit different from that in the great dining halls and ballrooms of England."

"I've heard similar things." Frederick's words tightened, so she looked up, but he'd focused his attention on his plate.

"Did you know that I packed one of the new split skirts just for the opportunity?"

He pinched his lips tight against the drink he'd just taken, his eyes narrowing as he looked at her. After a rather painful-looking swallow, he cleared his throat. "Split skirts?"

"Yes." Grace couldn't help but smile at the very idea of her newest fashion discovery—after all, fashion had never been her forte, so the idea of being forward thinking only added to her excitement. "I had purchased some when I went bicycling back in Virginia, but as I understand it, they can be much more suitable for climbing cliffs and riding camels."

His lips split into a soft smile. "And you plan on climbing cliffs and riding camels often while in Egypt, darling?"

"Don't you? Especially if we're searching for mummies!"

He coughed and set down his glass. "I doubt either of my cousins are searching for mummies, Grace. They are more likely to be *overseeing* such things, not actually doing them. Or in Timothy's case, he's taking in the social life of Cairo, so please, do not hang your hopes a great deal on actually seeing mummies in their. . .natural habitats?"

Perhaps she shouldn't mention the men's trousers she'd also purchased as an experiment. That would likely be too much to take in at one meal.

"I understand there will be plenty to see at the museum in Cairo, madam," Elliott offered, his lips almost tipping into a grin. "If it's mummies you're meant to see."

"Oh, I've seen photographs of the mummies in the museum,

and they look as if they came directly out of a horror fiction like *Frankenstein*." She attempted to bite back her smile but couldn't. A wonderful chill coursed through her. "Won't it be delightful?"

"For your sake, darling"—Frederick cleared his throat—"I do hope it is as delightful as mummies can possibly be."

"You wear a smile that lets me know you think I'm bordering on ridiculous, but I don't mind, because I know you don't really think I'm ridiculous."

"Not at all. I think your lively imagination brings all sorts of visible and invisible adventures to my extremely uninteresting life, and I am grateful for it." He placed his hand over hers on the table. "Though I hope nearly being killed by a murderer is well in our past and we can just enjoy the simplicities of seeing pyramids, riding camels, and. . .investigating mummies."

"Investigating mummies?" She shivered at the thought. "It sounds even more exciting when you say it. And maybe visiting a tomb or two? That seems only right in Egypt." She took a drink. "Do you know of the others who will be staying with your cousins? I would guess there must be an archaeologist among them and someone to read all the Egyptian ciphers and perhaps an artist on staff."

Frederick chuckled. "There was some mention of John Andrews as the lead archaeologist, and a man by the name of Charles Smallwood, who appears to be another financier of their excavation, along with Sydney, of course. But as to the other characters in this particular story, I have no idea."

"Is your cousin Georgia a beauty?"

His expression faltered for a moment. "She is, and I hope to find her still as kind as I've always known her to be. The wrong marriage can make all the difference in the world to a person's life and demeanor."

"As can the right marriage even if it seems wrong at first."

Frederick donned that tender look he reserved just for her.

"Indeed." For such had been theirs. When her father's arrange-
ment for Grace's older sister to marry Frederick fell through due
to Lillias's deceit, Grace had reluctantly taken her sister's place.
But it had all been a very lovely "mistake" that God took in hand
with His usual deftness and transformed into a providentially
designed fairytale.

They finished their meal, and Elliott left them for the evening.
Since Ellie was still sick, Frederick assisted Grace with her gown.
He'd become rather adept at helping her undress, despite the
intricate buttons and fasteners. In fact, he was able to undress her
much more quickly than Ellie ever had, especially when particularly
motivated.

At last, once Grace sat by the dressing table, Frederick began
removing her hairpins with such tenderness, she swooned from
her weakened knees upward. He was so very good with his hands.
It was a fortunate thing she was sitting.

How preposterous to think that she'd been so uninterested in
marriage before, when she really had enjoyed almost every part of
their union. Particularly the roguish ones, and a few of the near-
death parts too. In fact, he was so excellent in his marriage skills, she
couldn't imagine life without him ever again. And didn't want to.

It was a relief to know that not all marriages ended up like
the Bennets or Macbeths or—she cringed—Bovarys. And though
they'd only been wed a few months, the very idea of building a
family with him settled over her with a very different type of
love for adventure. She supposed it could be the most interesting
kind of all.

When the last strand of hair loosed from her pins, she stood
and began unbuttoning his shirt. . .since Elliott had already retired
for the evening, someone had to help the man.

Her grin slipped from one corner to the next in her own sort of roguish way. "Do you remember the last time we traveled on a ship together?" She'd become rather adept at buttons too and easily pushed his shirt from his shoulders. "You told me I could sleep with you every night, whether I was very good or very bad."

He lowered his lips to brush against her brow. "I did."

The depth of his cadence melted over her shoulders in delightful tingles. She slipped her palms around his waist, nuzzling her nose against his chin. "And does that promise hold true on this, our second voyage together?"

"I am a man of my word, darling." His lips smoothed a trail to her temple, then to her cheek. "And now that we are quite familiar with one another, I plan to enact some of the attentions I curbed during our first trip, if you are amenable."

She gave her answer in a rather nonverbal sort of way which was quite beneficial, since her lips were otherwise engaged for a very long time afterward.

The train shifted beneath Grace's feet as she awaited the great unveiling of Egypt's capital city of Cairo. From the moment they'd disembarked the ship in Alexandria, every sight, scent, and even the air itself held a foreignness to it. Warmth. Spice. Ancient ruins.

Of course she'd read dozens of books about Egypt, but as she was beginning to learn, not even her beloved novels could adequately paint the wonder of the world beyond the page. Oh, some of them came close—close enough that Grace recognized sights or sounds. But the feel, the scents couldn't be emulated in paper and ink. The vastness of the sea, the type of heat, the exotic scents and unusual clothing or structures.

And to think, a wonder of the ancient world waited just on the horizon. She stepped closer to the train window, peering out over the golden world for any sign. She'd read that the Great Pyramids were not incredibly impressive from afar, so she attempted to quell her expectations as the city of Cairo came into view. In several of the many travel books she'd consumed, the authors had described a first look from the window as the train neared the city, so Grace scanned the horizon intermittently in search of the famed wonders.

"Did you know that all of Egypt's pyramids are along the west bank of the Nile?" She glanced over her shoulder from the window as Frederick looked up from his paper.

"I did not, but I'm sure you wish to tell me why."

Her smile bloomed. "One travel writer said it's because the sun sets in the west, which symbolizes the realm of the dead, and since pyramids, at their very core, are magnificently adorned and created tombs, then it makes sense they are all on the west bank."

Frederick blinked a few times, his smile somewhat frozen on his face for a moment before relaxing. "Sometimes when you speak of things like the realm of the dead with such enthusiasm and delight, I. . .I'm uncertain how to respond."

"But it's all so fascinating and a world different from anything in ours." She turned back to the window, squinting toward the horizon. "And what are you reading about with such interest?"

"Nothing as fascinating as mummies and pyramids, I assure you." His voice held a smile. "But I am glad to say that Serbia and Turkey have signed a peace treaty."

She looked back at him. "I'd prefer peace over the opposite for certain." Her gaze roamed back to the window, unseeing. War? She'd heard her grandfather speak of the War between the States, a horrid affair of death and destruction. Families broken, landscapes decimated. Hopefully all of that horribleness remained safely in the past. After all, the world had gotten much smarter, hadn't it? Airplanes, automobiles, medicines. Surely the intelligence behind such inventions would lead to intelligence among countries?

Something caught her eye on the horizon. She gasped and

stood, holding to the wall to keep her balance as the train moved beneath her. "Oh, there they are!"

There'd been little variety in colors and hues along the Nile, though Grace sat captivated by it nonetheless. The greenery along the river, so rich and alive, marked a distinct contrast with the golden sands behind and the azure blue of the sky. She'd never recalled seeing such a blue before. Startling, really. Compared to the muted hues they'd left behind in Liverpool, this world of vibrancy kept her imagination on edge. It felt very much like looking at an artist's black-and-white sketch before he or she reveals the painted masterpiece.

Frederick moved to her side, his palm warming the small of her back as he approached. The pleasantness of his profile nearly distracted her from the very reason for her gasp, so she turned her full attention back to the window.

"They look so small, don't they?" Her mind plumbed the depths of her reading, trying to match what she'd researched with the tiny triangles in the distance. "Amber teeth against such an azure sky!"

"Those are the grand pyramids?" Frederick looked down at her, a smile in his words. "I thought they'd be. . .larger."

"Well, of course they're larger. We're miles away from them right now so they look. . ." The glint in his dark eyes stalled her defense of the ancient wonders. "You do like teasing me, don't you?"

"A little, but only with good intentions." He held her gaze a moment longer and then stared back out toward the site. "Though one does wonder how people can survive in such a desolate place."

"Desolate?" She shook her head at his comment. "I see life and beauty and colors I've never imagined before." She shot him a mock-innocent look. "Of course, after living most of your life in England, you may find all of this sunshine overwhelming."

"Not to contradict you, darling." He chuckled and slid his arm more securely around her waist. "But I've grown accustomed to a remarkable amount of sunshine on a daily basis since marrying you, so perhaps I'll be somewhat more prepared."

She nestled against his side, rewarding his sweet compliment with a quick kiss to his chin before a new sight came into view. A city like none Grace had ever seen. Box-shaped buildings with white-and-tan finishes interspersed by strange golden towers and smooth blanched domes, but before she could even absorb the intricacies of the foreign display, a grander building caught her attention. Perched on a mound above the rest of the city stood an intimidating structure of sandstone hues and silvery-white domes, with two golden towers jutting up into the brilliant blue sky.

Pressed at the foot of the grand citadel sprawled the rest of the city, as if each building proved a single worshipper bowing before its holy place.

"That must be the Citadel," she whispered. "I've. . .I've read about it but never imagined it would look so dazzling." She glanced up at Frederick. "But I suppose people of all faiths have wished to make their places of worship as dazzling as the person they worshipped, if they could. Just think of the beautiful cathedrals back in England with their extravagant stained-glass windows and magnificent vaulted ceilings." She sighed. "I suppose we do try to get as close to heaven as we can on earth in any way possible, don't we? It must be a remarkable place to inspire such beauty."

The train began to screech and drag into the Cairo Railway Station, so Frederick guided her back to their seats until the train shuddered to a final stop. After a few moments of gathering their immediate items, they followed other passengers from the train and stepped out into an open area, similar to the train stations Grace had been through before. . .except for two very distinct differences: the signs, which were written in the beautiful calligraphic style of Arabic, and the people. While Frederick and Elliott consulted about their travel plans, Grace watched the wide variety of new styles moving within the cavernous building. Some wore long white robes with matching turbans covering their dark hair. Others wore strange red cylindrical hats, which she later learned were called tarbooshes and signified an Egyptian official of sorts. A woman covered in black from head to toe with her black-rimmed eyes staring from her shrouds walked beside a boy in a simple robe. And of course, the Europeans scattered in all directions. Women flourishing their myriad colors of gowns and gentleman in either bowler hats or straw, some in more formal suits and others dressed more like Frederick in his beige slacks and jacket. She rather liked his more comfortable style.

Even within the station, the Egyptian heat made itself known, and the idea of wearing fewer layers and lighter fabrics brought a smile. With her less-than-ideal knowledge of fashion, keeping clothing choices simple, white, and light sounded wonderful.

"Freddie?"

A voice burst from the bustling crowd, drawing their attention.

From among the vast array of people emerged a young man whose smile practically split his face in half. He'd removed his straw hat to wave in the air, revealing a swath of chestnut-colored hair. As he approached, his hand out long before he reached them, he flashed a look to Grace and his smile grew even broader, if that was possible.

"I say, what a pleasure this is." Without hesitation, he took Frederick's outstretched palm and pulled Grace's astute husband into a hug. "It's been too long, good fellow. Much too long." He stepped back and placed both his hands on Frederick's shoulders, giving him a steady stare with brown eyes a little lighter than Frederick's. "What has it been? Four years?"

"I believe so."

Grace looked from the stranger to her dear husband, who seemed to be grappling with his words. Well, this was the first boisterous affection she'd noticed from an Englishman since her marriage. Aunt Lavenia proved quite affectionate, but she was an English*woman*, of course.

Perhaps manners were even more relaxed in Egypt than she thought.

"And this must be your lovely bride."

"Yes, of course." Frederick cleared his throat and moved to Grace's side, giving her a bit of a helpless look before gesturing toward the stranger. "Lady Astley, this is my cousin, Timothy Withersby."

At once, the man took Grace's hand into his and gave it a firm squeeze. "I have heard only the very best about you from your husband. He's not too liberal with his praise, but I read enough between the lines to know it's a very good match." Mr. Withersby shot Frederick a wink and then turned back to Grace, lowering his voice to a stage whisper. "Besides, Aunt Lavenia writes gallons."

Grace laughed. What a relief to find someone as distracting as herself. At least now her enthusiasm wouldn't stand out quite so much on its own.

"It's a pleasure to meet you, Mr. Withersby."

"None of that." He waved away Grace's words and patted Frederick on the back as he gestured toward the front of the station. "I'm your cousin now too, so you are to call me Timothy."

She cast a look to Frederick, who offered her his arm and a tense smile. Well, at least Grace had tried to prepare him for the less conventional world of Egypt by talking about split skirts and all.

"Georgia is beyond herself with excitement." Timothy waved away a small child who rushed in front of him, his palm out.

"*Baksheesh*," came his request.

Timothy continued on without so much as an acknowledgement, but Grace paused. Those large dark eyes peeking up from such a dirty round face held an almost mesmerizing quality. "Baksheesh?"

"A tip. Coins. They're always seeking baksheesh and once you offer, they'll never leave you alone about it." Timothy directed Frederick's attention forward, talking about some point of the architecture of the station.

Grace allowed the men to move ahead of her and quickly took a coin from her change purse and pressed it into the little boy's hand. His smile beamed within his beautiful bronze face. He dipped his head. "*Shukran, Sitt,*" came his quick response.

Grace followed his movements through the crowd until he disappeared, and then she looked up to meet Elliott's knowing gaze. "It was just one coin, you know," she added.

He merely pressed his lips together in such a way she knew he was attempting not to smile. Thankfully, Frederick's trusty valet had a soft spot for her theatrics, and he'd been incredibly useful for things like rescue missions and scaling walls, so an occasional coin here or there wouldn't bother him in the slightest. At least she wasn't asking him for permission to climb on his shoulders or something.

Ellie, her dear maidservant, kept close to Elliott, her gaze darting about like a frightened deer. Poor thing was still too pale for her own good, but hopefully keeping to land for a while would prove the best medicine.

"Our carriage waits just outside." Timothy's voice called from ahead.

The doors to the station opened. Sunlight and heat swarmed forward, stealing Grace's breath and nearly blinding her. She blinked against the change, attempting to correct her vision, as she felt herself being guided by hands over and upward.

"Are you all right?"

She focused on Frederick's face as he moved to help her into the waiting carriage, the rushing sound of hooves, voices, and calls of various types crowding in on all sides.

"I am." She covered his fingers on her arm with her hand. "But I don't think I've ever felt such heat before in all my life. I'm certain I chose the wrong gown now. I should have done more research on garments for Egypt, but I was really overwhelmed by the idea of tombs."

Timothy rounded the carriage. "No need to worry at all. Georgia is keen to take you shopping for whatever you'll need. We're gathering supplies to take back to the excavation site and copious shopping is on the menu at any rate, so she will be certain to lather you with too much fashion knowledge for your, or anyone else's, good."

Grace shot Frederick a look, her grin nearly unraveling again, before he carefully helped her to her seat.

"And we're staying at Shepheard's Hotel, the only real place to stay in Cairo," Timothy continued explaining in between giving directions to one of the servants in reference to their luggage. "Everyone stays there to see everyone else."

"So it's like a party?" Grace tried very hard not to frown. She'd had a little hope for a quiet afternoon in order to stare out her hotel window, write in her journal about everything she'd seen, and then make notes about anything of interest on which to do research. One could never do too much research, and several of the travel books had mentioned wonderfully unique bookshops in Cairo.

"Oh yes, every day." Timothy winked. "Most of the important people sit on the veranda of the hotel and examine passersby or arriving guests to appraise them, and you, my dear Lady Astley, will be sure to receive an ample appraisal with all the newsworthy information surrounding you and Frederick over the past few months." He leaned back against the carriage seat as the vehicle began to move. "Unexpected marriage, kidnapping, murder plot.

It's all very exciting."

"You've heard about all of it?" Grace looked from Timothy to Frederick. "Even here in Egypt?"

"News is news, and there are enough Englishmen here to get the latest, make no mistake. And they are all keen to share as much as possible, while adding a bit of their own elaborations. At this point, you may very well be as exalted as any Egyptian goddess and Frederick easily morphed into some sort of Greek hero."

Grace couldn't help but laugh. Timothy Withersby talked even more than she did and with as much enthusiasm. "I'm a little nervous to enter your Shepheard's Hotel now, Timothy. The thought of a group of people in wait for our arrival isn't my idea of pleasant."

"Pleasant, it may not be, but the vultures will soon find new victims, rest assured." He gestured toward the window. "Now, I've asked the driver to make a brief stop, and I'm taking you in with me, Freddie. I have to collect a few items of clothing for the journey, and I mean to ensure you have some appropriate accoutrements as well."

"I'm sure my purchases can wait, Timothy. It's been a long journey and—"

"Nonsense." Timothy raised a brow. "I know you lived in India for a few years and may be more accustomed to this type of atmosphere, but there are other things we can collect for you to have on the excavation site. A new hat for one, and since we must stop already, you might as well run in for a quick look. Isn't that right, Lady Astley?"

"It really is no trouble for me to wait in the carriage, Frederick." Grace touched his arm. "It will give me time to observe the people on the street. I might even attempt some of my Arabic."

Frederick stared at her for a few seconds and opened his mouth as if to ask a question, then firmed his lips back together before nodding and turning back to Timothy. "A *brief* stop, you said?"

"Yes, yes." He nodded. "And here we are."

Timothy exited the carriage, and Frederick turned to her, holding her gaze. "I won't be long. You should be safe here."

"Of course." She nodded and offered him a reassuring smile. "What on earth could happen in a carriage?"

His brow furrowed into a dozen creases, and he pinched his lips together even tighter. Perhaps he knew more about the dangers of carriages than she did.

With a deep sigh, he stepped toward the shop, leaving her to take in the world just beyond the window. She leaned forward, her vision now adjusted to the brilliance of the afternoon sun. It was a world of such brightness everywhere that even the many white robes seemed to glow. Some men wore darker robes with white turbans on their heads, others wore brilliantly colored and flowing gowns. Little boys rushed to and fro with. . .she couldn't quite make out what was on their backs, but it looked like it had legs. What on earth could that be?

And of course she'd never seen so many beards in all her life. Not that beards were necessarily a distracting thing, but when observed in such wondrous synchrony among the older, native men, it felt a little disarming. With the foreign curl and flow of Arabic all around her, the unusual sights, and the wild scents of spices wafting in on the heated air, Grace's imagination nearly burst with words.

She reached for her journal, loosening the top button of her blouse as she did. Already dampness cloaked her skin. The warm air swirled in from the windows of the carriage, giving no relief. She jerked off her gloves and took her pen in hand, jotting down a few descriptions. A beautifully ornate building in white and gold. A vendor with a canopy selling some sort of long pipe. A man pulling a two-wheeled carriage, the white of his tunic in contrast to his sunbaked skin as he ran through the streets.

And then, Grace heard a sound that rose above the tumbling chaos of animals, people, and movement. A desperate cry. In English.

"No!"

A girl's cry.

"Help me. No."

Grace's attention turned to the shop and then back in the direction of the cry.

"Please, no."

She pinched the notebook against her chest, and snatching up her purse, she dashed from the carriage into the crowd, following the sound of the frantic cries.

Chapter Three

The crowd seemed to recognize Grace's urgency, though why they weren't responding with the same level of resolve, she had no idea. Maybe they didn't understand English, but Grace felt certain *frantic* sounded similar in all languages.

Most people moved aside as she pushed through. She only paused once, to scream, when a little boy carrying a dead animal crossed her path. Admittedly, the scream embarrassed her. She should have recognized the goatskin water bag from her readings, but the sight of the leathery, bloated body with the animal's head replaced by a pouring spout hadn't been at all as she'd expected. Of course, she'd imagined a little less lifelike too. With the animal's leg stubs sticking out, it looked for all the world as if the dead goat was waiting for someone to come along and give it a set of new hooves.

Another cry shook Grace, this time in what sounded like Arabic and much more desperate. Grace's attention caught sight of a native girl, no more than ten or eleven years old, struggling in the arms of one man while another advanced upon her with a large knife. Both of the men wore robes with their heads wrapped in white cloth. The man holding the girl wore a rather ragged-looking light brown tunic, and the other sported a robe matching the stark white of his beard.

Without pausing to attempt to sort out what type of men they were or what on earth the girl was doing, Grace drew up her parasol and knocked the knife from the bearded man's hand. Shocked by the force of her own actions, she stared up into the wide-eyed man's face, his fluffy white eyebrows disappearing beneath his turban.

"Pardon me, sir, but it looked as though you had very ill intentions with that knife."

The older man's face froze along with his entire body. In fact, all three of them stood immovable, wearing the same shocked expressions. Clearly Grace hadn't been fully understood, so she must have spoken too softly.

"I'm sure we can clear up whatever misunderstanding this girl has caused." She shifted so that her gown covered the knife on the ground, just in case the older man had second thoughts. She offered a smile, but all eyes remained on the end of her parasol, which she'd forgotten to lower from its rather intimidating position of pointing at the man's chest.

The girl was the first to break from her shocked state. "I did not steal the meat."

"You didn't steal the meat?" Grace repeated the phrase, hoping clarity would come with the words.

"I did not," she repeated, her eyes a strange sort of green that stood out from her dark olive skin. "Another woman came before me and stole the meat, then left me to take the punishment. If they would search me, they would find no fish." And she turned to the man, repeating something in what Grace assumed was Arabic.

He made a quick response, his hands waving angrily, and the younger man tightened his hold on the girl until she grunted.

"I'll pay for it." Grace reached for her purse. "Whatever the fish cost you."

The older man's gaze landed on Grace's purse, and then his

eyes narrowed ever so slightly as his lips twitched into a toothless smile. He waved toward the girl and said something to which the girl responded in angry tones. He seemed nonplussed, gesturing toward the younger man who squeezed the girl so hard she coughed.

"He tries to cheat you." The words barely made it from the girl's lips. "Double the cost of the fish, the. . ." And she used some Arabic word that Grace could only assume meant something very scoundrel-ish.

"I will pay for it." Grace stepped forward, narrowing her eyes back at the man.

His attention didn't move from her hand as she dipped her fingers into her purse. "Let her go, first."

He seemed to understand and nodded toward the younger man, who immediately released the girl. Grace couldn't help but admire the way the little thing spat at the man. There was something rather impressive about her fiery disposition.

Without hesitation, Grace placed the coins in the man's hand and smiled her thanks, then took the girl by the arm and started back the way she'd come. . .only Grace wasn't quite sure which way she'd come.

People crowded on all sides. Whitewashed-and-gold stone buildings surrounded her, each looking the same as the next. And from a quick survey of the faces, not one Englishman was in sight. She blinked a few times and studied her surroundings, piecing together a plan. The sun had been behind her when she sat in the carriage, so they must have been traveling east. She turned away from the sun and realized she still had a hold on the girl's arm.

"Oh, forgive me." She released her hold. "Are you all right now?"

The girl stared up at Grace, those greenish-gray eyes wide. "Thank you, Sitt."

Grace smiled and opened her parasol, blocking them both from the brilliant sunlight. "I don't know what the man meant to do to you with his knife, but I'm sure it wasn't something good. Will you be all right now?"

As if on cue, a whistle sounded from their left, and a group of three men in navy uniforms charged through the crowd. Grace made to move out of their way when one of the men in the lead stopped and pointed toward them, shouting something in Arabic. Grace opened her mouth to respond, but before she could, the girl had grabbed her by the arm and pulled her into a run through the crowd.

"What. . .what are you doing?"

"They're after us." The girl called, tugging with more strength than Grace would have thought from her size.

"Us?" She glanced over her shoulder just before they disappeared into the crowd.

Perhaps the bearded man felt threatened by her parasol and had called the police? Grace breathed out a sigh. She'd only been chased by police once before, but that time she'd at least had on much more appropriate footwear.

"Follow me."

Without warning, they disappeared into one of the narrowest streets Grace had ever seen, and despite the daylight behind her, everything was suddenly shrouded in darkness.

Frederick's cousin Timothy adored clothes a little too much for Frederick's liking. Without a doubt, having the appropriate travel clothes for such a different environment would prove useful and smart, but Frederick made his decisions based on quality and cost, not adornments. Besides, he hadn't the humor to put up with his cousin's pandering for much longer. He could use a good bath and some rest after the journey, and he'd left Grace melting in the sun for much too long. Hopefully she brought a book with her in the barouche, because if she hadn't, his darling bride, if left too long without occupation, was much too likely to go in search of a way to expend her energies.

At the thought, he turned to his valet, Elliott, who held a few boxes of Frederick's purchases. "I think it's time we returned to the carriage."

"But we've only just arrived," Timothy argued.

"Half an hour is quite enough for today, Timothy." Frederick started for the door. "You forget. We've *newly* arrived, and Grace is waiting in the sun when we both can be resting in the cool of the hotel."

"Fine, but I have your word for tomorrow then?"

Frederick grunted a response and marched toward the door. The sun blazed bright, even more so than in Frederick's memories of his military outfit in India. There was a similarity in the dry air and some of the earthy and aromatic scents, but Egypt held its uniqueness as well.

Frederick looked up from mopping his brow to see Ellie running toward him. His gaze shot to the empty barouche, and he started into a jog to meet the servant. "Where is she?"

"I had no chance to stop her, sir." The poor woman was near tears and still pale from her sea sickness, so her red-rimmed eyes proved more pronounced. "She jumped from the carriage and dashed into the crowd, sir. I tried to catch her, but the crowd—"

Frederick turned to Timothy. "Do you have a man to interpret for me?"

"What?" Timothy's eyes grew wide, and he took in the situation. "Do you mean that your bride is missing?"

"Timothy? A man?"

"Yes, yes." Timothy blinked and then waved toward a small man who sat near the carriage. "Akeem, I need you to help Lord Astley at once."

Akeem stood, his dark eyes shining with readiness.

"Follow me." With that, Frederick ran into the crowd in the direction Ellie had pointed, Elliott, Akeem, and Timothy on his heels. Within seconds they were swarmed by people all around, and Frederick gave orders for Akeem to ask if anyone had seen an English woman with red hair.

What had to have been minutes passed like hours. One man gave no reply, another pointed in the opposite direction. When Frederick questioned an older salesman, his eyes widened, and though he wasn't forthright in his information, after a little forceful persuasion, the man divulged a little more.

"Police chased Sitt Haree and a thief into the carpet bazaar, Saiyid," Akeem translated and gestured in the direction.

"Police?" Frederick repeated, attempting to sort out how on earth his wife had already garnered the ire of the Egyptian authorities when they'd barely been in Cairo an hour. He exchanged one look with Elliott, who offered a subtle shrug and, if Frederick didn't know better, almost smiled. Well, if anyone knew the workings of Grace's mind besides Frederick, it was the valet she'd convinced to go on an adventure or two of his own.

Frederick took off in the direction, attempting to internally remind himself that his wife had the best heart in the world and had likely entered into this particular. . .mishap quite innocently.

This was not the way he'd planned on touring the bazaars of Cairo, however.

Some of the streets were so narrow they were barely passable in pairs. Others spread wide with vendors on all sides, offering everything from pots to hats to sweet meats and pastries.

Just as they rounded back to near where they started, the shrill pitch of a whistle broke through the crowd noise, followed by an eruption of chaos. A boy with a strange sort of bag on his back dodged out of the way. A shrouded woman veered to the side. Some sort of man wearing a blue cloak and tall turban threw up his hands and yelled something in Arabic, and out of the chaos, hair flying and hat dangling by its strap behind her, came his lovely bride.

Her sapphire eyes shot wide as she saw him, and she slowed her pace.

"You know, I felt certain we were circling back around to find you and here you are!" Her smile brightened her face so much he nearly lost a bit of the tension in his jaw. "I used the sky as my indicator just like a true adventurer would do."

"What on earth happened to—"

A loud call in Arabic pulled his attention to three men in navy uniforms taking a young girl in hand. Her dark hair fell about her shoulders, likely uncovered from the chase, and she pulled against the hold of one of the men.

"She didn't hurt anyone." Grace stepped toward the police, but Frederick took her arm and turned to the interpreter.

"What is all this about?"

Akeem stood tall, proud of his usefulness. "It seems the girl escaped from the orphanage." He gestured and shook his head to add some sort of emphasis to his declaration. "Again. And the police have been trying to locate her for two hours." Akeem's eyes grew wide and he turned to Frederick. "It is uncommon for a fatherless girl to have such attention from the police or the orphanage. She must be a favorite."

The way Akeem said the word *girl* with a bit of curl to his lip turned Frederick's stomach. He knew the tone, the disgrace associated with the fairer sex in certain parts of the world.

"Do be gentle with her, won't you?" Grace added, pulling against Frederick's hold.

"Tell them." Frederick nodded toward the police, his gaze fastened on Akeem. "Tell them I will reward them for their kind treatment of the girl."

Akeem interpreted, and the police suddenly shifted their holds, loosening them.

The girl looked up, her strange greenish-gray eyes focused on Grace. "I will repay your kindness, Sitt Haree. I promise you."

With that, the men took the girl away.

"Sitt Haree?" Grace murmured and turned to Akeem.

He stood taller at the sudden attention. "It is as you are called. Lady of Fire."

"Lady of Fire?"

"Yes, Sitt." Akeem patted his head. "You have fire hair and fire spirit."

Grace reached up to rub an absent hand across her errant curls, and errant they were. Long gone was the well-styled bun adorned with her broad-brimmed hat from the train; although, at least the hat wasn't a lost cause as many of his bride's other hats became. She had an uncanny ability to misplace hats. And gloves.

"I have an Egyptian name." Her smile bloomed. "I feel quite honored."

"Don't look so glum, Freddie." Timothy stepped forward, waving his straw hat in front of his pinking face. "I feel certain you will have a name before the day is out as well."

Frederick raised a brow to his cheerful cousin, but the man merely laughed it off. For being only a few years Frederick's junior, Timothy had an uncanny ability to behave as if he were much younger.

"Come on now." He gestured with his hat toward the way they'd come. "Let's get out of the blazing sun and find our way to Shepheard's."

Grace turned to look at Frederick as they followed Timothy. "Her name is Zahra, and I'm so glad she still has both her hands."

Frederick opened his mouth to reply, but nothing emerged, so he glanced at Elliott for clarification. The poor valet merely shrugged another shoulder, a habit he'd formed, curiously, about the same time Grace had arrived in Frederick's life.

At the moment, Frederick didn't care to take the time to sort out all the intricacies of what happened on the streets of Cairo. The most important part was clear: Grace was safe. Right now, he wouldn't mind walls, a door, and some privacy.

At Frederick's urging, Timothy rode on the front carriage seat with Elliott and Ellie so that Frederick might sit next to Grace and be free to discuss the entire situation with her. But as soon as they'd settled in the carriage and she braided her arm through his, she rushed ahead before he could start. "I'm sorry to have caused you worry, my dear Lord Astley. I know I'm terribly good at causing you concern, but the poor girl was going to wrongly lose her hand, and I just couldn't bear it, if I could help. You do understand, don't you?"

He released a long breath through his nose, giving himself time to calm a little more. Grace would explain the whole thing, he was certain, but at present, and especially in this unfamiliar place, he needed her to understand. More for the good of his peace of mind than anything else, because apparently, his little wife always seemed to come out of her "adventures" unscathed. "Darling, do you remember how you felt when I was taken from Havensbrook and held at ransom?"

"Of course I do. It was all quite exciting. Though I'm certain I should practice rope swinging with more seriousness for my next chance."

He pinched his eyes closed at the remembrance of her unorthodox rescue and drew in a breath. "I mean, at first. When you first learned that I'd been taken. How did that feel?"

Those large eyes rounded in such a stark contrast to her ready smile, he felt the pain of it in his chest. "Hollow." She blinked, her frown deepening. "That. . .that I might have lost you."

He wasn't certain why her simple declaration moved him with such severity. Perhaps it was the sharp difference in her usual cheerful demeanor, or the fact he'd rarely seen her so serious. . .or maybe it was the fact he hadn't felt as important to anyone as he felt to his wife at that moment. And the realization humbled him. She loved as completely as she did everything else, and God had allowed him to be the unexpected beneficiary of such a love.

"Is that how you felt about me? When you couldn't find me?" Her bottom lip dropped with a gasp, and she pressed her cheek into his shoulder. "I'm so very sorry. I thought for certain you would have worked out my only desire in leaving the carriage in such an unfamiliar place would be to rescue someone from a horrid fate." She looked up at him with such penitence. "Or fight an injustice." She frowned. "Or. . .well, I can think of at least three other reasons, but I will remember in the future to leave a note."

He nodded and released the last of his frustration. She loved with such abandon and purity, so much more than he'd ever known. The least he could do in return was allow her a few idiosyncrasies, even if they left him nearly mad on occasion.

"That would help."

She rested her head against his shoulder, her hair in unruly curls from her "adventure." Then, just before their carriage drew up to the hotel, Grace attempted to reorder her hair and dust off a bit of the dirt stains on her gown. He helped with the smudges on her forehead and chin. He'd hoped they'd discretely arrive at their hotel and have a chance to freshen up before meeting the throng of fellow travelers, but he'd not been prepared for the Shepheard's Hotel promenade.

The building rose a full four golden stories above them, stretching nearly the length of the street, it seemed. Its size dwarfed everything around him, both in height and length, giving off the very essence of opulence.

"I've read that it has over three hundred rooms *and* electric lights." Grace leaned forward, staring up at the building as their carriage drew to a stop. "And look, a garden of sorts just to the right of the front veranda."

And so it was. A rectangle of rich green with tall, bushy-headed trees growing to top the second story of the hotel. Steps led up to a wide portico, on which a sweeping veranda boasted tables and chairs for guests to look out upon the dusty city streets. And so they did. Dozens of collections and varieties of people, from well-dressed ladies to men in their top hats or even a few wearing their pith helmets. But one thing they all had in common? Frederick frowned. Flagrant curiosity.

Grace smiled at the crowd, so unaffected by her disarray that Frederick took the same approach. And as the curious gazes rounded in surprise and started a murmur of questions, they topped the stairs.

They'd barely made it through the front doors and into a high-ceilinged room of colonnades and two massive Egyptian statues, when a woman wearing trousers and a pith helmet of her own sauntered up to them. Her dark eyes glimmered, her lips curled, and Frederick's chest seized with a sudden warning. Something wasn't safe about this woman.

"I had no idea we'd be harboring a criminal." The woman sidled up next to Grace, her caramel-brown eyes surveying. Her manicured brow tipped. "But it does make the infamous Lady Astley much more interesting."

Chapter Four

"Amelia, don't frighten them as soon as they enter the hotel."

Grace pulled her gaze from the woman wearing the pith helmet and fixed her attention on the lady walking toward her from the grand staircase. And *lady* was the only way to describe the woman. She exuded elegance from the crown of her raven hair to the tip of her slippered feet. Grace wasn't well-learned in fashion yet, but the gown the woman wore cradled the woman's form in pale blue and held such delicate white embroidery along each shoulder and down the front of the gown. It reminded Grace of starlight.

Not to flatter herself, of course, but Grace felt certain she could wear such a frock quite well, and since Egypt stayed warm most of the time, she wouldn't have to worry so much about making the style match the season.

She frowned. At least, she didn't think so. Wasn't it always supposed to be two basic seasons? Hot and hotter?

"Frederick," the woman held out her hands, her smile blooming wide. "It's been much too long."

"It has, Georgia." He took her hands, his dark gaze searching the woman's face. Something in the way his brow furrowed for the briefest moment inspired Grace to give Georgia Withersby Archibald a closer study.

"I'd like to introduce you to my wife, Lady Astley."

"But do please call me Grace. It sounds so much friendlier than Lady Astley." Grace offered the woman a broad smile but noted the lines at the edges of the woman's eyes. Lines not meant for such a young woman.

What could cause them? Nerves? Worries? Grief?

"It is a pleasure to meet you, Grace." The woman's expression softened and took off nearly five years from her face. "Please, call me Georgia. I am happy to have you here." Her gaze flickered between Grace and Frederick. "I had heard your wedding wasn't quite as expected, but Frederick and Aunt Lavenia, of course, were quick to assure me of everything turning out well in the end?"

"I certainly hope we're not near the end at the very beginning, but it's been an excellent start," Grace added, glancing at Frederick and finding his gaze on her. Oh, she did love it when she caught him watching her. Although sometimes his look was more confused than endearing, but she just supposed that was because he didn't process certain types of information quite as quickly as she did. Especially if it was bookish information. Or the mystery type.

"I would make certain to live each moment then," the woman in the pith hat said, her large brown eyes holding Grace's gaze. "Especially in Egypt. Nothing is ever certain here."

Blond curls flipped from beneath the woman's hat, framing a face which was too tan to be considered fashionable. Grace had heard some older lady back in England mention how pale skin tone appeared to be the most appropriate, but Grace couldn't find anything wrong with a bit of sunshine on the skin. If she didn't burn like a baby herself, she'd have appreciated a little additional glow to her cheeks. Especially since she never remembered to apply rouge, and evidently that was fashionable too.

She held in a sigh. Why did everything have to relate to fashion? It was exhausting.

"This is Amelia Sinclair," Georgia offered, gesturing toward the woman in the hat. "She is one of our archaeologist's assistants and the resident artist for the digs."

"An artist for the digs?" Grace nodded toward the woman, who looked about Grace's age in every particular but her eyes. Something about her eyes seemed. . .old. And Grace couldn't help but admire her trousers with a bit of envy. Trousers. She only wore them when riding astride, but to traverse the deserts and excavations with such freedom? A little thrill worked its way through her. How daring!

And practical, but fashion didn't seem to prefer practical either.

"The best archaeological digs ought to have an artist," Georgia answered, sending a look to Amelia that didn't look as pleasant as the one she'd just given to Grace. "Should we ever discover anything of real note, an artist is invaluable in taking down likenesses of what we see. Paintings on the walls. Pottery. Statues."

"Mummies," Amelia added with a little twist of her lips. "In all states of decomposition. It's really quite fascinating."

"Amelia." Georgia grimaced, but the expression did nothing to Amelia's smile. "I am sorry for her manners. She's lived most of her life in Egypt with men."

Something flickered across Amelia's countenance at Georgia's last comment but was gone as quickly as it came.

"Well, I find it all rather fascinating." Grace smiled and looked over at Frederick, whose usually tender expression had stilled into something rather unwelcoming. She followed his gaze to Amelia. Was he upset with the fact she wore trousers?

"Until you've had to listen to men talk about finding nothing but broken pottery and centuries-old pieces of rock over and over again." Georgia shook her head. Her smile was soft, but her eyes held a sadness.

"It takes a great deal of imagination to understand the

importance of the pottery and the rock, I'm afraid." Amelia's gaze sliced in Georgia's direction before turning back to Grace and Frederick. "But I feel the two of you will bring ample imagination while you're here, and we could desperately do with a bit of imagination." Her attention settled on Frederick in a way that turned Grace's stomach. "New friends are always welcome."

Grace's attention flickered from Miss Sinclair to Frederick and back.

Grace hadn't experienced true jealousy before. Perhaps once, when her beloved dog chose to go for a walk with Lillias instead of herself, but that flicker of emotion was nothing like the sudden rush of heat rising into her chest at the moment. It wasn't anything like what she imagined from Katherine or Heathcliff in Wuthering Heights, but there was a distinct desire to poke Miss Sinclair's eyes out.

A gentle pressure to her back alerted her to Frederick's closeness, almost as if he knew she was internally breaking several of the Ten Commandments. The simple touch produced the most remarkable effect. First a swell of calm poured through her, and almost as an added benefit, Amelia Sinclair lost her smile. Perhaps the young woman had been much too confident in her lovely golden curls and her decidedly too-tight trousers.

"I am certain you both wish to rest and freshen up before dinner." Georgia's attention flickered from Frederick to the door as Timothy entered, dark hair waving about in wild disarray as it had been since Grace first met him. She couldn't quite place which character he reminded her of most, but perhaps a bit more swarthy Charles Bingley. Could Charles Bingley ever be considered swarthy? It was a delicious word, but she'd always considered Charles Bingley more like a golden retriever puppy, and that didn't match the word *swarthy* at all.

"I'm sorry to interrupt, sister-dearest, but Lord Astley is so popular he has already received a telegram." Timothy grinned and gestured with his head toward the door. "Unfortunately, I could not collect it for you as they are rather fiendish with protecting personal mail in this hotel, but I'll be happy to show you the way to the front desk."

"I'll escort Lady Astley to your room if you like, Frederick," while you collect your mail," Georgia offered, stepping between Amelia and Grace, as if *she* could read Grace's mind too. Oh dear, was Grace as obvious as all that? Or perhaps clairvoyance was a Percy family trait?

Her attention shot to Frederick. Is that how he always had an uncanny way of finding her?

He raised his brows as she looked up at him, his dark gaze searching hers. Well, if he had clairvoyance, it was likely a beneficial trait, especially if things ever turned willy-nilly again, as it had before Christmas with the man-napping and everything. She frowned. But wouldn't he have been prepared to be man-napped if he was clairvoyant?

His lips tipped ever so slightly, as if he was putting his clairvoyance to work, and he shifted his attention back to Georgia. "Thank you, Georgia. I know Grace was particularly interested in having time to locate her camera among the luggage."

Oh, he was very good. She hadn't even been thinking about her camera!

"Frederick bought it for me in preparation for our trip, and I've been practicing for an entire week so that I'm properly prepared for photographing camels."

A strange cough erupted from Timothy. "Photographing camels?"

Well, Grace had become much more accustomed to noticing a laugh over a cough, after all the practice she'd had at Havensbrook. "Oh yes, I'm rather fascinated with them. I think I first read about them in Herodotus, which, before you think my brain is much more clever than it is, I will admit to not completely adoring the book and at times not understanding it. However, there were mentions of camels, and after I saw one on display at a zoo back home in Virginia, I decided I'd like to know more about them."

"And when she fixes her mind to something, there is no getting in the way," Frederick added, with a stronger press to her back and a broader grin. He had an excellent smile—and lips.

"Until I'm distracted by something else, I'm afraid." She shrugged and offered Frederick a smile for his clairvoyant self. He would most certainly like the turn of her thoughts. They were kissably pleasant. "Besides, there is so much to remember. Photos will help me recall in vivid detail all the things I see on our trip, and I'm certain to see a great many new and wonderful things."

"And perhaps horrible and dangerous too." This from Amelia, whose unfading crooked smile and triumphant eyes proved she was not clairvoyant. "Egypt proves there is a great deal of peril hiding behind the most dazzling things."

"Amelia, you are going to frighten them." Georgia shot the woman a glare. A very impressive one.

"Not at all. I'm much better at these kinds of conversations than ones involving fashion or weather," Grace added.

Amelia blinked a few times and lost her smile.

Georgia's smile faltered and then she brought her hands together. "Let's hope for very few perils and more pleasant adventures. I think we've all had our fill of horrible things." With a lift of her hand, a man appeared from the corner of the room. He must have been there all along, but with his white robe matching the walls, Grace hadn't noticed. "Shakir, would you make ready Lord and Lady Astley's room?"

The man bowed his dark head, barely flashing Grace a look from his equally dark eyes before disappearing from the lobby.

Georgia turned her attention back to Grace, leaving the speculation from Amelia's comment hanging in the air like a ghost of Christmas past. With a lift of her dainty chin, she gestured toward the stairs. "Now allow me to show you the way, Grace. I think you'll find Shepheard's a suitable place for your imagination."

Grace shot Amelia another glance before following Georgia,

only to catch the young woman's gaze fastened on Frederick's retreating form as he followed Timothy from the room. Grace had little practice with real-life villains, though the practice she *did* have was rather noteworthy, but she felt well qualified to recognize one due to her extensive reading. Amelia Sinclair fit the list. And though Grace didn't doubt her husband's faithfulness, the very idea of a woman thinking rascally thoughts about him had Grace's imagination moving into a very villainous direction, complete with a few unique ways to use her ever-handy rope.

She desperately needed to reread *The Count of Monte Cristo* as soon as possible.

"I am so glad to have you with us, Grace." Georgia's words pulled Grace's attention back to Frederick's cousin, who led the way from the lobby, over the glossy floors. Massive white pillars lined their walk, rising to a ceiling two floors above, the splendor duly stealing some of Grace's ire.

"I've found few women here who I can aspire to friendships with and even fewer who I can abide." Georgia continued walking, as Grace stumbled behind, trying very hard not to become distracted by the splendor and uniqueness of the surroundings, but in all honesty, everything appeared very specifically designed for distraction. Colorful archways. Elegant rugs. Handsome furnishings. Men in white robes and strange hats serving the European collective at their elaborate chairs and tables.

"Why is that?" Grace muttered, wishing she'd had her camera on hand.

A large archway framed the entrance to the grand staircase where a pair of bronze statues stood on either side, holding electric lamps in the air. Grace slowed her pace to examine the artwork and blinked a few times to clear her vision. The statues were bare-breasted women wearing ancient Egyptian headdresses. They were lovely but. . .well, unexpected.

"Most women here hover between two extremes." Georgia had paused on the fourth stair, waiting, so Grace picked up her skirt to catch up. "Insatiably determined to prove themselves or wilting flowers in need of some dashing man's constant rescue, and I'm not keen on either."

"I should think that the men outnumber the women by a large amount at any rate, seeing that adventure and political unrest are the two main interests in Egypt at present, so I can imagine that the friendship pickings may be slim." Grace smiled, still attempting to sort out what could be wrong with insatiable determination. Lizzie Bennet would certainly fit the mark, and she was a fantastic creature. In fact, Grace had always wondered if Jane Austen wasn't a bit "insatiably determined" herself.

"I must say I'm looking forward to returning to England in a few weeks." Creases lined Georgia's porcelain forehead, deeper than expected for such a young woman. Surely she couldn't be much older than Grace's own sister, Lillias. Mid-to-late twenties, perhaps?

"Well, I'm happy to meet you. Frederick had so many nice things to say about you and Timothy and how you were close during your childhood." Grace glanced around at the opulence of the grand carpeted stairway they were climbing. At the first landing, the white walls along the stair gave way to glass, revealing a garden filled with a wild assortment of odd trees and shrubberies. Spiky-looking things, much like the few Grace had noticed in Alexandria.

"Lovely, isn't it?" Georgia offered. "A quiet place amid the city when the hotel is not hosting concerts."

"That smell? It's. . .heavenly."

Her face softened into a smile and something in the simple motion made her look even more beautiful. "Jasmine and narcissus, I believe."

A flutter of wings pulled Grace back to the garden to see a

large pink bird disappearing into a gazebo. "Oh my, was that a flamingo?"

"It was."

"I've never seen one in real life before, only in photos." She breathed out a chuckle, determined to find her way to the garden as soon as she located her camera. "They truly are that color pink!"

"You are enchanting, aren't you?" Georgia laughed. "I thought Aunt Lavenia was exaggerating in her claims about you, but I see she was not. Is everything an adventure or joy for you?"

Grace shrugged her shoulders. "Traveling to England as a bride was my first real trip to anywhere besides America, so I suppose I'm enamored by the newness of it all, but I must say, a healthy love of fiction can either tempt us toward happily-ever-after or a woe-to-thee horrible worldview, depending on the types we choose to read most often. I like to think that my view is framed by a solid faith, so it must tilt toward the former rather than the latter."

The woman studied Grace a moment and then nodded. "Indeed."

"Everything is so very elegant here." Grace waved toward the chandelier hanging above. "Of course, I expected elegant for a place which once served as a palace of Napoleon Bonaparte, but I never imagined something like this, and I have an extensive imagination."

Georgia's lips tipped wider. "I held your view when I first came, all the wonder of it. The exotic and beautiful." Her gentle look bowed to the weariness once again as she continued their climb. "You. . .you *are* very young."

Grace stifled her sigh.

"I suppose I am." Why was everyone always pointing out her age? Could they be any more original? Hair color and age. She had a high forehead and a narrow nose. Why not tease those a bit? It would at least provide some variety. "I hadn't planned to marry when I did, but it couldn't be helped, so here we are."

"You and Frederick have been married only a few months?"

"Yes, three." Grace slid her hand along the wooden banister and sighed out of sheer happiness. "I never expected marriage to be so delightful. Fiction rarely paints it so. Someone is always disgruntled or hiding their wives in attics or mooning over someone else's spouse, you know? So the very idea of finding marriage so wonderful is a delicious surprise. I'd always wondered if I'd die by piracy or a shipwreck long before I ever had a chance to be married."

Georgia's dark brows rose and she opened her mouth as if to say something but then stopped. She took a few more steps. "I'm glad the start is going so well. Those days are usually the most pleasant."

Grace wasn't quite sure how to respond, because she felt certain she'd heard from some lesson or other that asking personal questions to Englishwomen was considered rude, but since they were technically in Egypt, was the rule still true?

While she was contemplating what to say, Georgia continued. "I know this may seem untoward, my dear, but. . .but your dowry is what saved Havensbrook. Isn't that so?"

Well, so much for the personal-questions rule. At least Grace wasn't the one to break it this time. "Yes, and I'm so happy it has been such a relief for Frederick."

Georgia stopped at the top of the stairs and studied Grace, her brows furrowed. "Please tell me you were able to retain some control over your finances."

Grace knew very little about Georgia Archibald, but within the first quarter hour of introduction, a few concerns already came to light besides the hints Blake and Frederick had provided.

"No, I didn't." Grace drew in a breath and held the woman's gaze. "But Frederick and I have made many decisions together related to Havensbrook improvements as well as other things."

"Well, let's hope Frederick takes on more of the Percy disposition than the Withersby one." Her attention faded to the windows, expression turning distant. " 'Till death do us part' can be a very long time." She blinked as if from a stupor and her smile returned. "Forgive me. I always seem to turn pensive the longer we remain in Egypt."

Without another word, Georgia continued down the hallway where light-oak doors paralleled each other on either side, affixed with golden room numbers. Despite the somber turn of the conversation, the world of Shepheard's, and indeed of Egypt, boasted light and energy and airiness, a distinct contrast to the dark stone and cold gray skies of England she'd experienced since arriving there in December—though Grace held enough warm and exciting memories to endear Havensbrook to her forever. And Frederick assured her England's spring and summer were delightful.

"My rooms are across the hall." Georgia gestured in the direction. "So if you need anything, please feel free to ask." She pushed the door open to reveal a large space, as light and airy as the rest of the place. A sitting room welcomed them first and then a bed and en suite lavatory, all donned in the same fashion of dark rich furniture, Persian rugs, and colorful adornments. Two other doors on opposite sides of the suite led to servants' rooms, Georgia explained, but Grace couldn't remove her attention from the large bed shrouded in ghostly white from ceiling to floor.

"Ah, mosquito netting," Georgia commented from the doorway. "You'll become accustomed to it, but I advise you to rise carefully for the first few mornings, or you'll find yourself entangled."

Entangled? Oh dear, it was almost as if Grace could predict her own future.

"I'll leave you to rest and freshen up. I will send my maid to see to you should you need help preparing for dinner since I heard your maid is not well."

"Thank you."

With that, the door closed, and Grace walked to the large window which led to a balcony overlooking the garden below. It all felt very much like the sleeping princess's tower view, except for the busy city streets just over the garden wall.

And despite the color and wonder and brilliance of it all, shadows soaked the air in wordless ways. From Amelia Sinclair's warnings to Georgia's melancholy comments, it all reminded Grace how people carried darkness with them. They rarely needed to go in search of it.

With those thoughts, a little awareness pushed in beside the wonder. Fairytales were all well and good, but many of the characters could have done with a bit more sense to keep their troubles at bay. Grace nodded. And she'd ensure she ushered up as much sense in the middle of the fairytale-like world as she could, because everything was not as it seemed.

Her tingling scalp confirmed her suspicions.

And her scalp was never wrong.

Chapter Five

The telegram had not been for Frederick, but even before he delivered it to Ellie, he guessed at the news. Her mother's illness had worsened, which meant Ellie needed to return to England at once.

And Grace was losing her maid.

Frederick pondered the quandary as he moved up the grand staircase of the hotel. He'd been in many places, but few of his wanderings compared to this exotic and opulent place. Hopefully, Grace wouldn't have unearthed her camera and disappeared from their room already. They needed to discuss the current circumstances and sort out who could replace Ellie for the remainder of their trip, because based on Ellie's physical response to travel and her need to return home, she wouldn't be joining them for the remainder of the journey.

As he moved down the hallway, a familiar figure waited by the door Frederick presumed was his own.

Elliott straightened as he noticed Frederick's approach. "She's still in there," he said before Frederick made it to him. "Unless she happened to climb out the window, though with her history, I wouldn't put it past her, sir."

Despite the sudden twinge of concern knotting in Frederick's chest, his smile won out. "Well, she's promised to leave a note next time, so there's that."

"Prudent decision, sir."

Frederick released a sigh and studied his long-time friend. "I know you've said my dear bride has been a good influence on me, but I believe she's influenced you a bit too, Elliott."

"Sir?"

"Your confidence and sense of humor have become remarkably more apparent of late."

"It was either give in or go mad, sir." Elliott's lips twitched. "I chose the former, for your sake as much as mine."

Elliott's full grin stretched wide, but then his attention focused on something just over Frederick's shoulder. Frederick turned. Down the hall sauntered Amelia Sinclair. And *sauntered* was the appropriate word. She made certain to use every movement of her body to garner attention. Frederick nodded in her direction and cast a glance to Elliott, who didn't cloak his expression as quickly as the man usually did. Of course, how could Frederick blame him?

"Gentlemen," she said as she walked past, making sure to give each one of them a proper once-over.

Once she passed, Frederick's stiff smile faded into a grimace. "Dangerous."

Elliott's gaze shifted to Frederick. "Without a doubt." He cleared his throat and tugged at his collar. "She knows it too."

"Come on then." Frederick gestured toward the door. "Let's take our conversation elsewhere."

Within the finery and the quiet of the room, a faint whirring drifted forward. Frederick stepped farther into the suite, following the sound, and found Grace fast asleep on a couch by the balcony.

He paused long enough to admire her, auburn hair in contrast to the pale cream of the couch. He'd learned through fire the importance of a steadfast heart, the oft-fleeting nature of attraction, but God in His mercy had given Frederick a woman who was beautiful throughout. Young? Yes, with much more of life to learn, but mature and constant in many ways that mattered most. The rest could be learned in time. And she was intelligent. She'd learn.

"I'm happy to report the window theory is not a concern at present," Frederick whispered and tilted his head toward the couch. He gestured for Elliott to follow him back toward the entry room to give distance from Grace.

Frederick offered Elliott the telegram he'd received downstairs. "Would you take care of the arrangements for Ellie on the first available steamer from Alexandria?"

Elliott skimmed over the telegram, his frown deepening. "Of course." His gaze came back to Frederick's. "And Lady Astley's needs?"

"I'll enquire after options from Mrs. Archibald." Frederick released a slow breath, and his quick valet noticed.

"What is it, sir?"

"I'm not certain, but I think we ought to keep our guard up."

"You felt the tension too, sir?" Elliott lowered his voice even more. "I already heard a few conversations among the servants that hint at financial and. . .personal struggles with the Archibalds." His grin tipped. "Maids and housekeepers know everything."

"Well, keep those ears open and"—Frederick glanced back toward the door—"there's something about Miss Sinclair that I don't like."

Just the memory of the way she surveyed him and her sardonic responses reminded him too much of one of the least favorite women of his past: Celia Blackmoore Percy.

"I'll keep a keen eye and ear out for anything, sir."

"Well, your eyes may get you into trouble with that one."

Elliott caught Frederick's teasing tone and brought his other brow up to join the first. "Now sir, you know my past well enough to count on me to recognize a counterfeit from the real thing, don't you?"

Frederick's grin broadened at Elliott's allusion to one of the many "talents" from the man's past. "Very good, then."

"You used to dabble in counterfeiting?" Both men turned to see Grace staring at them from the other side of the couch, blue eyes wide. "I thought it was boxing?"

"Perhaps someday, Lady Astley, our good Mr. Elliott can fill your mind with all sorts of sundry tales from his former days. He made an excellent thief too, as I recall." Frederick tossed his valet another grin, grateful for the comradery of the man he'd considered a friend now for more years than not. "But for now, I believe we are meant to be ready for dinner *after* we share some news with Ellie."

Dinner proved a parade of the rich and unusual. Knowing Elliott was somewhere in the vicinity gave Frederick a sense of comfort, but from the moment they took their seats at their table, the cast of characters, headed by Sydney Archibald, secured all the more the concerns he'd felt for his cousin Georgia.

No wonder Timothy had left his London College position to join her here.

Of course, they'd already met Amelia Sinclair, but along with her there was her unusual aunt, Mrs. Eloise Casper, a woman who wore pale blue eye powder and too much jewelry. . .and boasted the ability to tell the future. Grace found her fascinating, and proceeded at several intervals to inquire after the rumored clairvoyance.

Charles Smallwood, Sydney's friend and businessman, who by all accounts had some financial stake in the expedition, proved a most amiable sort. White hair and matching beard revealed him as the senior of the trip in age. In fact, the man had been a military commander in the Boer War at the end of the last century, which was the way Sydney and Smallwood knew one another.

"You must take the time to see the Cairo Museum while you're here." Mr. Smallwood gestured for the server to refill his glass. "The sheer age of some of the artifacts is astounding."

"The place is a disaster, if you ask me." Their host, Sydney Archibald, growled his answer, barely offering anyone at the table much attention—though he seemed to offer an inordinate amount of attention to one of the ladies at a nearby table.

Frederick's stomach turned.

"Disorganized, mismarked." He sighed. "No wonder thieves can steal antiquities with such ease and no one knows for weeks or months that something's gone."

"Sydney, please," Georgia's calm voice did little to turn her husband's attention.

"I could do with a bit of those artifacts, since we can't seem to locate any on our own dig." His voice rose to a heightened volume, drawing a few glances from those nearby. "Three seasons and nothing to show for it. I'm beginning to think Professor Andrews isn't as good at his job as he professes to be."

Frederick hadn't liked him from the start of his courtship with Georgia. Of course, he'd had little to say about it and, with his own broken past, felt he had little right to voice his concerns, but four years later, the man had only devolved. Boorish, without one kind word to say to his wife as she attempted to soften the blows of his poor behavior.

"You well know, Sydney, that John is doing everything you asked of him," Amelia shot back, looking much more dangerous in her green gown than she ever had in her trousers. "Is there anything left to find with all the discoveries in Thebes? At least anything that hasn't already been ransacked by tomb robbers?"

"Do you mean tomb robbers are still active?" Grace asked from beside him, the pale blue of her gown bringing out not only the hue of her eyes but also the vibrance of her hair. "I thought they were only from long ago."

"Not at all, my dear," Smallwood responded with a twinkle in his eyes. "Which is why we are still in hopes of finding tomb treasure to this day." He chuckled. "If the thieves can do so, why not us, right, Sydney?"

"Yes, why not us," he ground out. "And with that in mind, we leave for the dig site in two days' time. I must see how much the sandstorm has ruined my investment. This is the last straw, I tell you."

"A sandstorm?" Grace asked. Those sapphire eyes of hers had carefully studied each person with much more fascination, but no less care than he had, he guessed, and the thought almost inspired a smile.

"Yes, I'm afraid we received news this afternoon that a sandstorm swept through the dig site yesterday." Georgia offered a sad smile. "I had hoped to stay in Cairo a few more days so that the two of you could experience more of the city, but I'm afraid Sydney will not be deterred."

"Well, I'm certain we'll experience wonders on the field that can't be emulated here." Grace's quick and gracious response softened the worry lines around his cousin's eyes a little.

"You're very kind, but you must make certain on your way back through Cairo that you avail yourselves of the additional wonders here, such as the palaces, mosques, churches." She opened her mouth to say more, but Sydney interrupted.

"I find myself tiring of Egypt," Sydney grumbled, downing another shot of whiskey. "Those wonders and discoveries seem plentiful for everyone else, but me. I don't mean to return after this season."

"Now, now, Sydney," Smallwood waved a palm toward the man as if soothing him. "Let's not be rash. There are other places to—"

"I don't care for it any longer. In fact, I'm tempted to quit the entire thing early."

"And you haven't the money to waste on a fruitless endeavor at any rate." This from Timothy, whose friendly countenance had taken a sober turn. In fact, the man's expression bordered on menacing. "I think the sooner *you* leave, the better for everyone else."

In Frederick's periphery, he noticed Amelia Sinclair flinch. Why? Did she have some connection to Sydney? Frederick stifled an inward groan. Or Grace's overactive imagination and her love for mysteries were beginning to rub off on him.

"Who has the money to waste on fruitless endeavors? None of us, I should think," Georgia quickly responded, her face paling. "I think we will all look forward to a respite from Egypt after this season."

"I've read that most Egyptologists believe they've only scratched the surface of the treasures housed within the deserts here," Grace offered, her eyes glittering with what Frederick could only imagine. Her mind never ceased searching for adventures.

"I'll leave it to the other poor souls with a keen sense to waste time and money." Sydney tapped the side of his glass and a server quickly refilled it.

"It would be a poor decision to leave now, Sydney." This from Mrs. Casper, whose blue-tinged eyelids made her pale blue eyes look ever larger. "I foresee gold." She gasped. "The ancient sands will part for you. The fate of the ancients is waiting for you, unless you accept their gifts. If you dishonor them by abandoning their offerings, they will only bring you death."

"Death?" Grace repeated, as if the word hung in the air.

"I haven't had enough whiskey to put up with Eloise's nonsense." Sydney waved toward her as if trying to make her disappear.

"The fate of the ancients is death," Grace whispered, her large eyes staring back at Frederick. "Do you think she meant that?"

"I'm not certain we should put much stock in what Mrs.

Casper declares."

The corner of Grace's lip tipped, and she kept her voice low. "Well, I didn't believe she was foretelling anyone's future, but she may have planned to slide in an insult. You should have seen the way she glared at Mr. Archibald. I imagine Bertha Mason could have done no better to Mr. Rochester."

It only took him a few seconds to follow her fictional analogy, but he caught on. . .and was getting a bit quicker at them after having been married to her a few months.

"Who all is a part of your expedition, Sydney?" Frederick offered, attempting to quell the tension a bit for Georgia's sake.

"There is John Andrews, the lead archaeologist, and very passionate about his work," Georgia answered.

"And Daniel Graham, the philologist," Smallwood offered. "Good man. Excellent at his job."

"Philologist?"

"An expert in reading ancient languages and hieroglyphs," Amelia offered, shifting her gaze to Frederick, her smile tipping with not-so-subtle allure.

He didn't return the expression.

"Oh, I cannot wait to see true hieroglyphs." Grace touched Georgia's hand in her enthusiasm, and once his cousin got past her shock, she seemed to soften at the affection. "I've attempted to study some of them from books, but I feel certain I will learn more quickly in person."

"I have only learned a few symbols here and there but feel my time is better used in serving the neighboring village." She lowered her voice so that Frederick had to lean a little to hear. "I've befriended some of the women and children there, and they've allowed me to read to them and help with hygiene lessons at times."

Georgia caught Frederick's gaze and the color in her cheeks deepened as she turned to Grace. "You see, Father would not allow me to pursue medicine, but I've done my own bit of study to help in small ways."

No, her father would not have borne a daughter of his going to university. Why were so many people in his family so broken?

"I believe that you and I are going to become very good friends." Grace gave Georgia's hand another squeeze. "And Frederick can warn you of all my vices so you can be sure to avoid me if you don't think you can bear them."

A laugh burst from Georgia so suddenly, it drew the attention of several people at the table. "I believe, Lady Astley, your arrival in Egypt may have been just the medicine *I've* needed to make it to the end of our season with my sanity intact." She met Frederick's gaze. "Having you both here will make the rest of the trip much more bearable, I can already tell."

Just beyond Georgia's head, Frederick noted a look pass between Sydney and Amelia Sinclair. His gaze settled back on Georgia. His cousin had always been one of the gentlest sorts of women, and to see her chained to such a man as Sydney Archibald nearly brought Frederick's blood to a boil. He couldn't imagine how much more furious her own brother must be. No wonder Timothy had followed her to Egypt. If anyone needed the support of someone who loved them, it was Georgia Archibald.

And if anyone needed a healthy dose of justice, it was Sydney.

Chapter Six

Grace had barely escaped from Georgia with her life. The woman had taken Grace from one shop to the next, choosing scarves or dresses or hats of every shade of white, blue, and green known to mankind. Why not other shades? Grace sighed. Because these colors were the only ones that would do, Georgia had said.

At first, Grace thought that disagreeing with her might shorten the shopping experience. After an hour, she decided simple submission was her only course of survivable action. Thankfully, they had secured a meeting with some of the others at the Cairo Museum at noon, so their shopping excursion came with an end in sight. In all honesty, Georgia proved a lovely person. Not quite as keen on talking about books or mummies, but if Grace set her mind to listen rather than talk, she and Georgia got along quite well. And Grace had to admit she learned a great deal about hat styles, perfumes, and some famous French designer named Paul Poiret. Securing a nice set of day dresses, shirtwaists, and skirts that fit the fashion requirements of Egypt certainly added peace to Grace's mind as well. She took copious notes on Georgia's descriptions and directions on which outfits would work best with what hats, so as not to embarrass her dear husband.

Grace's favorite part of the entire morning was walking among the vendors in the streets. Vendors of all kinds, selling everything imaginable. She even purchased Frederick a leather vest and cowboy hat like the ones she'd seen in Buffalo Bill's Wild West Show. Oh! What a roguish cowboy he'd make! And though Grace had seen some of the shops while she had run through the streets with Zahra being pursued by the officers, taking her time to actually enjoy them made all the difference. The taste of *kushari* or sweet *fiteers,* the scent of jasmine mixed with the smoke of the *shisha* pipe or the savory aroma of roasted meat. The myriad rugs or slippers or beaded necklaces and pottery. In fact, anything from a European hat that met even Georgia's high standards to the latest kitchen utensils managed to find its way to the Cairo vendors. And each and every salesman offered a smile as big as his ready willingness to bargain.

Grace never realized how energizing the process of bartering could be, though she stopped waving her arms as forcefully as the native salesman when she noticed Georgia's obvious look of embarrassment. Women with pale skin had the most difficult time hiding embarrassment.

The bartering bit *did* remind her of the moment she tried to convince Frederick to marry her. Not her favorite memory, but invigorating, nonetheless.

After such an energizing and sometimes tedious morning, the Cairo Museum came as a rewarding balm to Grace's fashion-weary soul. Frederick and Timothy had gone on their own shopping adventure, though Grace had the sneaky feeling Frederick enjoyed the process as much as she did, so it was left to Mr. Smallwood and Amelia to join them.

"Mr. Smallwood has a wealth of knowledge about all of these things," Georgia whispered as they descended from the carriage. "Sydney attempts to compete with him, but he just hasn't the capacity Mr. Smallwood does." She nodded toward Amelia. "And Amelia isn't a novice either. She can even pronounce some of the names as if she's a native."

The large building stood out from those around simply by its color. Grace couldn't decide whether it was a rose pink, coral, or a pinkish-golden hue, but based on the way the light hit it, it could be any of those.

"Welcome, ladies." Mr. Smallwood stepped forward in his white linen suit, his matching hat tipped just enough to be fashionable. "I hope your morning proved fruitful."

"Very much so, Charles." Georgia placed her hands in his and tossed a look over her shoulder to Grace. "Lady Astley shall not only have a trousseau of practical breathability for this Egyptian climate, but she'll look splendid in the process."

Amelia did nothing to hide her eye roll, but Grace felt certain Georgia was relieved that Amelia had donned a simple white shirtwaist and brown skirt instead of her standard trousers. Georgia had mentioned Amelia's penchant for wearing trousers quite a bit that morning and never with the same admiration Grace felt toward them.

"Wasn't Sydney joining us?" Georgia's attention went from Mr. Smallwood to Amelia.

"I believe he had a rather late night, I'm afraid," Amelia tossed the statement out as if it was nothing serious, but the way her gaze lingered on Georgia's a little longer made Grace wonder at the real reason. The man had consumed a great deal of wine at dinner. Perhaps, that had been the problem?

"No matter." Mr. Smallwood waved toward the museum. "As usual, Sydney will miss out on the delights hidden within these walls. I've been here no less than twenty times and each visit offers new discoveries."

"I. . ." Georgia shook her head and sent a tight smile to Grace. "I wonder if I should see if Sydney is well." She looked toward the carriage.

"I'd leave him to the consequences of his actions, if you asked me." Amelia folded her arms across her chest and frowned. "Like most men in the world, he doesn't deserve your compassion."

"Now, now, Miss Sinclair," Mr. Smallwood crooned out the gentle reprimand. "Let's not step into the private affairs of others, shall we?"

"Private affairs?" Amelia released a humorous laugh. "They're anything but private."

Georgia paled all the more, her gloved hand coming to her throat.

"Amelia." An edge crept into Mr. Smallwood's voice, and Amelia sighed, the tension in her stance gentling.

"I'm sorry, Georgia." She shook her head. "I'm sure you'll do whatever is best, as always."

"Yes." Georgia took a step back. "I need to have our parcels delivered to our rooms anyway, so I can ensure they are placed where they ought." She turned to Grace. "Will you forgive me for abandoning you, my dear Grace?"

"Abandoning?" Mr. Smallwood tsked, his brow creased. "Lady Astley will be with two individuals who are quite happy to lead her into a great discovery of Egyptian history." He offered his arm to Grace, and in contrast to his magnanimous welcome, Amelia's frown produced an opposite response.

Grace slid her arm through Mr. Smallwood's, keeping her smiles for him, since Amelia seemed indifferent to any positivity from her. Or perhaps she just didn't care for attention from another woman. Grace wasn't certain yet.

The matter resolved, Georgia disappeared into the carriage and Grace was left at the steps of the Cairo Museum with two new—and mostly friendly—acquaintances.

"How does she bear it?" Amelia groaned. "I would throttle the man in his sleep if he treated me with as much disregard as he does her. In fact, I'm tempted to do it for her. Insufferable scoundrel." Amelia turned on her heels and marched toward the museum entrance.

Grace adjusted her idea of Amelia Sinclair a little to add "compassion" to the list, a character trait she would not have thought to pair with the woman from their first few meetings. Her general response toward men and her passionate protectiveness of Georgia didn't match the little seductress or indifferent observer from yesterday. Who was she, really?

"Let's not allow this alteration in plans to dampen your visit, Lady Astley." Mr. Smallwood rubbed his white chin and chuckled with the same enthusiasm she imagined Santa Claus possessed. "I feel I can distract you with one step through those doors. I overheard you are quite interested in Egyptology?"

"Yes, I didn't have enough time to properly prepare my reading list before arriving, but I did get through a few books. I read mostly fiction, but some of the stories in Egyptian history come very close to sounding fictional."

"Quite so." He walked with her up the steps to the large wooden double doors of the entrance. "And did anything in particular garner your interest?"

Did he really want a full answer to that question? In her experience, few people wanted a detailed list of all the things to interest Grace from any particular category, so she decided to summarize. "Well, I find the idea of hieroglyphs fascinating and mummies and of course the vast types of artwork and stories, then there is the entire dilemma surrounding King Akhenaten and his lovely Nefertiti."

"Akhenaten?" Mr. Smallwood's brows rose. "Then you should be even happier to learn our dig site is at Tel el-Amarna, the very site of Akhenaten's city."

"Which only piqued my interest the more, you understand."

"Excellent." Mr. Smallwood's grin grew. "I know exactly where to take you."

The doors opened to reveal a two- or three-story entry of white walls and floors. A dome rose in the center of the space with halls stretching out in each direction. White stone balconies from the story above allowed people—or statues—to peer down onto the floor below and gave the space a cavernous feeling.

Sand-colored or dark granite statues stood at points along each wall, in various styles of dress, some wearing pointed headdresses, others with curved. One similarity among most of them was that the hands were fisted at the statue's side, and each figure had its left foot out as if taking a step. Grace asked Mr. Smallwood about it, and his pale eyes glimmered with his grin.

"Very observant, Lady Astley. It is my understanding that each of the pharaohs or religious men portrayed here are holding the Book of the Dead in this hand, a manual to assist him in the afterlife." He guided them down a single corridor away from the center of the building. "Not everyone is certain of the left foot forward idea, but it is consistent with some other cultures. Some say to show the king stepping forward with power, others think it depicts him in motion as if still alive." He shrugged. "I would ask Professor Andrews when you meet him. He may have more information on things than I do. I'm afraid my knowledge is more broad brush strokes than details."

Smaller artifacts were displayed in glass cases. Everything from brooms and kitchenware to weapons and mummification tools. At one point, Mr. Smallwood leaned close and pointed to a beautiful amulet of gold with markings within the gold and in the center a red stone.

"I'll tell you a secret. That is a forgery."

"What?"

He lowered his voice even more. "Professor Andrews is excellent at picking out forgeries, but he's taught me a thing or two. With this one, some of the markings are in the wrong order if you study it closely. It's fascinating, really." His brows lowered with his frown. "And a lucrative business the natives engage in on a regular basis, which makes those of us who are truly trying to locate authentic treasure work all the harder. Nasty way to treat artifacts, if you ask me."

"Have you found anything on the dig so far?"

He sighed. "Not yet, but this is my first season with Sydney and Professor Andrews, and though this dig hasn't been as productive as we'd hoped, I feel our process is very good. I mean to carry on with them again next season."

They rounded a few sarcophagi, the blank faces staring up to the ceiling.

"How did you come to know them?"

"Ah, another excellent question. Sydney and I fought in the Boer War together." He nodded. "Well, I was more of a commander at that time, and Sydney was one of my riflemen. A good shot. Trained him myself." He sniffed as if proud. "We reunited in London last year, and he told me of his plans to return to Egypt, but was searching for someone to help fund the trip. So as I was in need of a new adventure after too much idleness, I took it on, and I'm glad I have, or Sydney would have spent everything on the wrong people."

"He seems to make a great many wrong decisions." The picture of Sydney as an honorable man kept growing dimmer with each passing day. Poor Georgia. Perhaps pretending all was well helped her manage the disappointment of it all?

Grace tossed up a prayer of gratitude for marrying so well.

"Yes." Mr. Smallwood shook his head. "I'm afraid I'll have to find another partner next year if he can't pull himself together. It's an embarrassment really."

Grace started to respond, but the view ahead stole her attention. Towering above them sat the massive statue of a man and woman looking over the room as if holding court. Grace stared up at them, trying to understand the difference here. In some of the paintings and statues she'd already seen, either in passing or in books, the king had been carved or painted as much larger than the queen or his children. She hadn't seen many, except those printed in Weigall's book on Akhenaten, where the partners touched, but here the woman had her arm out as if placed on her husband's back.

"It's difficult not to notice Amenhotep III and his wife, Tiye, isn't it? Some of the largest ever discovered."

"She's the same size as him," Grace whispered.

"Another clever observation." Mr. Smallwood raised his cane as a pointer. "By all accounts, theirs was a shared throne. She held as much power as he, and he let her, so he honored her by displaying his admiration to the world, so to speak."

"As any proud husband should, I think." Grace grinned.

"Quite so, Lady Astley." He tucked his chin in acknowledgement. "And since you are so fond of fiction, I should suspect their union and apparent marital bliss may rival some of the best we have."

"Like?" Some people spouted fictional knowledge in general, but it was a very different matter altogether when specifics were involved.

"Well"—he cleared his throat and leaned back, hands on his cane—"what would you say of the Garths in *Middlemarch*? Or Lucie and Charles in *A Tale of Two Cities*?"

She blinked a few times before nearly drawing the man into a hug. "Excellent examples, Mr. Smallwood. I'm glad to know you enjoy fiction."

"Why of course. Dickens is one of my favorites."

They wove through the cases of mummies, which were a little

horrifying to see up close, speaking of Dickens and Hardy and even a little about Shakespeare. Mr. Smallwood told stories of his lovely wife, who he'd lost while fighting in the Boer; his son, who wasn't as thrifty as his father wished; and his pleasure in studying old stories and "trinkets," as he called them. They continued through aisles of scrolls and rows of glorious wall paintings with colors so fresh they looked as if they'd been painted recently instead of thousands of years ago. Then they reached a familiar visage.

Akhenaten, the heretic pharaoh. His statue looked so different from the other statues she'd seen that it stood out. Instead of the flatter lips and generic face, his face took on more curvature, his lips larger. Even his body, instead of the more square-shaped and stiff alignment of the previous statues, showed imperfections of a protruding lower stomach. Nearby, a relief depicted a picture of Akhenaten and his famed wife Nefertiti as they openly showed affection to their little daughters.

What made him so different?

Grace preferred the paintings and reliefs of a couple openly showing care for each other and their children, but why did this particular pharaoh not only break away from the art style, but also be named the heretic pharaoh for turning away from the historic polytheistic rule of Egypt to enforce a monotheistic one?

"He is a curiosity, isn't he?" Mr. Smallwood murmured, shuffling down a row of funerary goods and leaving Grace to pull out her sketchbook.

She'd almost finished her quick sketch of the statue when she felt a presence beside her. "Nothing is in any order here." Amelia released a deep breath and rolled her gaze to the ceiling. "New Kingdom is mixed with the Middle Kingdom. The Fifth Dynasty is alongside the Seventeenth Dynasty."

"How did you learn all of this?"

Amelia glanced down at Grace's work, her lips crooking. "Not bad." She turned her attention back to the room. "When you live in the middle of archaeology long enough, you either learn it or hate it." She shook her head. "Or both, at times."

"You've been in archaeology a long time?"

"Most of my life." She squinted up at a nearby relief. "Professor Andrews and his wife took me in when I was orphaned as a young child. I think I learned to read hieroglyphs along with my alphabet."

"How fascinating." Grace smiled and placed her sketchbook back in her bag.

"There are times. . ." Her voice trailed off. "And a certain wonder to it all. But I would give anything for one day in an ordinary world of pleasant people and peaceful silence than the—" She shook her head. "You're trying to learn, are you?"

Grace stuffed down her questions at Amelia's vague response and nodded. "I've tried, but it looks too complicated to learn in such a short period of time."

Amelia studied her and gestured toward a glass box where a set of small, oval-shaped stones about the size of Grace's hand lay.

"These are cartouches. They're like"—she waved her hand in the air as if trying to find a word—"nameplates for royalty. And this one in particular is Akhenaten."

Grace wasn't certain what caused Amelia's change of heart, but she'd take advantage of it. She stepped closer to the glass case to get a better view of the cartouche.

"These symbols quite literally mean the Spirit of Aten."

"The sun god disc. The god Akhenaten worshipped as the only god."

Amelia's lips tipped higher. "Been reading, have we?"

"A little." Or more than a little, but having visuals certainly helped with comprehension.

After another pause, Amelia broke apart the symbols to show how each symbol, starting with Aten at the top of the cartouche, represented each word.

"Thank you, Amelia, for the lesson."

Her expression remained neutral. "You are free to learn as readily as anyone else, aren't you?"

The woman nearly brimmed with barely held fury, but in Amelia's simple act of teaching Grace about the hieroglyphs, Grace recognized a difference between Amelia and the deadly Lady Celia. A desire to help. It may have been only a small flicker, but it was there.

Perhaps Grace had been placed in Amelia's life at just this time to keep her from going in the direction of Celia Blackmoore Percy. Perhaps a little kindness could be exactly what this woman, who was much too hardened for her age, needed to see.

Mr. Smallwood called to them from down the corridor, and Grace started to follow when Amelia caught her arm. "Stay clear of Sydney." Her golden-brown gaze held Grace's. "If he finds you agreeable at all, he'll attempt to win you over."

Win her over? The meaning took a moment to make it to comprehension. Heat rose into Grace's cheeks. "I wouldn't worry about that, Miss Sinclair." Grace looked back toward the statue of Amenhotep III and his wife. "Lord Astley and I are not only equals, but friends. I'm as devoted to him as I am certain he is to me."

"We're just pawns in the chess game of the men in our lives, Lady Astley. They use us until we aren't useful anymore." Her lips dipped into a sneer. "The sooner you learn how to play the game, the better for you."

Chapter Seven

By the time the carriage finally stopped in front of the famed pyramids of Giza, Frederick had learned more about Cairo's social connections, Sydney's financial missteps, Georgia's marital disaster, and the Withersby family strife than any woman of his acquaintance could have relayed under the same circumstances.

Timothy Withersby outperformed them all. His ability to switch from light-hearted banter to a detailed explanation of how Sydney Archibald had recklessly depleted Georgia's dowry put the energy of the whirling dervishes to shame. Though there was a sort of desperation in Timothy's behavior, as if he attempted a cry for help without even knowing it.

Frederick's uncle on his mother's side, John Withersby, had never been the sort to lavish praise or mercy. Rising through the ranks of his job as a solicitor, he'd invested money in schemes that had proved successful, raising his family's status through trade, not ancestry, which meant Uncle John always seemed to have something to prove. The youngest of his four children, Timothy and Georgia had felt some buffer from their father's harshness by the protection of a mother and two older brothers, but their mother's death and subsequent marriage of the brothers left Timothy and Georgia exposed to their father's deepening anger.

It had been a house as cold as Frederick's.

Georgia had searched for escape through marriage.

Timothy, through society and "information."

And both seemed to succeed with the efficiency of draining a bottomless glass.

What few words of comfort or guidance Frederick was able to eke into the conversation barely made a pause in Timothy's obfuscation. So when he saw Grace standing at the edge of the Giza plain, her smile spreading with welcome as he approached, he determined to keep her nearby for the rest of their trip. At least he knew the conversation would be interesting. And hopeful, except for those occasions where she mentioned in detail how ancient Egyptians were mummified or the best ways to steal a jewel without being caught. He frowned. Or the most potent poisons.

He shook his head. Thankfully her imagination proved much more dangerous than her intentions, and a small adventure learning about excavation and Egyptian history might provide just the touch of daring she needed to not seek anything else of the mystery or detective nature.

He tipped his hat to Miss Sinclair, who stood nearby, and then searched for anyone else from their party.

"Georgia had to return to the hotel to check on Sydney," Grace answered at his inquiry.

"Who was likely in a drunken stupor still," Miss Sinclair added.

"And Mr. Smallwood had already made plans to meet one of his business friends so he escorted us here, then left for that meeting."

"Well, I'm glad we've come along," Timothy interjected, coming up alongside Frederick and lifting his hat in greeting. "Climbing the pyramid is a perilous endeavor."

As Timothy paired with Miss Sinclair, Frederick offered his arm to Grace and they followed. Any idea that these pyramids were small or insignificant vanished from Frederick's mind. Even from their distance across the plain from the road, they towered tall enough to block the afternoon sunlight, their golden tips jutting up into the blue sky.

"I read that they used to be covered with a limestone casing, like the bit you can see there, so they'd shine like sunlight to anyone who saw them." Grace pointed to the center pyramid, whose top third boasted a distinctively paler hue than its bottom portion. "I think the tallest one is Khufu's pyramid."

"Sultan Hassan took much of the limestone from the pyramids to build his mosque in the 1300s." Amelia tossed the information over her shoulder. "What's a pharaoh to a sultan? I suppose."

Grace slowed her pace enough to allow Timothy and Miss Sinclair some distance ahead of them. She worried her bottom lip, released a sigh, and then tugged at the glove on her hand wrapped through his arm.

"What is it?"

She looked up at him, narrowed her eyes, and then turned back toward the pyramid. "Probably nothing."

"But. . ."

She bit down on her bottom lip again and stopped their walk to face him. "Are most women just pawns to the men in their lives?"

"What?"

"I thought it was just an idea used for villains in books, but Amelia suggested the characteristic was a common occurrence, and I"—she looked up at him—"I suppose you wouldn't tell me if you thought I was a pawn in some vast game of your life, would you?"

He attempted to curb his smile while fighting the urge to throttle Miss Sinclair. Then compassion bled through the annoyance. If she held such a distorted view of men or marriage or both, perhaps there was a painful reason why. It hadn't been so long ago that Frederick had taken a very dim view on a great many things, women's motives included. He sighed, placing his hand over his wife's on his arm. Until Grace.

"If I thought of you in that way, darling, I'd be the last person to admit it to you, don't you think?"

"You're probably right." She looked ahead, the lines on her brow deepening.

Hmm, what could he do to assure her, because if he didn't try, her imagination was likely to take her down roads he'd never wish her to travel. "But since you are training to be a detective, I suppose you could come up with the answer yourself."

They resumed their walk, her chin bobbling with a nod. "That's an excellent idea."

"Because there are always clues to the truth, of course."

"Exactly." Her nod became more emphatic, and the sparkle returned to her eyes. "And if you were using me like a pawn, I'm afraid you would be a very poor chess player."

He chuckled. "Why do you think that?"

"Well, you tried to talk me out of marrying you in the first place. That doesn't seem like a game player at all."

He pinched his lips together and nodded with as much seriousness as he could muster.

"And marrying me led to you almost being killed three times and blackmailed once."

Not exactly the way of it, but if it helped her come to the proper conclusion of his undying devotion to her, he'd hold his tongue.

"And you chose to come to Egypt for *my* sake when we could have waited and only traveled to Italy, and I can't think of one benefit you could obtain from coming to Egypt when you'd rather stay and make renovations to Havensbrook."

He quelled the desire to touch her face and simply tilted his head in response. "So, detective, what is your conclusion?"

A smile played across her lips. "That I'm rather dangerous to have around, my lord."

He laughed, and her lips tipped wider as she continued chattering on in her happy state of mystery finding, whether a mystery was present or not.

"Amelia Sinclair must have had a very poor sampling of men in her life to make such a bold statement to someone she barely knows."

Bitterness has a tendency to speak in a loud voice.

"But after my little investigation, of which I only took a small sampling of clues, I feel certain that my heart and my future are in very good hands."

He gave her hand a squeeze. "There's my clever girl."

She stopped and beamed up at him. "I would kiss you right now if we weren't in public, but alas, I'll have to make up for it tonight."

He raised a glance heavenward in silent gratitude for a wife who loved so liberally. If her imagination had to run the same course as her heart, he would bear the "clue finding" without one complaint. His shoulders dropped. Well, perhaps with a rare complaint. Especially when near-death instances followed some of her "investigations."

They continued forward, the massive pyramids growing in triune grandeur as they approached.

Ruins led the way forward, remnants of a valley temple and smaller tombs. The sphinx rose above the ruins as a welcome, or deterrent to continue, but continue they did. The sunlight glowed with less brilliance as late afternoon waned but created a spectacle of varied colors unseen in earlier parts of the day.

Though he had planned this trip for Grace, he couldn't deny the fascinating majesty mixed with ancient images that Egypt already introduced in only their two days so far.

"I expect you'll want to climb to the top?" Amelia held her hat and looked upward to the pinnacle of the Great Pyramid.

"What about inside?" Grace asked, her gaze following a few tourists who disappeared behind a torch-wielding guide into a tunnel near the bottom of the pyramid.

"Good night, inside?" Timothy grimaced and looked down at his suit. "I didn't wear my climbing clothes and have little interest in traversing the depths of a bat-riddled, stifling corridor, thank you."

Grace bit down on her bottom lip and looked back at the entrance.

"If you don't wish to go, Timothy, I'll pay a guide to take us." Frederick looked to Grace, and her smile flashed wide.

"What?" Amelia barked out the word, her eyes wide. Perhaps it was the first unguarded expression he'd witnessed from her. She looked at Grace. "*You* plan to go?"

"Of course." She nodded, slipping past Amelia to move nearer the entrance. "Why come all this way to merely observe from the outside when you can actually enter a tomb that's over four thousand years old?"

"Are you serious?" Timothy gasped, looking from Grace's retreating form back to Frederick, who took a few steps in Grace's direction.

Amelia followed alongside him. "You're. . .you're going to let her do it?"

"Why would I hinder her?" He shrugged a shoulder. "She's capable, and I'd much rather share the experience with her than have it on my own."

"But. . .but. . ." Amelia stumbled through her response. "She's a countess?"

"Yes, and a curious tourist, like any other tourist." He slowed his pace to match Amelia's. "My wife has an exuberance that is infectious, and a great deal of imagination, not to mention heart. Why would I keep her from living all the good or fascinating things in life, while I have the power to give them to her?"

"How very magnanimous of you." Her eyes narrowed with the suspicion he'd come to expect. "I suppose money can cover a multitude of vices, can't it?"

The poor woman truly had no concept of a healthy relationship between a man and woman, did she? A good, wholesome shared camaraderie between equals.

"We all have vices, Miss Sinclair, and no amount of money eliminates them." He turned his attention back to Grace, who was speaking with one of the guides, likely attempting to use her very poor Arabic to do so. "And if my wife's greatest vices are an overactive imagination and a desire to throw protocol to the wind in order to climb through a pyramid, I consider myself a fortunate man. I'm afraid my past vices have not been as benign nor as forgivable. But, I might add, the right person sees beyond all that." He took a few steps, then turned back. "You're welcome to join us, if you like."

She followed, almost as if entranced, remaining mostly quiet during the climb. And climb, it was. From the "newer" ninth-century tunnel into the original, which required crouching to continue forward. This was followed by a large open passage called the Grand Gallery, which had an incline so sharp on the hand-hewn stairs that Frederick had to keep Grace from tumbling down backward twice and Amelia once. And within the vast silence of the tall-ceilinged corridor came the night noises of the bats above.

Grace took it all as a marvel, whispering little statements like, "This is the perfect place to hide treasure"; "Don't you think it resembles a massive vault much more than a tomb?"; and "Can you imagine how many people died building this colossus?"

The heat and air inside pressed upon them as they walked or crawled by torchlight through the ancient space. To think they were near the center of the monstrous piece of architecture, surrounded on all sides by meters of stone, inspired the strangest sense of both awe and trepidation.

"Are there any traps for this tomb?" Grace asked from ahead, her breaths coming in bursts. "I've read about them, especially in Rider's books, but wondered if they were only the creative expressions of an adventurous imagination?"

Silence followed for a moment, and then Amelia responded, her words echoing in the darker recesses of the Grand Gallery's shadowed ceiling. "Most tombs have traps to deter robbers."

"What sorts?"

Frederick thought Amelia might not answer, it took her so long to reply. "Carefully placed rocks that fall on the person when triggered, shafts placed in locations where the robber can easily fall into them, or a great deal of debris to block the corridors."

"Oh." Clear disappointment in Grace's response.

"And of course, curses." Humor tinged Amelia's words. "Things like horrid deaths, no offspring, lose your way to the afterlife, and all of your funerary goods destroyed."

"I doubt those created a great deterrent, did they, Miss Sinclair?" Frederick interjected into the massive stillness around them.

"From the lack of ability to locate an intact royal tomb, Lord Astley, I would say the thieves may have already known their eternal fates and decided they'd enjoy the current life to the fullest as they waited for the future one."

"How horrible to live as if the actions of this life don't impact the other." Grace tried to look back at them but almost toppled again. She quickly righted herself. "Of course, we'd all be in terrible trouble if Christ hadn't taken our many horrible actions on Himself so that we don't have to worry about the curses." She chuckled and then stopped. "Do you think it's wrong to mention one religion while climbing through a tomb for a very different one?"

Frederick would have laughed if the thick air didn't require focus on breathing.

"I suppose since God is everywhere, anyway, He doesn't mind," came her happy reply to her own question, and then they finally reached a summit.

With only the torch from a guard before and behind, they crawled on hands and knees through the final passageway to enter the king's chamber. Unlike the rest of the pyramid, which was built of limestone from the surrounding plain, the pharaoh built this rectangular room of granite. On the far back wall of the room stood a sarcophagus that was said to have held the body of King Khufu, the purported possessor of the pyramid and ruler of the land at the time.

"How remarkable to think we are at the very heart of the pyramid!" Grace said, her voice echoing against the granite walls. Then she turned to him. "I must say, Frederick, that I prefer European and American means of burial over these. Though it's incredibly grand, it's also incredibly lonely. And there's something a little comforting in the fact of being buried next to someone who loves you, even if your soul isn't really there anyway."

She squeezed his hand and walked over to the sarcophagus.

Amelia moved to his side, her gaze fixed on Grace as if watching an exotic creature. "She really believes all that."

"All what?"

She looked away from him and back at Grace. "I knew someone who believed in God and faith too. A long time ago. I. . .I didn't realize there were other people like her."

He studied the woman's pensive profile, taking in her declaration with a sudden, sobering awareness. Perhaps Frederick and Grace had come to Egypt on a whim, but just as Frederick had been learning since Grace entered his life, God meant their plans as something very different indeed.

It was gone. Where could it possibly be?

Grace checked her dressing table again and rummaged through her clothes closet. She even dug into the couch cushion where she'd napped earlier in the afternoon, followed closely by an afternoon romantic interlude with her dashing hero, but the bracelet wasn't anywhere to be found.

"What on earth are you doing?"

Grace nearly hit her head on the underside of a nearby table at the sound of Frederick's voice. Of course she likely looked ridiculous in her dressing gown, crawling around on all fours, but some things could not be helped. Not when her precious bracelet was involved.

"My bracelet is missing."

Frederick crouched down to her side and offered his hand, his brow creased. "Your bracelet?"

She slipped her hand into his, and he helped her rise. "Yes, the one you bought me in London on the eve of our trip." She rubbed her wrist and glanced around the room again. "If you recall, I wore it every day we traveled because I wanted to keep it near me just in case we were forced to get into a life raft to flee a sinking ship or some other disaster which might cause us to lose our luggage. I only chose not to wear it the past two days because we were somewhat settled for the time being."

He stared at her a moment, and his lip twitched before he answered, "And you couldn't find it this evening before dinner?."

"No, and I chose the blue gown for the very reason it would match the sapphires in the bracelet." She nodded up to him. "You see? My fashion sense is growing by very slow degrees."

"Let's not worry about it just yet." He tugged her to him and placed a kiss on her cheek. "Perhaps after a good night's sleep and some help from Ellie, you'll discover it in the morning. But if not, we'll alert the hotel staff to keep an eye out." His thumb traced a gentle trail down her cheek before he led her to their bedroom. "I'm certain with all the excitement of the day, it's simply been misplaced, and when we pack our things for the journey tomorrow, we'll find it."

She didn't correct him. Yes, there were times when she was forgetful, but not about this. When had she last remembered seeing it? On the train? Yes, she remembered admiring the way the sun glinted off of it through the train window. And then it had caught on her dress sleeve when they'd gotten into the carriages to start for Shepheard's.

But then. . .she couldn't remember. In fact, the last time she remembered seeing it was their first day in Cairo. Right after they'd returned from helping the little falsely accused theif in the street. Grace's breath caught.

The falsely accused thief? Cold splashed through her. What if the young girl hadn't been falsely accused at all? Grace shook her head. No, surely not. She would have noticed someone stealing a bracelet from her very own arm, wouldn't she? Though the pickpockets in Oliver Twist were supposedly very good at their jobs.

"We should get some sleep." Frederick drew back the mosquito netting surrounding their bed so Grace could slip beneath the blankets. "Our entourage is set to leave by lunch so we can make it to the dig site before nightfall."

He secured the netting back around Grace's side of the bed, checked the lock on the door of their room, and joined her in bed. She snuggled up to his side, as she did every evening, and placed her cheek against his chest, often falling asleep to the soft thrum of his heartbeat. It was amazing how soothing and relaxing the sound and position could be. He never seemed to mind. Even if they rolled away from each other throughout the night, or even in those moments where she accidentally kicked him, they'd begin this way, with his arm around her and her head resting on his chest.

"Do you think Sydney is financially strained?"

Frederick's chest descended with a long exhalation. "I've heard he's mishandled the money he gained when he married Georgia, and some of his current investments are not doing well."

Grace smoothed a palm over his chest. "Then that explains why she questioned me on our first day here. She wanted to know if I'd kept any control over my finances. It seemed, she was concerned I'd have the same fate as her, but I assured her that you have been very good to go over finances with me."

"I wouldn't have the fund without you, and I'll not take that lightly. Besides, we are equals." He covered her hand with his, holding her palm against his chest. "I'm grateful for the money you provided so we can save Havensbrook. Your opinion matters to me because *we* are the future of our home."

For such a wonderful answer, she kissed the spot on his chest nearest her lips. "Even though I am not equal to you in life experience, which I feel certain is extremely helpful in situations like dinner at Shepheard's Hotel in Egypt. When Mr. Smallwood started speaking of how much England has helped secure the modernization of Egypt, you were so clever in taking up defense of the native culture here." She sighed and buried closer to him. "You must have learned so much when you lived in India. About different cultures and peoples. All I know of them is from books, and I don't believe *The Jungle Book* gives an accurate accounting of things." She yawned. "And animals don't talk."

"Not our language at any rate." She felt his grin more than saw it. "And there are beauties worth preserving in every culture. I understand the desire for improvement, but some people force change and lose good things in the process."

"You are such a good man." She sighed, allowing her eyes to

drift closed. "I'm so very glad you are not like Sydney. We are so well suited, even if I am distractible and think in fiction. I don't feel as though you think less of me for it."

"We are well suited. Perhaps, God help me, I needed a little more fictional thinking in my life."

"You did!" Her eyes shot wide and she pushed up from her sleeping position, hand poised on his chest as she peered down at him. "You lived in a very dreary nonfictional world, so I brought you whimsy."

His expression softened, and he cupped her cheek. "You brought much more than that, dear Grace. A very nonfictional sort of love I'd craved for a long time. So if you are distractible or whimsical or whatever else, I know you have a very good head and an even better heart."

"That was a very lovely thing to say." Her eyes stung just a little so she lowered her lips to his. "Much better than any book."

He chuckled, and she returned to her position, nestled up against him. "I feel certain Mrs. Casper must have been excellent in theatricals when she was younger, but. . .there's something odd about her and Amelia's relationship."

"What do you mean?" His voice took on a sleepy quality.

"I don't know." She closed her eyes and succumbed to another yawn. "I don't think they like each other very much. Amelia kept glaring at her."

"Perhaps her niece was attempting to get the woman to stop talking about whatever curse was placed on the last archaeologists she met who had mistreated a mummy."

A little shiver traveled up Grace's spine at the thought, though it wasn't necessarily a scared shiver. More like a shiver of intense expectation. Like. . .Christmas, only with mummies.

"Do you truly think there are such things as mummies' curses?"

His chest trembled with a chuckle. "Do you?"

"No." She smoothed her cheek against his warm skin. "But that doesn't mean I don't imagine them being real every once in a while."

"Of course."

"It's not difficult to do with such a group as we have here, is it? I believe the only people who really seemed to like each other at all were you and me, and Georgia and Timothy. And Mr. Smallwood seemed to generally like everyone." She blinked her eyes open. "Where was Timothy this evening anyway?"

"He'd gone to collect someone from the station. A friend from America, I think."

"Oh." Grace's eyes fluttered closed again. "It certainly takes a lot of people to find a mummy."

The room grew quiet, and the sound of Frederick's breathing created a soft lullaby to her busy mind. There were so many things she needed to write in her journal in the morning so she wouldn't forget, and she needed to rise early so she could investigate the garden in search of flamingos since she'd not had a chance to locate them yet.

She wasn't certain if she'd drifted off to sleep or not, but she turned on her other side with her body positioned toward the windows and the balcony door. A sudden rustling slipped into the rhythm of Frederick's breathing and disrupted her mental attempt to recollect where she'd placed her missing bracelet. She almost ignored the sound, until it happened again. Closer.

Pinpricks of awareness skittered across her shoulders and up her neck into her tingly scalp. She could almost feel someone's eyes on her. For a second, she pinched her own eyes tighter, determined to ignore the sensation as just another exaggeration of her imagination. It had happened so many times before, she ought to be able to ignore it. But this time, the sound didn't go away. . .and a quiet thump followed.

Frederick had locked their bedroom door.

Elliott's room was just through the sitting room, and he was a light sleeper.

It really was no good to talk about mummies' curses just before bed.

She swallowed through her dry throat and opened her eyes just a little. Air congealed in her lungs at the sight. Poised in the balcony doorway, haloed in moonlight from behind, stood a dark-robed figure staring directly at her.

Chapter Eight

A sudden shift in the mattress followed by a whimpered gasp shook Frederick from his sleep. He blinked open his eyes and looked in Grace's direction. The mosquito netting softened the room into a hazy white, and the moon's glow only added to its otherworldly hue. Grace was turned away from him, her body quivering against his, and then he saw it. A dark figure standing in the doorway of the balcony, its unmoving stance jolting him full awake.

Almost in synchrony, he shot from the bed, Grace at his side. The figure flinched, and Frederick dove headfirst into the mosquito netting along with his wife. The netting wrapped around him like a spider's web, restricting his movements, so in his attempt to vault from the bed, his legs became entangled and he crashed to the floor with Grace falling directly on top of him as the netting popped free from its fasteners and fell to the floor with them.

They were sure to be killed now, like flies awaiting the spider's sting.

"I have a corner of it," Grace called. "I just need to—"

"Here let me—"

"My leg is twisted in the—"

"That's my arm—"

"I can help you," came the unfamiliar voice from the dark

figure. A young voice. Childlike, even.

Frederick froze. Grace stilled at his side, her foot pressed into the back of his knee. Through the mesh netting, a pair of strange pale eyes met his. Black hair framed the face, but now, as his eyes adjusted to the dimness, he made out the young face, and the eyes were not as dark as expected. A girl.

Without waiting for Frederick to regain his voice, the girl went to work untangling them from the netting, her dark hair long and loose around her face.

"Zahra?" came his wife's cry. "I'm so glad you're not a ghost."

The girl's head turned away from Frederick and her lips tipped ever so slightly. "No, Sitt, I am no *efreet*." Her dark gaze came back to Frederick, searching his face with an apology in her pale eyes. "Sitt Haree, she save me. I will serve her."

Frederick finally detangled himself and stood, grabbing for his nightshirt to cover his chest from the girl's curious eyes. Moving between the girl and the netting, he helped Grace to stand.

"What are you doing here?" Grace asked as Frederick moved past her to the balcony. The moon shone so brilliantly, Frederick could almost make out some of the colors in the floral bushes below them in the garden.

"As I said, I will serve you."

Frederick turned from the doorway. "How on earth did you get into our room? We're three floors up."

"I am a good climber." Her white teeth shone in the moon's glow. "I saw Sitt Haree standing on the balcony and waited for the sun to fall before climbing. It took me two days to find you."

"What do you mean by serve me?" Grace shot Frederick a wide-eyed look. "You are a child."

"You climbed up three levels on the outside of the building?" Frederick stared down at the girl's bare feet. "How?"

Her toes wiggled. "When you are a street child for years, Saiyid, you learn many things."

Saiyid? Yes, he'd heard it before. It meant something generic like "sir" or "lord." He turned on the room light just as a knock came to their bedroom door.

"Forgive me, sir, but are you all right?"

Frederick released a long sigh and unbolted the door, then drew it open to reveal Elliott and a wide-eyed Ellie—hair in wraps with her robe pinched to her neck—by his side. Frederick met Elliott's gaze and, after ensuring Grace had donned her own robe, waved the two bewildered servants into the bedchamber. "Our unexpected midnight guest."

Ellie gasped and Elliott's brow rose to his hairline. "The street girl?"

"Who happened to scale the outside wall and find her way to our balcony door."

"Good heavens!" This from Ellie who retreated a step as if the girl would sprout claws of some sort and attack everyone.

Now that Frederick could examine the girl by the electric lights, his annoyance ebbed slightly. She wore a tattered robe of sorts, and her hair lay in a tangled mess around her shoulders. Scratches marked one side of her face, as if from fingernails or perhaps from her climb. And her narrow shoulders stood to attention as if she was either preparing to fight or flee. How many times had she been forced to do either?

"I suppose the real question, Zahra, is why did you steal my bracelet?"

All three of the other adults turned toward Frederick's wife, whose flushed cheeks and bright eyes either hinted to her uncommon anger or a dangerous idea. To be honest, he was hoping for the former.

"No, Sitt Haree. I am no thief." The girl shook her head and scanned each of the other faces, before turning back to Grace with a slight shrug. "I mean, I steal food before, but not such things as your bracelet. No."

Grace seemed uncertain how to continue, and if he knew his wife, she was desperately hoping the girl was telling the truth.

Frederick took a turn. "So you didn't come to our room to steal more things, Zahra?"

"I tell you, Saiyid. I came to serve the Sitt. I can help." Her eyes widened. "I speak both language of English and Arabic. I know how to listen to get information." She waved toward the balcony door. "I can climb."

"And what of your orphanage? Will the police come fetch you again?"

"They will not look for me." Her body gave the tiniest flinch at his question. "I am a street child again."

Grace stepped forward. "Why is that?"

"I run away. They would marry me to an old man. That's why the police came before." She sighed. "I escape during my beating to find you. The old man not want me after I bite him."

And now Frederick noticed the red welts on her arms. Where else did those scars hide?

"If I can serve you for food and shelter, I won't have to be like a street child." She fastened those large eyes on Frederick. "I eat little. And I learn fast. I can fetch and carry and hide when I need to."

Frederick felt Grace's gaze burrowing into the side of his head, and truth be told, he didn't have the heart to toss her out into the street in the middle of the night. So what was to be done? He drew in a breath and gestured with his chin toward the sitting room. The whole group followed.

"It is the middle of the night, and I don't care to continue this conversation, so here is what we will do." Frederick gestured toward one door. "Mr. Elliott sleeps there, and he is a very light sleeper." He pointed to the small couch by the window. "You may sleep here tonight until we can decide what to do with you." He held the girl's gaze, forcing as much warning into his expression as he could. "Sitt Haree and I will have our door bolted, as will Mr. Elliott and Miss Miller. If when we awake, you are gone and have taken any of our belongings with you, we will find you and not be so gracious."

Her little lips puckered.

"Otherwise, we will have a clearer answer for you in the morning." Frederick surveyed the others. "If any of you have other ideas, let's leave those to the morning as well."

After Ellie had provided a blanket for the girl and Grace had given her one of her own nightgowns, which nearly swallowed the tiny child whole, Frederick ushered Elliott into their bedroom with Grace. As the two men worked to replace the mosquito netting, Frederick nodded toward his friend. "I'm sorry to lay this at your feet, Elliott, but do keep an ear out, won't you?"

"Yes, sir." The valet's lips twitched. "Though she doesn't have the makings of a thief, in my opinion, sir."

"No, I don't think so either." Frederick nodded. "And you would know what to look for."

Grace shifted her attention to Elliott. "It's not quite fair that everyone in the room knows of Elliott's former escapades, and I'm left in the dark." She looked over at Elliott with narrowed eyes. "Though knowing you were once a thief is an excellent bit of information. Have you ever read *Oliver Twist*, by any chance?"

Frederick squeezed his eyes closed to keep his chuckle under admirable control. Why was he surprised at this point that his wife rarely responded in a typical way about anything?

"No, my lady. I don't think I have."

"You ought to, Elliott." Grace walked over to the balcony and looked out, trying to sort out just how Zahra made it to their room. "But since you're a former thief, I am curious. Your perspective could become quite useful, especially in relation to my missing bracelet."

Frederick caught Elliott's gaze as they finished restoring the netting into the hooks on the ceiling. "A subject which we can discuss in the morning."

"Indeed, sir." Elliott grinned and walked out the door.

Frederick peeked around the corner of the doorway to see Zahra curled into a little ball beneath the blankets. She was a petite thing and thin. Frightfully thin.

With a deep breath, he closed the door and bolted it behind him.

"I cannot even imagine scaling that wall," came Grace's quiet response from the balcony. "Of course, I scaled the lattice back home when I was younger so that the governess wouldn't see the state of my clothing after a day of playing with the village children, but nothing like that." She turned those large eyes on him as he flipped the overhead light off and moved toward the bed. "Do you think she is so desperate?"

"I think time will tell." He removed his shirt and drew back the netting, returning to the comfortable position he'd been jerked from only a half hour before. "If she waits around long enough."

Grace took her time joining him, her thoughts clearly trying to work out the whole situation, but at last she took up residence in her usual position: cheek against his shoulder and palm over his chest. It was one of his favorite moments of the day, feeling her all soft and warm pressed against his side.

His eyes had just started to drift closed when Grace stirred just a bit.

"If she is so desperate, it would be rather heartless to leave her on the street."

He released a long stream of air through his nose but didn't reply.

"And she seems rather clever, doesn't she? I imagine she could learn new things quickly, so having her around might prove very fortunate, assuming she's not a thief."

"Let's discuss it in the morning," he murmured, attempting to make his voice sound even sleepier than he was.

Grace pressed in closer, touching a kiss to the place where she rested her cheek. "I imagine Ellie could teach her how to do a few lady's maid things." Grace yawned. "Wouldn't that be helpful on our journey into the desert?"

Her ability to fall asleep while talking was staggering.

"We can't send her back to be beaten." She nuzzled her nose into his skin and sighed. "It's all very *Oliver Twist*, isn't it?"

With a hum of something unintelligible, everything grew quiet.

Frederick stared at the ceiling, listening to the night sounds and replaying all the events of the day. They'd entered something unusual among the cast of characters in his cousins' lives in Egypt, and he wasn't too comfortable with the idea that he'd brought Grace into the middle of it.

If Zahra proved to be as genuine and ingenious as she appeared to be, perhaps an extra set of eyes would be exactly what he needed.

Zahra was still on the couch when Grace checked first thing in the morning, so after a rather intense discussion with Frederick in regards to the biblical importance of taking care of orphans— even possible thieves—they decided to keep Zahra with them as a companion of sorts for Grace. Ellie didn't appreciate the idea, but since she had to leave, she really had little reason to argue, so with quiet (and somewhat annoyed) resolve, she gave Zahra a few lessons on tending to frocks, styling hair (though Grace could mind her own hair), and other tasks that Ellie felt Zahra should know.

Elliott kept a steely watch on the girl, though Grace couldn't find anything of concern about her, except for the way her skin barely seemed to cover her ribs. Grace had insisted on a bath for

Zahra, which only revealed more of how little flesh she had covering her small body. She did have the most beautiful, thick black hair, especially when it was clean, and Grace kept getting caught in those strange, greenish-gray eyes of hers. They held knowledge beyond her years. Pain even, but mostly, well, gratitude. . .and curiosity. She seemed to absorb everything going on around her, but those eyes hinted to a possible parentage beyond her Egyptian roots.

There was little time to attempt to unearth this knowledge, with packing and planning happening so quickly. Sydney Archibald urged everyone into a hurried fashion, his patience as thin as his hairline, though Grace felt certain at one point or other he had sported a very nice swath of golden-brown hair.

At Ellie's clever suggestion, they sent a hotel staff member to fetch some suitable clothes for the girl in order for her to look the part of a serving girl instead of a street urchin.

They were to leave soon after breakfast, and if Grace wasn't smart about her time, she'd never have a chance to take a photograph of a flamingo. She wrote a quick note for Frederick and left it in their room, then alerted Zahra of her plans, because Ellie was off finalizing her own packing and Elliott was likely with Frederick. The girl took the notice to stay in the room quite soberly, so Grace snatched up her treasured camera and slipped out the door.

She'd barely made it halfway down the hallway when the sound of raised voices paused her steps. A door nearby stood slightly ajar, allowing sounds from the room to carry out into the hallway. Clearly the people arguing had no idea their conversation had escaped, and a bump in the carpeted floor proved the reason the door hadn't fastened all the way. Grace should have kept walking. It was the proper thing to do. And if she'd only continued at the pace she'd begun, she would never have overheard the phrases she did that made her stop altogether, but just as she made it to the door, a woman said, "I could strangle the both of you and not feel an ounce of remorse right now. How dare you bring him here!"

Did that maleficent voice belong to Georgia Archibald?

"How dare I?" came a male's response. "I dare because I'm watching my sister waste away in a loveless marriage, and I'm determined to rescue her."

Timothy. But of whom were they speaking? Hadn't Timothy been off to the train station last evening to collect a long-time friend? Grace moved a step closer.

"Rescue me?" A humorless laugh erupted. "How do you propose Trent Anderson can rescue me? I am a *married* woman!"

"Married to a man who flaunts his dalliances as much as his false money," he replied with as much venom. "I hate him, Georgia. And I hate seeing what his heartlessness is doing to you. I won't stand by any longer."

"I cannot believe you!" Her voice broke. "Bringing Trent here only makes things worse for me. Don't you understand? I loved him once. I would have given anything to be with him, but his parents wouldn't allow it. Now, to flaunt what I might have had in front of me? How could you?"

"I'm doing it so you will leave Sydney and start really living your life," Timothy answered, his voice lower as if he'd drawn closer to her. "The only thing you love about this place is that precious village of yours. And you can flee to America. Start afresh. I don't think Trent has ever stopped loving you."

Grace covered her mouth to keep her breaths quiet. What on earth was she overhearing? A philandering Sydney? An unrequited romance from the past? A brother who was attempting to break up a marriage? This sounded much too fictional to be real. She gave herself a little pinch to make sure she hadn't lost herself in a daydream again.

"Do you truly think anyone in our society will judge my actions fairly, Timothy? Regardless of what Sydney has done, I will be the one who is destroyed in the end no matter which choice I make, and I would never bring Trent down with me." A sob shook from the other side of the room. "A widow will receive mercy. But a woman who abandoned even the most base man will not find the same compassion, Timothy."

"Georgia." The pain lacing his one word nearly brought Grace to tears. "I will not continue to watch you hurt. Trent could take you away from it all."

A noise to Grace's left drew her attention to Amelia Sinclair standing on the other side of the doorframe, one of her golden brows arched high. "Chess games and all that?"

Grace frowned and pulled her camera into her chest. How had Miss Sinclair slipped up so quietly, and how long had she been standing in that position? Without a response, Grace turned and walked down the hall toward the grand staircase, her pulse hammering in her ears. Oh, how she wish she'd brought a few copies of her Sherlock Holmes books, but she hadn't expected to need mystery-solving inspiration on her honeymoon. Her eyes popped wide. But she *had* slipped *Mr. Bazalgette's Agent* into her trunks along with some romance novels, as well as a few Dorcas Dene mysteries. Perhaps she wasn't so ill-equipped for a mystery after all.

Just in case one happened upon them, of course.

With lighter steps, she made her way to the gardens in back of the grand hotel. Already, the heat of the day brushed against her face and had her giving a little tug to the high-collared blouse of her dress. Those lovely white tea dresses with the open neckline that Ellie had packed at Grace's insistence would suit this weather much better than a choking collar. And all the new things Georgia had encouraged her to buy as well. Her lips tipped a little higher. Once they made it to the desert, perhaps she could convince Frederick of the virtues of her wearing the bicycle trousers she'd packed.

Of course he'd agree once he saw the sense of it.

Even though she knew the sun was the exact same sun that shone in England, its rays appeared more brilliant here. The sky seemed bluer. And the greenery of the garden bloomed with more vibrancy than she recalled from her past in England or America. Of course the only season she'd experienced in England so far had been winter, so an accurate comparison was likely impossible at the moment.

But as she stepped into the garden, she felt very much as if she'd fallen down her own little rabbit hole into a wonderland of lush greens and brilliant reds and birds of varied type and color. She found an excellent sitting spot on the grass and remained perfectly still, watching the birds with her camera at the ready, but her mind still buzzed with thoughts of the overheard conversation. If Sydney was such a scoundrel, why didn't Georgia stay in England as many other wives seemed to do when their husbands traveled? At least then she wouldn't have to bear witness to her husband's betrayal.

Grace's heart pinched at the thought. What a terrible thing to witness! She couldn't even imagine what sort of pain it would feel like to discover her dear Frederick in a passionate embrace with another woman. Heat branched through her chest into her cheeks. No wonder women flew into rages over such things. Grace looked down at her white-knuckled grip on her camera and gave her head a little shake.

Frederick was not Sydney Archibald.

He adored her and showed his adoration in many wonderfully appealing ways. And she'd already listed very clever clues to prove his devotedness without even delving into the extremely romantic ones.

She cleared her throat and blinked out of her thoughts to find a very strange bird staring at her. Its long legs took up most of its white body and a black stripe slid from just above its eye back to a long feather, almost like an extended eyebrow.

Grace grinned at the creature and steadied her camera, taking a photograph or two.

The bird tilted its head as if examining her as much as she examined it, those strange yellow eyes holding a wealth of curiosity. Grace lowered her camera and smiled.

"Have you ever felt like you were living inside a story?"

The bird's head twitched, its long neck curling back.

"Well, I feel like I am, and I know a great deal about stories." Her smile fell, and she sighed. "I'm afraid something bad is getting ready to happen. I know this because it always happens at the beginning of a story. It's what makes the story worth reading. And I hope it's not too bad, because I've met such lovely people so far." She nodded. "But I'm at least happy for one thing."

The bird blinked as if waiting for her response.

"I brought some of the right books to help us along."

Chapter Nine

The carriage came to a jolting halt not far from the Nile. Grace had been watching the winding river as it weaved in and out of view outside her window, barely keeping her grin under control. The Nile! She'd imagined seeing it a dozen times but had only expected to travel via the written word. Now here she was, in the very flesh! Oh, how she wished Ellie could have come along, but she had left on a northbound train only a short while before their own train had departed south.

And perhaps with Ellie's general dislike of boats and water, she wouldn't have enjoyed following the Nile at all. But the river wound in fascinating turns and swells, narrow at some points and extremely wide at others.

Of course Grace had seen paintings of the Nile done by Florence Nightingale in her famous book about her travels, but not even those lovely replicas could do the actual river justice. Much wider than she'd anticipated and framed in by foliage and structures so foreign to her eyes, everything about the scene exuded the sense that Grace had walked into a dream. An exotic dream.

She'd had no chance to meet the mysterious Trent Andersen, for breakfast was served in their rooms to ensure they were able to leave as soon as possible. Of course she'd told Frederick of the entire conversation, including the uneasy appearance of Miss Sinclair, and though her husband wasn't as detective-minded as she, he found the coincidence unsettling. Well, she supposed he did. His brow furrowed and his lips pinched to one side enough to form a dimple in his cheek. She'd only recently discovered the dimple and had the overwhelming desire to kiss it whenever it emerged. Lucky for Frederick's peace of mind, her current distraction with a mystery prevented her falling prey to her own temptation.

Evidently Timothy and Mr. Anderson were coming a few hours behind due to arranging the transport of last minute supplies, but Grace wondered if it was Georgia's way to keep her distance from her former beau.

Grace's heart fluttered. When this many mysterious people came together, certainly something tragic would ensue. She gave her head a little nod and smoothed her skirt down to where her palm felt the hard edge against her leg. Her knife. She may not have mastered pistols yet, but she'd become excellent at throwing knives. Mr. Reams' lessons certainly paid off. Even Elliott had seemed impressed—well, more impressed than Frederick, who'd looked a bit paler and blinked repeatedly at the four knives she'd sunk into the target.

Perhaps he wasn't quite used to knife-wielding wives.

They'd spent a few hours traveling south via rail to a city called El Minya, where they traded their train car for carriages that would take them to their residence on the outskirts of the city. Grace supposed the refurbished house Georgia referred to as the Alfurn House was to be a real residence, though she'd envisioned sleeping inside ruins of an ancient tomb or in a desolated monastery, staring up at the sky from their roofless room.

When they reached their destination, a house unlike any she'd ever seen met her gaze.

"Welcome to the Alfurn House," Georgia announced, descending from her carriage and looking up at the structure. Sydney followed, with Mr. Smallwood at his side.

It stood two-stories tall with a covered entrance hanging over an arched double door opening. The house was built of mudbrick, shaped like a large box with a flat roof, and Grace wondered if it resembled the homes of biblical times, for it did look ancient.

"One of Sydney's acquaintances renovated the place and allows us to use it while we are in Egypt," Georgia continued, gesturing for them to follow. "You'll find it's quite comfortable." She shot them a look. "We would not have you spend your honeymoon in some tent in the wilderness when we have such accommodations."

There was an exuberance in her voice, a brightness that didn't seem to match her eyes. Was it due to the arrival of Mr. Anderson? Or did she truly love this house more than the opulent hotel they'd left? According to some of the most recent detective stories Grace had just finished, she'd guess the former rather than the latter.

Though there could be some respite for Georgia out here. Fewer women for Sydney to meet.

Mrs. Casper left her carriage and moved directly to the doors of the house, her oversized blue gown swaying around her. A far-off look, which Grace was beginning to notice as a regular expression on Mrs. Casper's face, remained intact as the woman entered the house.

Perhaps seeing the future kept one in a constant state of awe? Dread? Grace rolled her eyes heavenward. Of course Mrs. Casper couldn't see the future, but something incredibly odd about her otherworldly countenance remained, as if she was entranced.

"Welcome back to El Minya."

The entreaty came from their right, where a tall man in some sort of uniform that reminded Grace of a constable approached. He removed his corresponding hat to reveal a wealth of blond hair to match his abundant mustache. Beside him walked another man, younger and in a less decorated uniform.

"Inspector Randolph?" Sydney stepped forward, placing his hands in his pockets. "To what do we owe this visit?"

"Sergeant Lane and I saw your carriage pass and felt we ought to inform you of some unsettling reports in the area." He tapped the brim of his hat as his attention fell on Grace and Frederick.

"These are my cousins, Inspector." Georgia offered. "Lord and Lady Astley. They're recently arrived from England."

"Welcome to Egypt." He bowed his head and Sergeant Lane followed suit. "I'm sorry to dampen your visit with some recent news, but I feel it my duty to make you aware so that you can take proper precautions."

"What is it now, Inspector?" Sydney groaned. "It's always something around here, isn't it?"

The inspector stared at Sydney for a moment, as if garnering some patience, and continued. "We have received several reports of valuables being stolen in the area, particularly, as you can imagine, from the homes of people like yourselves." He gestured toward the house.

"Well, Sydney and I are rather adept with guns, and I daresay Lord Astley is as well. I'm not certain about the rest," Mr. Smallwood offered. "But we're certainly not unprotected."

"Are they stealing certain valuables in particular, Inspector?" This from Frederick.

Grace looked over at her dashing hero. Excellent question.

"Yes, my lord. Antiquities." He focused on Frederick with raised brow. "In fact, we discovered a crate of several priceless artifacts in an abandoned house near the river. Things our antiquities expert had never seen before. We're not certain from where they had been stolen, but we are keeping an eye out for dealers."

"And possible tomb robbers," Sergeant Lane added, focusing his attention on Sydney. "All archaeological finds are to be reported."

"Well, I'd gladly report them if I had the chance to find any,"

Sydney growled his response. "This only confirms my decision, Charles." Sydney turned to Mr. Smallwood. "Blast it all!"

"Your decision, sir?" The inspector's gaze sharpened.

Sydney released a long stream of air. "Mr. Smallwood and I have discussed the financial expectations of this dig and agree it's best to end everything within the week."

"What? Leaving?" Amelia stepped forward. "But we have three weeks left."

"Three weeks of the same results will only cost more money for nothing at all." He shoved a hand through his pale hair and started forward. "No, I am finished here. There are several important investments I need to secure back in England, and they require immediate attention." He nodded to Georgia. "Your cousin and his wife can benefit from the last few days here, but I expect the house to be packed up within the week."

Amelia paled and then turned and ran in the opposite direction.

"Blast!" Sydney dashed toward the house without another word to the police.

Georgia looked back at the way her husband had gone and offered a trembling smile. "Thank you, Inspector." She tipped her head toward Lane. "Sergeant."

They took their leave, and Georgia kneaded her fingers into her forehead. Grace moved to her side, offering a gentle touch to the woman's arm.

"Where did Amelia go?" Grace asked.

"She plans to outrun Sydney, if I guess right. Get a head start on telling our archaeologist of a change in schedule." Mr. Smallwood gestured with his chin toward the direction in which Amelia disappeared. "She went directly to the stables. Sydney's off to change into his riding gear first, so she'll have an ample head start."

"Oh Charles!" Georgia said, pressing her fingers into her

forehead. "I'm not looking forward to the confrontation, even if I can return to England sooner than planned."

"Professor Andrews will be none too pleased with the news, I can assure you. It's a great grievance for an archaeologist to have his contract cut short." Mr. Smallwood rubbed at his chin. "But perhaps fortunes could change within the next few days. I'm ever hopeful for a good change of fortune, aren't you?"

"I think all of us could do with a change of fortune," Georgia sighed.

"I did try to reason with him, but he was dead set on leaving." He tapped his cane against the ground. "And I can't say I blame him with the debts piling—"

"I think our guests should like to refresh themselves after the journey," Georgia interrupted, sending Grace a tight smile and gesturing toward the house. "Come, let me show you to your home away from home, for the next few days at least."

Mr. Smallwood followed. "I think I will go and try to reason with Sydney again. See you both at dinner."

Frederick ushered Grace forward, his gaze taking in the house and surroundings, as if he was scouting the area. Had he been taking notes from Detective Miracle's book for the amateur sleuth? Oh, how fantastic! And with the news of possible thieves and stolen antiquities, a thorough understanding of one's surroundings could prove invaluable. What a very dashing man! Adding sleuthing skills only made him even more endearingly rascally. And she was quite fond of his rascally side.

The arched doorway led them into a small foyer which opened into a large courtyard surrounded by two stories of doors. The upper-level doors led out onto a porch that looked down upon the courtyard and covered the doorways on the bottom level. A long table stood in the middle of the courtyard, and wicker chairs and green potted plants dotted various areas of the open space.

"Your rooms are upstairs." She gestured toward the doors on the left. "There are servants' quarters downstairs for your man and"— Georgia paused, looking back the way they'd come as if trying to remember something—"the girl. The street child?"

"Zahra?" Frederick offered.

"Yes, there's a closet in your suite that I suppose could be refurbished as a room for her."

"A closet?" The words popped out of Grace's mouth before she had a chance to stop them.

"Does our suite have a separate sitting room, Georgia?"

Georgia looked from Grace to Frederick before answering. "A small one but yes."

"Excellent." Frederick smiled. "Then we will make do with that."

Her smile resurrected. "Our rooms are on the opposite side of the courtyard from yours. Amelia and her aunt, Mr. Graham, and Professor Andrews, as well as Charles Smallwood fill out the other guest rooms, though Mr. Graham and the professor's rooms are on the lower level. I refused to allow the women to keep a ground-level room. Higher is much safer." Her smile fell and her hand moved to her neck. "And. . .and Timothy sleeps on the north side of the upper level. I believe they're refitting his parlor as another guest room for our"—she swallowed audibly—"for our newest arrival."

A chill swept up through Grace despite the heat of the day. She scanned the courtyard and examined the railing from the upper level which overlooked the area. If someone was pushed from such a height, it would likely kill them. If the walls were mudbrick, would they muffle the sound of a scream? And those stairs were made of stone. A hazardous place to fall.

Grace shared her concerns once she and Frederick were alone in their suite.

He took her by the hands and led her to the little couch in the center of their small parlor. "Darling, I recognize that there are quite a few unexpected situations going on among the people here, but I pray you are searching for danger where there is none."

He hesitated, and she raised a brow. "You feel it too. Something isn't right here."

"Your intuition is correct. There are many things that aren't right, but lucky for us, murderers and thieves and many of the other dangers you have floating about in that head of yours do not travel about as often as they do in fiction."

"But you do sense the disquiet?"

His gaze sobered. "Yes, and I've alerted Elliott to keep an extra eye out as well. There is always some risk when traveling, but the unrest among this group is a bit more than usual. And Sydney's behavior and choices concern me." He touched her chin, holding her attention with those dark eyes of his. "Be smart, my dear girl." His grin tipped. "For my heart, if not for your own."

She smiled and breached the distance between their lips. "Your heart is very important to me, Frederick, and I hope to take better and better care of it."

"Then don't run off without alerting someone." The pad of his thumb tapped her chin in time with his words. "Please?"

"I already promised." She blinked up at him. "And once I promise, I am very good at keeping that promise."

"Good." He kissed her again as if to seal her declaration.

"But should I have to make a very quick decision to save someone's life, you would understand if I didn't leave a note, wouldn't you?"

He sighed and his shoulders sagged, but the smile lingered on his lips. "Hopefully, I will be right there with you as you dash off to save the day."

"That's perfect!" She gave him another quick kiss. "You're much better with fiends and pistols than I am anyway, but I feel certain I'm better at climbing. I've been practicing since the last time I had to scale a wall so that poor Elliott will not suffer the consequences of my inexperience."

"You've been practicing—"

A cry broke into their discussion, and Grace rushed with Frederick to their door. From their viewpoint on the balcony, they saw a small group rush through the archway carrying someone on a stretcher.

"Hurry. He's fading," came the call of the man at the front. A tall, sun-tanned man with dark hair and a mustache of the same shade. He wore dusty clothes and a set of strong boots. "Call the doctor."

The demand echoed through the courtyard, and as the men passed beneath where Grace and Frederick stood, there was no mistaking the red stain darkening the white sheet over the wounded man.

"Frederick?"

Her husband met her gaze, his face pale. Perhaps he wouldn't admit it, but she read it in his eyes. The mystery had begun.

Frederick took off at a run, Grace on his heels as he moved down the stairway to the main level. Two Arabs in their white robes carried the cot, with Miss Sinclair helping to support one side and the other Englishman, presumably Professor John Andrews, leading the way.

"What happened?"

"A rockslide," came the professor's quick response.

Miss Sinclair's head came up for only a moment, her brows raised in a look of confusion, but she made no response.

"The sandstorm must have loosened the earth," the man continued as they navigated the cot into a small bedroom. "And as Daniel attempted to excavate, the rocks collapsed on him."

Grace made an empathetic noise at Frederick's side, drawing the man's attention up from the body.

"Not the best way to welcome you to El Amarna, I'm afraid," he said grimly and then turned to the cot as the two workmen transferred the wounded man from the cot to the bed. A cloth wrapped around the unconscious man's head already was dark with bloodstains.

"I just heard." Georgia entered the room and gasped when her attention landed on the unmoving figure on the bed. She turned away, her palm pressing against her stomach. "Oh, is he. . . ?"

"Not yet, Mrs. Archibald, but he has lost much blood," Professor Andrews added. "We came here as quickly as we could, but the journey is still almost a half hour, at least."

"I'll send for a doctor." Georgia started for the door.

"In the meantime, could I call for my valet?" Frederick offered. "He has some experience tending such wounds."

"He does?" Grace whispered, and when Frederick's gaze met hers, she nodded. "I shall go fetch him right away."

She dashed out the door.

"I do not see what there is to be done." Professor Andrews stood looking down at his comrade on the bed, his head shaking slowly from side to side. "Time is the only measure we have at this point."

"Time and good care, I should think," Frederick added, moving to the other side of the bed. He'd seen head wounds before while in the military. Nasty things, they were. Unpredictable. But as he examined the makeshift head bandage, the size of the bloodstain gave a little hope. Either the bleeding was slowing or the wound size hadn't been as large as Frederick had originally thought. Lantern light had a way of magnifying shadows.

"He is a good man," Andrews sighed. "He should not have this fate."

"Let us hope, then, he will not." Frederick met the man's gaze, holding it for a second longer than necessary. Miss Sinclair's shocked look when the professor had relayed the cause of the injury didn't sit too well with Frederick—or maybe Grace's suspicions were starting to rub off. Either way, a little caution couldn't hurt.

"You needed me, my lord?"

Frederick turned to see Elliott at the door, Grace just behind him. "Would you take a look at Mr. Graham? I know in your past. . .er. . .employment, you've managed such wounds as this, and until the doctor arrives, I think you could offer assistance."

Elliott peered around Frederick to take in the scene. "I will be happy to help as I can, sir."

"Excellent. What do you need?"

Elliott scanned the room. "Hot water, some fresh cloths, and brandy."

"Morphine, do you think?" came Grace's question.

"Not at present, my lady." Elliot shook his head. "Nothing to encourage a deeper sleep than he's already in. He may not come back to us if we do."

"I have no skills in healing, so I shall excuse myself to clean up." Andrews gestured toward his bloodstained shirt. "Please alert me if I can be of assistance."

"Thank you. . ." Frederick offered his hand.

"Ah yes, Professor John Andrews." He took Frederick's hand in a strong grip. "And thank you for trying to save my friend."

He bent his head in benediction and left the room.

Quiet stilled the room, except for the wisps of air coming from the unconscious man. Elliott moved to the bed and began slowly unraveling the makeshift cloth.

"Elliott." Frederick leaned closer. "Do you think we ought—"

"Miss Sinclair," Grace said, much louder than the quiet room required. "Would you mind helping me retrieve some cloths and hot water? I don't know where to find them."

Frederick hadn't noticed the woman standing in the shadows of the far corner of the room, but Grace's quick intervention kept him from revealing his deeper concerns in the presence of someone he didn't know, let alone trust.

The woman shifted into the lantern light and looked from Grace back to Mr. Graham's body, less composed than he'd ever seen her. But it only lasted a second. Right before his eyes, with a tilt of her chin, her expression turned placid. "Of course."

Frederick pulled the door closed behind the women's retreating forms and joined Elliott at the bed.

"I take it you think something underhanded has taken place here?"

"I don't know." Frederick ran a palm down his face. Was he letting Grace's concerns influence him? "There was something in the way Professor Andrews and Miss Sinclair exchanged a look. As if the professor isn't telling the full truth of the incident."

"Why lie?"

Frederick held Elliott's gaze. "Exactly."

Elliott succeeded in removing the cloth, revealing a rather nasty cut.

"It's certainly the blunt force of something." He kept his voice low. "Rock is possible from the sharp edge in the cut. I don't like the compression in the skull, sir."

"Is there any hope?"

"I don't like to think of there ever being no hope, sir." Elliot offered a small smile. "I know what it's like to be at the end of my rope in life and have someone believe in me just enough to bring me to the right."

Frederick nodded at Elliott's reference to Frederick finding him in a gutter in London after the man had been beaten to the edge of death and left for the elements to finish the job. Frederick may have never physically been to the point of Elliott's destitution, but he'd known it at the heart level. Abandoned. Rejected. It had taken a heavenly hand and a mistaken marriage to rescue him and give him the right perspective.

"If he makes it through the first night, he may have a fighting chance," Elliott sighed, pushing back the unconscious man's pale hair, darkened by the blood. "I may ask for a needle and thread too. I could stitch up the gash."

"I'll see to it." Frederick started for the door and then stopped, lowering his voice. "You'll stay by him until I relieve you, won't you? No one else, just until we can learn more?"

A look of understanding firmed Elliott's features. "Yes, sir."

Frederick opened the door to find Miss Sinclair preparing to enter, her hand laden with cloths. "Lady Astley may need your help with the water. The pail is nearly as big as she is."

Frederick stepped back to allow the woman to enter and then dashed toward the kitchens. Perhaps he should encourage Elliott to supervise any liquid or food delivered for Mr. Graham? He groaned at the thought. The next time Grace asked to read one of her mystery books aloud to him, he was going to politely and thoroughly distract her.

Elliott studied the wound, dabbing at the blood with the remnant of the cloth he'd taken from Mr. Graham's head. Elliott knew all too well the damage of severe force at the temple. He'd lost a brother that way. One hit. And by their drunken father. The fact his brother was protecting Elliott from the brunt of their father's anger only made the loss more painful.

Elliott supposed that's why the truth of scripture had pierced him with such force. Someone dying for him. No, his brother hadn't been anywhere near a saint and nothing close to God's own Son, but the idea of sacrifice mattered to Elliott deeply. So when Lord Astley had rescued him, restored him to health, and even given him a job, Elliott had embraced true gratitude for one of the first times in his life. Someone had shown him grace.

Then when Elliott had begun visiting the little church on Lord Astley's estate and he'd not only heard the story of the Good Samaritan but also of the sacrificial Savior, it seemed stupid not to embrace the offering. Lord Astley may have cleaned up Elliott's cuts and set him right with upstanding employment, but Christ had gone to Elliott's heart. He'd cleaned up the sin stains and set Elliott's broken life right before a holy God.

He didn't reckon many people with his past were given two rescues, and Elliott never wanted to take either for granted.

The door creaked open. Elliott looked up, expecting Lord Astley, but instead Miss Sinclair entered.

"I brought cloths," she whispered, her gaze moving from his face to Mr. Graham's.

Her eyes were a strange, marble-like shade of moss and gold, and they shimmered in the flickering lantern light. Something about her put Elliott on his guard. One wounded soul recognized another, his mother used to say. Something haunted this woman.

"So you're a valet who treats head wounds?"

He took one of the cloths she placed on a nearby table, the shadows hindering his view. "Would you bring the lantern closer?"

She hesitated and then complied, moving to his side. "The bleeding is slowing."

Hope lilted her voice. An unexpected response from the picture he'd created of her in his mind. Not that he'd thought much about her since the few instances he'd seen her, but she didn't seem the gentle, caring sort.

"Yes. That's a good sign. He needs all he can keep to help him stay as strong as possible."

The room grew quiet again as Elliott took out a small knife from his pocket.

As he raised it to Mr. Graham's head, Miss Sinclair's hand snatched his wrist. "What are you doing? He is an innocent man in all this."

Her fingers tightened. Strong. Nails biting into his skin. *"Innocent man in all this"*? In all what? And who was guilty? And guilty of what?

Without flinching he looked up at her. "I'm cutting back some of the hair around the wound so that I can clean it more easily and then stitch it if necessary."

She blinked, and her gaze flickered from his before she released his arm. "I'm sorry. I'm afraid I'm quite on edge about all of this." A false sad smile turned her lips as she looked back at him. "It was rather dreadful to see him all crumpled to the ground and lifeless."

Lantern light flickered against her sun-touched face, and golden tendrils of her hair fell loose against her cheeks. Elliott looked away and began to gently cut back some of Mr. Graham's hair. "Did you see what happened to Mr. Graham?"

He thought she might not answer, but after a long pause, she released a quiet sigh. "I was barely twenty feet away, on the other side of a rock formation, when I heard him cry out." She swallowed and the lantern shook. "By the time I reached him, he was already unconscious."

"Were you the first to find him?"

Her gaze flashed to his. "Why should I tell you anything?"

He slowly placed the loose locks of hair on one of the cloths on the bed and looked up at her. Her attention had followed the movements of his hands and now she stared at the small clumps of gold lying within the folds of white.

"Is there a reason you shouldn't?"

She stared at him, and the quiet lengthened. Her eyelashes were dark and long, framing those mysterious eyes. For a moment, the facade fell away and her pinched lips loosed. Then she blinked, and the expression disappeared. She raised a manicured brow. "How is it that a valet knows how to stitch wounds?"

"Perhaps I've not always been a valet."

"Mysterious," she cooed, but her attention flickered back to Mr. Graham.

"How is it you were barely twenty feet away and didn't see anything to give clarity to Mr. Graham's condition?"

The door opened and in walked Lord Astley carrying a large pail of steaming water with Grace following directly behind, bottle in hand. "Water and brandy." Grace raised the bottle. "What else can we do to help, dear Elliott?"

Miss Sinclair stiffened at his side. "You, Lord and Lady Astley, would help a wounded man you don't even know? Surely you would leave the dirty work to the servants."

"Surely, we would not." Lady Astley pushed up her sleeves and approached the bed. "Compassion doesn't adhere to social standing, and I'm very good with blood. Always have been, so I would make an excellent assistant for Elliott, should he need one."

Miss Sinclair's bottom lip relaxed a little. Elliott attempted not to grin.

"What else can we do, Elliott?" Lord Astley placed the water at Elliott's feet. "Mrs. Archibald sent Mr. Smallwood for the doctor and expects him to be here within the hour."

"If Lady Astley will assist me, we will clean the wound, but I wouldn't mind, sir, if you'd fetch another pail of water so we'll have fresh for the stitching." Elliott cleared his throat. "Supposing one of you is willing to retrieve my sewing kit from my room."

"You can use mine," Miss Sinclair said, offering the lantern to Lady Astley and moving to the door.

She'd barely made it to the threshold when a wail erupted from the courtyard.

"The gods tried to warn you!" came the haunting voice. "They warned with sandstorms. And then falling rocks."

Through the doorway, Elliott made out the pale garbed form of Miss Sinclair's aunt. What had her name been? Mrs. Casper?

"You planned to reject the gods' offerings of gold, and now the gods are displeased with you." Her voice rose. "Beware, those of you who do not heed the warning. Who do not respect the offerings. Beware! There is only death in their displeasure. Death!"

Chapter Ten

Miss Sinclair attended her aunt, taking the woman, who was still bellowing about some ancient catastrophe befalling them all, to her room. Georgia, for her part, made a poor attempt at turning the conversation away from the series of unexpected interruptions and encouraging everyone to enjoy dinner, which was currently being set on the dining table in the middle of the courtyard.

The entire situation set Frederick's nerves on alert. Whether from Grace's influence or not, so many unsettling incidents and disgruntled people made it impossible to shrug off the events of the day. As they gathered for dinner, all dressed as if dining at some London party instead of out in the Egyptian desert, a facade of normalcy appeared much more on the menu than the roasted chicken or potato puffs.

Elliott remained with the unconscious Mr. Graham, while Mr. Smallwood, Georgia, Grace, and Frederick made up the small dinner party. The others hadn't returned from the dig site yet. Another unsettling turn.

Dining under the open sky, however, provided a suitable distraction from some of the events of the evening, with the deep blue sky swirling through a rainbow mixture of golds, reds, and ambers above them. An added vibrancy brightened the hues into myriad watercolor streaks leading to the striking silhouette of jagged mountains in the distance. Mountains, Sydney had said, that led to the tombs of the ancients. The brilliant sunset appeared to recognize the significance of the place, for as it sank beneath the golden hillsides, its light bathed the mountains in a gentle umber hue before finally casting the tombs into shadow.

Frederick had never seen any landscape equally dazzling and desolate, a dichotomy of beauty and want. And as he sat at the dining table, listening to his cousin redirect the conversation away from stolen antiquities, Mr. Graham's accident, and Mrs. Casper's dramatic "prediction," he couldn't shake the idea he'd stepped very much into a story with as much a competition of beauty and want as the landscape's history itself. He released a pained sigh and sent a glance to his wife, who sat across from him. Heaven help him! He had to stop reading the novels Grace kept giving to him. He was beginning to hear her descriptions of things in his head.

The empty chairs around the table didn't help. "Will the others be joining us?"

"I think so." Georgia adjusted her serviette in her lap and smiled up at him. "Professor Andrews and Sydney were having another conversation about our plans to leave." She graced the table with a tense smile as she sliced into her roasted chicken. "But let us enjoy our time while we have it here. Just because we live on the edge of the desert doesn't mean we can't benefit from fine dining and excellent atmosphere. And the weather always cooperates. It's one of the saving graces of life in Egypt."

"I find it all very romantic," Grace added. "And I'm not certain how I'll sleep tonight with the expectation of visiting tombs tomorrow. Pyramids are one thing, but the tombs carved into the side of the mountains—there seems something unique and personal about those, I think." Her shoulders trembled with excitement. "I can't tell you how much I've read about the subject, so to experience the places to which I've given so much of my mental energy is rather exciting. I can't wait to see mummies."

"Grace, dear." A soft laugh bubbled up from Georgia as she placed her glass to her lips. "You are interested in the most peculiar things."

"And why not?" Mr. Smallwood added. "The world of Egyptian history is fascinating for anyone who has a mind for it."

"How long have you been interested in Egypt, Smallwood?" Frederick thanked the server for filling his glass and turned back to the man.

"Let me think." He looked up at the sky and stroked his chin. "Well, my brother was actually the instigator. He'd started studying the place years before and pulled me into it, I suppose. I thought it was a load of old tosh at first, but joined him on a few visits, and then, when he passed on unexpectedly, I . . ." He cleared his throat. "Well, I'm certain it sounds sentimental, but I felt a connection to him here." He looked up and sent Georgia a smile. "And once I heard of Sydney's endeavors, I approached him about joining in on the fun, and he and his lovely wife greeted me with open arms."

"You've been a welcome addition, Charles." Georgia swept the table a look. "And it was Charles' contacts that helped us find Alfurn House as well as most of our workers. He's incredibly popular in archaeological circles."

"Well, it's really my brother's connections. We made a very good team, I think." He sighed. "Which is why I'm a bit disappointed in Sydney's decision to leave early, but I understand it. I do." He nodded. "I've been hard pressed before and can't blame him."

A crash erupted from the doorway. Sydney marched into the room with Professor Andrews on his heels, the latter man's voice booming into the open space.

"You can't do this, Sydney. My permit is approved for three more weeks."

"*My* permit," Sydney corrected, barely looking at the man as he took his place at the table. "Funds I have been wasting for much too long."

"I don't need long, Sydney. A week? Perhaps a week and a half." Andrews shook his head and dropped into a nearby chair. "The natives know of more sites. More tombs. They cannot recall exactly where they uncovered a cave or a set of stairs, but they all swear another tomb rests not far from where we are digging. We are so close—"

"You've been preaching a possibility for the entire season, and all we have to show for it are some pot shards and a few minor antiquities. You know as well as I that we can't trust these natives. All they want is more baksheesh for dead ends." He shook his head. "No, I have tired of this."

"Gentlemen." Georgia's voice broke into the argument, her eyes pleading with her husband. "Can you continue your business conversation in private so as not to ruin this lovely meal?"

"You have until the end of the week to clear the site and relieve your workers," Sydney continued without a glance to his wife. "I will not pay you beyond."

Frederick caught Georgia's gaze. The apology in her eyes twisted his insides.

"You hired me to finish this season, and I intend to—"

"*I* hired you, and when I say we are finished, we are finished." He growled out his response and slammed his palm against the table.

"Speaking of treasure"—Georgia attempted another distraction, sending Frederick another look of apology—"have any of you happened to see my diamond broach? I only wore it last week, and now it's gone missing."

The distraction worked its magic. Professor Andrews relaxed back into his chair, and Sydney shot his wife a look of pure confusion.

"Didn't you misplace a set of emerald earrings a few weeks back?"

"I did not misplace them." She shot Sydney a severe look.

"Perhaps they were mistaken for some of the antiquities." Sydney laughed at his own joke and took a drink from his glass. "Weren't they your mother's or some such?"

"Last week, weren't you in Cairo, Georgia?" Frederick asked. "Did you take them with you there?"

"Yes." She blinked up at him. "Yes, I did. But the earrings went missing here."

Odd. Missing jewelry in two different locations. Frederick's attention scanned the table. But the same people?

"Just in time for dinner, I see." Timothy sauntered in from the front doors, followed by a taller man of much more distinguished presentation than Frederick's cousin. Donned in an impeccable linen suit, the stranger removed his hat to reveal a wealth of blond hair left in disarray quite in contrast to his pressed clothing. "Anyone know why there's a bobby outside sniffing around?"

"What?" Sydney began to rise from the table, but Mr. Smallwood waved him back.

"Perhaps one of the police noticed a possible thief in our vicinity." He stood. "You haven't even eaten yet. I'll see to it."

As Frederick's attention moved back to Sydney, he caught Georgia's expression. Her face had paled, her gaze fixed on the tall stranger, but Frederick didn't need that clue to work out who the stranger was. What he had not expected, however, was his darling wife's response.

"Richie?"

The stranger shot a look at Grace, and a broad smile split his face. "Grace Ferguson?" Then his attention scanned the others at the table and focused on Frederick, who'd stood from his place with the other men. The stranger's jaw grew lax and his smile spread as his attention returned to Grace. "You're Lady Astley?"

Grace flashed Frederick a smile so broad, it nearly knocked him over.

"I am. And happily so, though I can understand your shock." She shrugged a shoulder. "Lillias was supposed to have married him, but I. . ." Her brow furrowed, and Frederick could only imagine she sought a tactful way to state how her elder sister had been caught carrying another man's child before the wedding, so Frederick cleared his throat.

"She won me over with her charm, and I would settle for no one else." It was true.

Her smile softened with her gaze, warming him through, and she turned back to the stranger. "But. . .but I thought we were to meet a Trent Anderson, not a Richard Anderson?"

"And you are." He stepped forward, gracing the room with another smile, his gaze taking a momentary pause on Georgia before fastening back on Grace. "After stepping into my inheritance and taking over the family business, I began going by my renowned grandfather's name. My middle name." He leaned forward, encouraging a camaraderie with Grace that Frederick wasn't too certain he liked at all. "And with my daring past, a separation from Richie Anderson became necessary."

"How. . .how is it that the two of you know one another?" This question emerged from a breathless Georgia who was doing very little to hide her discomfort in the entire situation.

"Our families traveled in the same circles back in Virginia," Grace offered. "And he would find a way to sneak away from the parties and spend time with me and Lillias, though I do believe his sights were much more set on my sister at the time."

Mr. Anderson's smile faded for a second, but he recovered. The man certainly brought a distinguished air that had been missing from most of the other male counterparts at the table. "We all have our childhood romances, Lady Astley, though I should think yours bordered along the fictional realm more often than the nonfictional."

"Mr. Anderson." Sydney returned to his chair and reclined

back, his expression impassive. "I do not recall inviting you to our excavation."

"It's because you didn't, Sydney." Timothy stepped forward, making a nonchalant presentation with his hands in his pockets and his grin crooked, but there was a challenge in his eyes. "Trent is here at my invitation. He's a collector of antiquities and quite well known in the field, so I thought he'd appreciate a first-hand treasure hunt."

"I know exactly why he's here." Sydney raised his chin. "And it's not for the excavation."

"I beg to differ, Mr. Archibald," Mr. Anderson offered, his smile unwavering, though his gaze never failed to stray in Georgia's direction now and again. "I spent last season in Haraga with renowned Egyptologist Reginald Englebach where we uncovered some Middle Kingdom artifacts. The year before, I joined a team in Luxor at the Valley of the Kings, so I have quite the track record for being invested."

"And you expect me to believe you'd leave those opportunities for a chance to crawl around in this barren wasteland of the heretic pharaoh?" Sydney blew out a stream of air from his nose. "Well you've wasted your time. We're ending the dig this week." Sydney's gaze locked with Mr. Anderson's. "Nothing here of any sort for you to find."

"Sydney, I believe there is still—"

"You've already heard my plans, Andrews."

"Well, at least that will give Lord and Lady Astley a chance to have the grand tour of the tombs." Timothy offered, his grin challenging Sydney. "And Trent would make an excellent companion for them with his knowledge of Egyptian history and antiquities."

Without another word, Sydney rose from his chair and tossed his serviette to the table. "Enjoy it while you can. We are finished here." His gaze landed on Andrews. "All of us."

Frederick was mulling over the events of the day while he and Grace readied for bed, when his darling wife turned from her dressing table and sighed. "You know what all this means, don't you?"

Such a question from her left him in a bit of trepidation as to how to answer. "An unfortunately shorter visit to Egypt than planned?"

Her brow crinkled with a frown, and she stared at him for a second before answering. "I suppose so, but that's not what I meant, though now I'm a bit disappointed at the idea of our shortened visit."

"No worries, darling. As I said before, we will spend some time on the Nile before we leave for Venice in order to explore those other sites you wished to see."

Her smile resurrected. "I do so want to see Karnak. And the famous Queen Hatshepsut's mortuary temple." She turned back to her dressing table to finish readying for bed, evidently completely forgetting her initial statement. Her long hair fell in fiery tresses down her back, a pleasant contrast of ginger and white. Frederick pulled back the mosquito netting to allow her to climb into bed, and then he followed suit on the other side.

She sat up against the pillows, book already poised in hand. "I'm so glad we were able to keep Zahra in our sitting room. Somehow I feel she's safer there than in another part of the house with servants she doesn't know."

Frederick nodded and nestled down against the pillow. The last thing they needed was another dangerous accident, but from what he'd gathered about Zahra thus far, she knew her fair share of ways to avoid trouble.

"You think Elliott will be all right?"

Frederick turned to Grace. "He can hold his own, I assure you, but I mean to go and see to him after a few hours' sleep."

"Well then, I shouldn't keep you awake any longer than necessary." Grace closed her book and blew out the lantern, then snuggled up against his side. "But I am very glad to hear you are going to ensure Elliott is fine. I know he's strong and brave, but if an entire caravan of tomb robbers or sheikhs or reanimated mummies barge into the house seeking retribution, it's comforting to know he won't be alone."

Frederick pinched his eyes closed to steady his humor.

"And I know there are no such things as reanimated mummies, but it's very exciting to say."

His grin unfurled, and he squeezed her close by his side. "Much better to say than see, I should think."

"Most certainly." She yawned and smoothed a palm over his chest as was her custom.

"Is that what you meant by knowing what all this means?"

Silence followed his response, and for a moment he thought she'd gone to sleep, but then she rallied with a shake of her head. "Oh no, I was referring to Mr. Graham."

"Mr. Graham?"

"Yes, the whole situation with him." She sighed. "I'm afraid he's going to die."

"We can certainly hope not, Grace. The first night is always the trickiest for a head wound."

"I don't mean from the head wound, Frederick." She pushed up from his side, her palm on his chest and her hair splayed all about her shoulders. Truly she was beautiful, but the glint in her eyes incited more concern than amour at the moment.

"You don't mean Mr. Graham will die from the head wound?"

"The signs are all there, Frederick. If you recall from Detective Miracle's book, it's nearly a perfect stage." Her eyes widened, glistening by the light of the moon. "An 'accident' to make the victim unable to speak, a strange reaction from Mrs. Casper, a highly contentious cast of characters, a remote location where police and doctors are scarce?" She nodded, as if he understood perfectly. "Isn't it perfectly clear? Poor Mr. Graham is going to be murdered, and we must find a way to stop it from happening."

The bedroom door gave a tiny squeak, barely a sound, but enough to pull Elliott from his doze and have him slipping his knife from his pocket. He didn't truly expect trouble from such a posh lot, but after overhearing the low row between a few of them on the floor above him, he didn't doubt tempers rose to the dangerous spot.

Elliott had gone to the bedroom door at one point and peered out into the courtyard, only to note a woman slipping through the shadows of the courtyard and disappearing in the direction of the kitchens. Her movements had been too lithe and young for Mrs. Casper, and he'd become so accustomed to Lady Astley's walk, he felt certain it wasn't her. The clothing style didn't hint at one of the servants either. And though it wasn't unusual for one of the residents to walk about at night, the form's deliberate movements to remain in the shadows cast a great deal of suspicion. Had it been Miss Sinclair? Mrs. Archibald?

Only a few minutes later, a man descended the stairs, keeping to the shadows as well.

Lord Astley had been right to raise the alarm. Something wasn't right about this place and these people. Trouble and danger lurked in every house, rich or poor, but the people in this house wore their trouble differently, especially the rich.

Elliott sent a glance over the unconscious man's form. The newest cloths had remained white, confirming Mr. Graham's blood loss had stopped, and there was additional color in his face. Another good sign.

Around the doorway peered a set of large grayish-green eyes. Elliott's shoulders relaxed.

"What do you need, child?"

"Sitt Haree wanted you to eat." Zahra slipped through the slightest opening, plate in hand. "She went to the kitchen and made this plate for you."

"And she sent you here?"

Zahra nodded, looking wide-eyed at the unconscious man on the bed. "Is his spirit weak or strong?"

Elliott returned his knife to his pocket. "I'm not certain, but he's survived the night, so that is a good sign."

He took the plate she offered him and placed it on the nearby table. Zahra scanned the room, those curious eyes of hers taking everything in. He wasn't sure what he thought of the girl yet, but *scrappy* fit his initial impression. However safe or trustworthy she may be was yet to be seen.

A thud broke into the silence from above, followed by another round of raised voices. Zahra's gaze found his. "They have been arguing for too long."

"You've heard them?"

She raised her chin. "When you live on the street, you learn to listen."

"I thought you were in an orphanage."

She nodded, running her hand over the cloth of the curtain as she walked past. "I was on the street before."

He studied her a moment longer before relaxing back in his chair. "They're quieting down now. You should go back to bed."

Her chin raised a little higher. "I will wait for Sitt Haree."

Elliott quelled his grin, determined not to show the girl how he approved of her loyalty to his mistress. A good sign in her favor.

The voices rose again. Two men this time. Only a few moments earlier, Elliott had thought he'd heard a woman's voice as well, but almost as quickly as it began, a door slammed and all went silent.

The door to the room shifted again, and in walked Lady Astley, her ginger hair in complete disarray around her shoulders. Elliott felt certain Lord Astley had no idea his wife had slipped down the stairs in the early hours of the morning in her dressing gown to serve Elliott tea.

"I thought you might be awake." Her blue eyes brightened with a smile, and she moved forward, all the tea accoutrements on a tray. "Of course, I'm not sure how you could sleep with the noise upstairs anyway."

He stood, moving to take the tray from her, but she shook her head. "Now Mr. Elliott, you have been at work all night and deserve a little care." With great ceremony she placed the tray on the table and poured his tea. "I'm not certain how long the fight had gone on, dear Elliott, but I hope you were able to get a little sleep."

"Yes, my lady." His smile softened. "The argument is fairly recent. Mostly the night passed quietly."

"At least it's almost morning and someone can come to relieve you."

"I'd rather remain at my post until Mr. Graham regains consciousness, if I may, my lady. It would make me feel better."

She held his gaze a moment, those intelligent eyes of hers catching his meaning. "Of course, but we must ensure you don't tire out, dear Elliott." She waved toward the food. "So you might as well eat an early breakfast and enjoy a second one later as reward for all your longsuffering." She touched Zahra's head in such a way that Elliott knew for certain his mistress had already accepted the girl as part of their family. Of course. "Zahra is willing to help run errands for you today as Lord Astley and I are taken to the tombs, unless you'd rather us remain here in case something"—she glanced behind her—"unfortunate comes to light."

"I expect all to be well here, my lady."

"Good." She nodded. "Because I mean to have a look around at the accident site in case someone left clues behind."

He steadied his expression. Should he alert Lord Astley of Lady Astley's sleuthing plans? Elliott released a long sigh. It was likely his master already knew full well.

Lady Astley clasped her hands together and rounded the bed, scanning over Mr. Graham. "How long has it been since you last changed his bandages?"

Elliott's lip tipped slightly. "Two hours, my lady."

"And has he moved at all?"

"He murmured some, only a short while ago."

"Oh!" Her eyes widened with a smile. "That's very good news, isn't it? Perhaps that means he'll recover consciousness soon." She mumbled almost too quietly to hear. "Time enough to name his assailant."

Zahra's head shot up, her eyes like saucers, but Elliott merely shook his head to calm her.

Lady Astley returned to her perusal. "There's a bit of color in his face that I didn't notice last evening."

Elliott nodded.

Her expression suddenly sobered, and she glanced back behind her toward the door before closing the distance between the two of them. "I hope, very much, that whatever misfortune came upon Mr. Graham was a simple accident." She held his gaze. "But I must say I'm happy to have your skills and attention on hand, Elliott. And I feel certain you'll keep an eye out even when the nurse arrives."

"You can be sure, my lady."

"Well then, I'd better return to the room before Lord Astley worries about me." She turned and made it to the door before she stopped. "And Elliott, I made the tea myself to ensure all was. . .in good order."

He tried to hold his smile. He'd had Lady Astley's tea before, and it was quite clear the woman wasn't English.

As if reading his thoughts her grin slid wide. "It's much better than the last time. I had Aunt Lavenia teach me how to make it correctly so that you wouldn't have to look so pained when you took a drink."

With a little wink and a gesture for Zahra to follow, Lady Astley slipped from the room.

Elliott gave another look to Mr. Graham, and then, with slight hesitation, he brought the teacup to his lips. The liquid moved over his tongue, smooth and warm, steeped to perfection, and then he tasted it. Sugar. And his grin unfurled. Lady Astley was notorious for sweetening her tea beyond comprehension, and evidently, she'd thought Elliott would appreciate the same abundance.

With a chuckle, he topped off the cup, effectively watering the tea down to a more digestible sugar content and made quick work of his meal.

Chapter Eleven

A camel!

Grace held her head high, her palm wrapped around the handle on the camel's saddle and the reins intertwined through her fingers. She was currently living one of her most exotic dreams. In fact, her whole ensemble matched the exoticness of the moment, and she knew down to her pulse she was born to be an adventurer.

With dust goggles, a broad hat complete with scarf covering it, breeches beneath her skirts, and a pair of sturdy boots that almost reached her knees, Grace felt certain travel writer Amelia Edwards or novelist H. Rider Haggard would be duly impressed. Dressed as she was, if she didn't discover something, she might be rather disappointed.

Though she and the camel had gotten off to a slightly rocky start—clearly he needed more acquaintance with her before she took his photo from such a close angle—once they'd started following the caravan, everything moved so smoothly. She particularly liked the hint to fold one leg up while riding to help more evenly balance her body weight on the creature.

She couldn't help but send her darling husband the largest smile as he rode nearby. As ever, he looked dashing, but sitting atop his own camel while wearing a crisp, white button-up, linen slacks, and a large-brimmed tan hat, he held an additional attractiveness. Very heroic, the likes of Haggard's Alan Quartermaine or Doyle's Lord Roxton. And he'd left the top buttons of his shirt loose. She found something incredibly pleasing about an open-collared shirt on an extremely handsome man. Especially if that extremely handsome man happened to be one's husband.

She shivered with delight.

Or perhaps it was from the heat.

Maybe both.

Their little entourage comprised of Professor Andrews at the lead with some of his men running alongside, followed by Mr. Smallwood, then Grace and Frederick, with Mr. Anderson coupled with Miss Sinclair. Unfortunately Sydney had slept in, as Georgia shared at breakfast with a sigh, saying he was "tired out" from all the frustration in the last few days and was wont, at times, to exhaust himself from pure fury.

Grace felt keenly the special exhaustion associated with fury. She'd only experienced it a few times, but each experience left her a little quivery and tired. How much more should it impact Sydney, who'd fairly erupted with fury most of yesterday related to one thing or the other, only to reach a tipping point with Mr. Anderson's presence. The vein in his forehead had bulged a considerable amount, and she'd never seen anyone's nostrils flare with such determination.

The rust-colored mountains rose before them in the distance, contrasted against the brilliant azure sky, and within those mountains hid the history of the infamous Akhenaten. For some reason, she'd expected broken columns and half-buried statues to rise out of the dust, as she'd seen in Florence Nightingale's travel book, but a great wide plain stretched out in a vermillion and rocky landscape, barren and dusty, with an intense sort of beauty.

The mountain range seemed to curve around the plateau, as

if on guard, and a strange awe poured through Grace. An ancient feeling. An awareness of millennia buried among the sands. Stories waiting among the dust. Whispers of lives and loves and dangers.

Had this been similar to the landscape the biblical Joseph traversed after his brothers sold him into slavery? Had this been the world he helped rescue from famine or the one where his namesake fled to keep baby Jesus safe from murderous Herod?

What a desolate place.

"I don't know why you encouraged me to come with you, Andrews. I've already seen your work, or lack of it," Mr. Smallwood grumbled from his place on his camel. The round man looked rather uncomfortable, and the expression on the camel indicated it wasn't extremely excited either. Of course, Grace hadn't noticed a varied array of facial expressions on the camels, but she assumed that was because she hadn't studied them well enough yet.

"We do have progress to show," Andrews responded, an edge in his tone. "It is proof enough to keep up the excavation. I would have brought Sydney with me, but since he was unavailable, I wanted to prove it to you."

"I am sorry for the way things have turned out for you, truly," Mr. Smallwood continued. "But there's simply nothing I can do about it."

"I wouldn't be surprised if there weren't more tombs in this area to discover." This from Richie. . .er. . .Trent. "All this vast land and centuries of dirt covering history. About the time we think we've discovered them all, we find more."

"Though many call the place Amarna, its ancient name was Akhenaten, which is made up of two words: *Aket* and *Aton*," Amelia interjected, tipping her head to Grace. It was difficult to ignore how fabulous she looked atop that camel with her golden hair, partially covered by a hat, glistening in the sun. Trent seemed to appreciate the vision too, for he kept close to her side. The fact that

Amelia donned an excellent set of trousers only made her entire appearance more fascinatingly unbearable, because she looked a little more the part of the adventurer than Grace.

The next time they planned to enter a tomb, Grace was determined to wear trousers.

"*Aket* which means 'horizon' and *Aton* which refers to a cycle of the sun. Put together, many think it means "the rising of Aten.""

"And since King Akhenaten worshipped said sun god," Trent offered, "if he named his city after this powerful god, it would in turn mean that building his city here was a holy ordinance of sorts, wouldn't it, Professor?"

"Indeed, and an important beginning to creating followers of a new religion. He also made himself and his wife the only ones who had direct access to this new and singular god, which, as you can imagine, upset the other religious leaders by threatening to make them impotent." Andrews increased the pace of the entourage but continued talking. "As I show Mr. Smallwood our hopeful progress, Amelia will take the rest of you into the tomb of Meryra, Akhenaten's high priest and one of the tombs with the most intact reliefs on the walls."

"Is it true that most of the likenesses of Akhenaten and Nefertiti were disfigured after he died?"

Professor Andrews turned on his camel to look at Grace, his brows raised. "You have done some reading of the heretic pharaoh?"

Frederick's grin spread, and Grace bit back her own smile. "I've tried to do a little. I find the pharaoh fascinating as he's so different from others of his time."

"I have always found him a fascinating study, and the city of Akhenaten is an archaeologist's dream. Few cities have been so well preserved, giving us the opportunity to explore the daily life of a group of people who lived over three thousand years ago."

Professor Andrews waved to a long stretch of flat land in the distance to their right, a vast space littered with boulders but not much to note that a great city once stood there.

Grace could make out only a few rectangular raised areas in the distance, perhaps of remaining mudbrick walls. "But as to your question, yes, Akhenaten's views were so contrary to the previous generations that, once he passed on to the afterlife, the rulers after him attempted to destroy any depiction of him in hopes of destroying his influence."

"And what about him caused them to have such hatred for him?" This from Frederick, though Grace was fairly certain she'd told him everything she'd read on Akhenaten. Of course, that could have been one of those times when he was listening with his eyes closed.

"What usually causes such strife among people? Religion and politics," the professor offered, his grin crooked. "Akhenaten, who was formerly known as Amenhotep IV, had taken some of the ideas of his father and brought them to the extreme. You see, his father, Amenhotep III, worshipped all of the many Egyptian gods, but had a favorite: Aten, the sun god."

"And when Akhenaten became pharaoh, he took his interest in Aten and created a monotheistic religion, rejecting the long-held polytheism of Egypt." Grace grinned as Andrews gave her an approving nod.

"But despised by the religious leaders in Thebes," Professor Andrews added, sitting a little taller in his saddle. "So much so, that after Akhenaten died, his entire city was destroyed by a later generation, and many of the wall paintings and statues of him and his queen were defaced."

"Finding anything intact from this period is not only a treasure of the financial sort, but a historical goldmine," Mr. Smallwood added with a deepening frown. "Which is why Sydney and I were in such hopes of a real discovery, but I don't see it happening unless we miraculously stumble upon something in the next few days that we've not been able to locate for the past three months."

"Well, Mr. Smallwood," Trent laughed, "that's exactly how most archaeological discoveries happen. Unexpectedly and quite by accident."

"Quite right, Mr. Anderson," Smallwood chuckled. "Quite right."

Silence followed them for a few moments, and the mountains grew nearer.

The sun's heat beat down on them, with a warm wind bringing the only reprieve. Not a single tree or bush dotted the view ahead for miles. When they reached the base of the mountains, all dusty and sharp, Grace looked increasingly forward to disappearing inside the shade of a cave or a tomb for reasons beyond fascination and possible reanimated mummies. Shade meant cooler air.

They began climbing a trail up the mountain's side, single file, with Andrews leading the way. As they rose, the valley spread out below them, stretching all the way back in the direction they'd come and farther.

In the valley below, Grace made out the outlines of what looked like a small village with the same square-shaped, mudbrick homes as she'd seen along the Nile. The little city where they'd traveled situated just beyond with its more congested buildings. And then the glistening Nile slid between lush green land, like a shining serpent among the grass. It was a fascinating site. The rich verdant area along the river cut a defining line with the dry, brown earth of the desert. Two contrasting worlds, side by side. Life and death?

Her gaze shot forward toward the rectangular indentations in the mountainside ahead.

Tombs.

The camels made the slow ascent up a set of stone stairs to a plateau with another trail that stretched along the mountainside to the right. Deep indentations into the rock wall along the trail noted other tombs. How many had already been discovered? How many more waited within the rock?

A collection of white tents fluttered in the breeze in the distance, seemingly at the edge of the mountain trail.

"My team is still trying to excavate as long as we have any time left," Andrews announced as he brought his camel to a stop in front of one of the large rectangle indentations in the side of the rock wall. "We will take refreshment here, and then Amelia will lead you into the tomb." He moved to help Amelia off the camel that had sat so easily upon the woman's first instruction to "tut tut."

Grace had listened intently to Ali Hassan's instructions, so surely she could get the camel to sit as nicely.

She gripped the reins in one hand and braced her other against the handle before giving a very firm "tut tut." Nothing happened. The creature didn't quiver. She repeated the command a few times to no avail and finally acquiesced to Ali Hassan helping her and eventually dismounting. The camel stared at her without emotion, and for some reason, she felt he didn't quite like her. Well, they just needed more time together.

"It's all right, darling." Frederick came to her side, a smile in his eyes. "If anyone could win over a camel, I feel it is you."

"I know you're making fun." And though she tried to hold her frown, she couldn't. The idea of trying to win over a camel really was a little silly.

Grace had imagined going down a long flight of stairs to enter the tomb. After all, if her research proved true, Akhenaten's own royal tomb followed a long stairway into the earth and she hoped to visit it while they were in Amarna before Sydney called off all the excavation.

But even with only a step, entering inside a mountain in the middle of Egypt brought a certain sense of awe. A small overhang from the mountain made the tiniest of entries. Amelia lit a lantern, and Trent followed suit.

"As we pass through the entry," Amelia instructed, "you will notice on the lintel of the doorway some intact carvings. These are hymns unique to Amarna which praise not only Aton but also the king and queen, Akhenaten and Nefertiti." She waved the light farther inside, letting the glow fall on the carving of a prostrate form in the wall. "And this would be Meryra facing the doorway and the sun, bowing in worship."

She focused the light on a small set of oval carvings, each oval filled in with other markings.

"Cartouches!" Grace exclaimed.

Amelia's lips quivered ever so slightly, and she nodded. "Exactly, Lady Astley. The nameplates of the important people in ancient Egypt."

"I see one is the name of Meryra," Trent said, running his finger along the carvings.

"You read hieroglyphs?" Amelia asked.

"Only a little, but I'm learning."

"Are the two destroyed cartouches meant to be the names of the king and queen?" Grace reached out toward the decimated forms but couldn't quite bring herself to touch the markings.

"Yes."

They stepped farther in, daylight still giving off enough glow to see the entry room.

"Always remember to look up when one is in a tomb," Amelia said, and everyone obeyed.

The ceiling still held color and was broken up into three rectangles, each framed by a checkered border that held a pattern of diamonds and something that looked like flowers in faint hues of blue and yellow.

They followed Amelia into a small room which boasted carvings on every wall, almost bursting with confusing markings. A hand here. A face there. Rows of cartouches and symbols which looked like layers of various types of crowns. What did it all mean?

"Here is an excellent depiction of Aten." Amelia pointed toward the top of one of the doorposts where a circle marked the center and a dozen "rays" came down from it. At the end of the rays were tiny hands, as if the sun was reaching down to the people worshipping below.

What a lovely thought! And a wonderful way of imagining how the God of the Old Testament seemed to do that very thing so often. Visiting Abraham and Jacob and Moses. And then, of course, the idea became much more obvious with the way Jesus actually took on hands and feet to enter the world as a human.

What a remarkable way two very different religions could find a similar truth in a god reaching down to man.

They moved on to the next room, a little less grand than the previous, but still the unique artwork of Akhenaten's time depicting family and everyday life. The pharaoh and his bride were portrayed as the same size as each other, while in other Egyptian art, the queen was usually much smaller in size to her husband to denote the power difference. Not here. Not with Akhenaten. He and Nefertiti were represented as equals.

As were Meryra and his wife.

Grace approved and offered her dear husband a hand-squeeze in the shadows just because she could. The next room held two large columns on one side, and the darkness made the columns loom larger against the shadows. The most fantastic part of the room, however, was that pictures covered every wall. Stories. The rays of Aten shone down over and over again upon people bowing or eating or serving the faceless king and queen, with resemblances of their little daughters untouched by the haters' hands.

Myriad of cartouches mingled with the beautiful markings of

hieroglyphs shown in forms of birds, serpents, bowls, and various lines. It was all so beautiful, and Grace couldn't wait to return to the house and retrieve her book on hieroglyphs. As it was, she kept trying to draw what she saw into her little notebook and felt certain she'd hardly be able to recognize any of it when they reached the sunlight again.

"When we visit the royal tomb, we'll see some excellent reliefs representing the royal family, particularly in the mourning room of their daughter Meketaten."

The crowd moved on ahead, but Grace lingered in the room, surrounded by paintings on every wall. The stories surrounded her. Trent had been kind enough to leave his lantern behind when he'd noticed Grace attempting to sketch some of the paintings into her notebook. She was determined to study them later, maybe even learn more about the curious Akhenaten and his wife. And though her drawings were no masterpieces, she was pleased enough with the fact that she'd actually be able to decipher them later. As Grace finally emerged from Meryra's tomb, the spectacular view before Grace nearly stole her breath. Even in its barrenness, the land revealed an intense beauty from the lush green paralleling the Nile contrasted with the golden-brown of the desert. The vistas stretched to the horizon and beyond, giving one a sense of the bigness of the world. How very much God had to take care of! She was ever so glad it was up to Him and not her. She had a difficult enough time keeping up with her gloves.

She caught sight of the last remnant of someone's garment as they entered another tomb down the trail, but what truly caught her attention was her camel. He'd come out from the other camels, who were reclining, and marched directly over to her as if he wanted something.

"Are you going to be nice to me now?" Grace stuffed her notebook into her bag and stared up at the creature. "Because I would like to get off to a better start."

He only stared back at her, his big lips pinched in a chew.

"Well, I don't think it's on my account we started off so poorly." Grace nodded to him. "I was the epitome of friendliness. I even gave you a piece of melon before you sat for me."

As if the creature understood everything Grace said, he sat down in front of her.

She blinked and glanced down the trail at where the archaeological tents stood in the distance. Ali Hassan was likely there, assisting Professor Andrews.

She looked back at the camel, who'd kept staring relentlessly at her.

"Do you want to go for a ride?"

He lowered his head as if in answer.

Grace bit her bottom lip and looked back toward the tomb where the others had gone. She was an excellent horsewoman after all. And it wasn't as if the animal moved very fast. And, she'd listened intently to Ali Hassan's instructions on how to mount and guide the camel. Surely she could give it a go on her own. Just once. And if it didn't work, she'd quickly return to the group.

She looked over her shoulder toward the tombs one last time before reaching for the saddle handle. Wouldn't Frederick be proud!

Chapter Twelve

"I must say, Lord Astley, I'm a bit envious of you."

Lord Astley turned from following Miss Sinclair and moved in step with Mr. Anderson. "To what do I owe your envy?"

"Your happy marriage." Mr. Anderson offered a ready grin. "It isn't often to find wealth, good looks, and happiness rolled up into matrimony. Timothy told me a bit of how your situation came to be, and I'd say, despite Grace's eccentricities, you came out on top."

Discussing his personal life with a stranger, no matter how accurate the stranger may be, wasn't among Frederick's favorite things, so he offered a smile and a quick change of subject. "Where is Timothy this morning? He seemed well enough last evening."

"He's too afraid we'll put him to work." Miss Sinclair moved deeper into the tomb and cast a look over her shoulder. "Is that it, Mr. Anderson?"

Mr. Anderson laughed and removed his hat, wiping back a rivulet of sweat trailing down the side of his forehead. The shade of the cave did little to curb the heat in the afternoon air. Miss Sinclair appeared unaffected, but of course her body had likely adjusted to the temperature.

"I have no doubt, Miss Sinclair. He's a good-hearted sort but always seemed to find a way to weasel out of the harder work." Mr.

Anderson placed his hat back on his head and laughed. "But in this case, he is actually running an errand for his sister. Evidently she sent him off this morning to their hotel in Cairo to see if he could locate her missing jewelry."

"And which jewelry was it this time? She does appear notorious at misplacing things."

The sarcasm in Miss Sinclair's tone was undeniable.

"I'm afraid my hopes in convincing Mr. Smallwood of our continued excavation was in vain." Professor Andrews entered the tomb, his hat in his hands, head down. "If only my benefactors cared for the actual art of the dig!"

"I'm sorry to hear it, Professor." Trent shrugged. "If we had time to transfer the dig to me, I'd happily take over the cost."

"I appreciate the sentiment, Mr. Anderson."

"And what of Mr. Smallwood now?" Miss Sinclair gestured with her lantern toward the doorway. "Is he sitting outside in the sun as protest?"

"I'm afraid we had a row about Sydney's choice to end the dig." Andrews shoved his hands in his pockets and shook his head. "He retrieved his camel and started back to the house."

Even in the shadows of the tomb's front chamber, Frederick could see the fall in Miss Sinclair's smile. Her attention shot to the entrance of the tomb. Had she grown paler? Why would Mr. Smallwood's reaction surprise her so much when he'd made his opinion extremely clear already?

"Is it safe for Mr. Smallwood to travel the distance alone?" Frederick asked, attempting to ascertain the reason for Miss Sinclair's reaction.

Professor Andrews' gaze shot to Frederick, frown deepening. "I should think so. Evenings are when the thieves make their appearance, and he's well acquainted with this area and the people." His lips softened into a smile, but his eyes remained alert, cautious.

"Besides, I sent Akeem along with him to assist with the camel."

The idea of Mr. Smallwood traveling back to the house alone suddenly brought to attention Grace's prolonged absence. He'd recognized her delay in leaving the last tomb due to attempting some drawings of the reliefs, but shouldn't she have rejoined them by now? His stomach tensed, and he stepped back toward the tomb entrance.

"I'm sorry for you, Professor. Truly." Trent shook his head. "I know too well the discouragement of having to end a dig when one feels close to a discovery."

"Yes." The professor sighed. "But what can be done but wait for another benefactor to take my cause next season and pray that no one else makes the discovery before I can."

"Perhaps after you've cleared out your team, we could talk about next steps?" Trent offered. "My funding may not be as grand as Archibald's or Smallwood's, but—"

A cry broke into the conversation from outside. A strange sort of sound. Animal?

"Tut, tut," came a much more familiar and frantic cry. "Tut means stop, camel."

Frederick dashed for the entrance of the tomb and made it over the threshold in time to see his wife, clinging to the camel's reins for dear life, as the creature ran past him down the trail.

Her gaze caught his. "I'm terribly sorry, my dear Lord Astley." She turned back toward him as she passed, her voice unnervingly calm as the camel ran headlong across the trail along the cliff. "Apparently, he's afraid of parasols."

Frederick blinked a few times and looked back in the direction she'd come, only to see her parasol blowing down the trail in the opposite direction. Without hesitation, he took off at a full run in pursuit. Workmen jumped to keep from being trampled. A tent canopy fluttered off the hillside and floated toward the plateau below. Frederick dodged past a few yelling men, following in the camel's wake. They were much too far ahead for him to truly catch up, but at some point either the camel would slow, Grace would jump, or something worse would happen. He closed his mind to whatever "worse" could be.

In the distance near where the cliff took a curve to the left, the camel appeared to slow, and his wife shifted in the saddle, then slid off the moving creature. At first she appeared to have her footing. Then she stumbled. He increased his pace as she waved her arms in quick succession in an attempt to regain her balance. Her gaze met his. Eyes wide, she teetered backward and, without a sound, slipped over the edge of the cliff.

The camel looked over the mountainside and turned to resume his walk back the way he'd come, sans his rider. Frederick's legs burned as he pushed harder.

Too many long seconds passed before he made it to the edge, every conceivable disaster playing through his mind in gory, bone-chilling detail. Would she be a broken heap on the rocks below? Beautiful body severed, skin torn?

He skidded to a stop at the edge of the hillside. Rocks skittered from his shoes and danced over the ledge, but it was not a steep-cliff ravine that met his gaze. The hillside sloped downward to the base, as boulders jutted here and there and small ledges protruded like teeth all the way to the bottom.

He took in a deep breath, his pulse pounding in his ears. She could have slid down to a stop, perhaps? Much better than plunging to her death. But she wasn't anywhere along the slope, no matter how much he looked. Something white fluttered. Her scarf. It danced along the breeze, occasionally snagging on a boulder or rock before blowing loose again.

"Where is she?" Trent appeared at his side, breathless.

"I don't—" Then he saw it. A small sliver of blackness within the rock. He slipped over the edge, barely keeping his balance as he slid down the rocky incline. Dust flew in all directions, and he used his left palm against the earth to help keep erect.

The sound of voices behind him alerted him that others followed. Trent. Professor Andrews. Some workmen. But he only had eyes for the cave-like break in the rocky wall. It was the only answer for where she could be. . .and depending on the depth, whether she was alive or not.

He slid to his knees when he reached the jagged hole, and his suspicions were confirmed. Her hat dangled on the edge, hooked on one of the rocks at the entrance of the cave.

"Grace." His voice sounded weak, raspy to his ears.

Silence and darkness greeted him.

His throat tightened. "Grace. Can you hear me?"

"I'm. . .I'm afraid I may have sprained my ankle," came the small reply.

He released a burst of air, and his whole body weakened from a rush of relief.

"I'm terribly sorry, Frederick." Her voice gained strength. "If I'd known the poor creature was so terrified of parasols, I would never have retrieved mine to help block the sun. I can assure you, Ali Hassan said nothing of the phobia when he gave us instructions about the creatures."

She couldn't be too far, though her voice echoed as if she was in a large space. Trent slid to his side, his gaze going from the cave entrance back to Frederick, eyes wide.

"But I'm so grateful my injuries are not more severe. My bag strap caught on a rock at the cave entrance for a split second and slowed my speed enough to render only a twisted ankle instead of. . .well, worse I suppose."

"She hasn't changed a bit since we were children," Trent gasped out a laugh.

Frederick hadn't made it to laughter yet. He was still attempting to breathe; however, from the few stories Grace had told him of her upbringing, it appeared that his bride had developed a very specific talent for miraculous survivals.

"I need to get to her." Frederick turned to find Professor Andrews and his men standing nearby. "Do you have any idea about this particular cavern, Professor?"

He looked past Frederick, then back to his men. "I don't know how we could have missed it, but it's possible the sandstorm shifted the earth so that its placement was revealed."

"Have you a rope?"

The professor's brows rose, and he looked back down at the cave opening. "Yes, but it would be better if I or one of my men entered the cave, instead of—"

"I will be the one entering the cave first, Professor Andrews." Frederick held the man's gaze, brooking no refusal.

The man hesitated, his gaze traveling back to the cave entrance, before he turned to one of his workmen and gave directions in Arabic. The workman rushed up the hill, passing Amelia Sinclair on her way down.

"What on earth is going on here?"

"Naji has gone to fetch a rope," Professor Andrews explained, his tone surprisingly harsh. "Lady Astley has fallen into an unexpected crevice in the mountainside."

Miss Sinclair's expression stilled and she looked from the professor to the opening in the rocks. "And. . .and is she. . ."

"She's alive, yes." The professor answered before Frederick could. "And well enough to speak." He turned to Frederick. "Thankfully, yes."

"Yes," Frederick responded, attempting to make out the man's odd behavior.

"Ah, here comes Naji. It would be wise to retrieve Lady Astley as soon as possible." Professor Andrews turned back to the cavern. "In many cases, the air in these darker places is unhealthy to breathe." He waved toward the servant. "Naji, the rope. Quickly."

"A rope?" came a voice from within the cave. "That's terribly smart of you."

Another snicker sounded from Trent.

Within a few minutes, Frederick was being lowered into the cave, and the last thing he saw before the darkness surrounded him was the equally dark gaze of Professor Andrews. Frederick had the sudden sense that the professor was not all he seemed.

In truth, more than Grace's ankle stung. Her backside ached from a solid impact on stone and her palms were likely scratched, if not bleeding. But in all honesty, her situation could have been a great deal worse. And Frederick was coming for her. She smiled in the dark, thankful for the bit of sunlight shining down into the space.

If only she could see a little more, perhaps she could make out where she was.

She sat up straighter and pulled her satchel close, digging into it until her fingers found what she sought. A candle. It was a very good thing she'd read about undiscovered tombs. Someone or other always seemed to need a candle.

With quick movements, she lit the tiny wick, and the glow blazed against the deep shadows surrounding her. Immediately she realized two things. One, she was much closer to a wall than she realized. And two, a pair of eyes were staring back at her. She opened her mouth to scream, but then logic kicked in. How could a pair of eyes be staring at her from a wall?

She blinked and the wall cleared before her. Paintings. Hundreds of them. And hieroglyphs.

She pressed her hand against the wall and pushed to a stand. The paintings continued on each wall, and though the room was small, she could see it bled into another. She turned back to investigating the paintings with what light she had. They were of the same style as the paintings she'd seen in Meryra's tomb, with the sun disc on display as well as the royal family. Yet these looked even more vibrant. Was it because they'd not been uncovered in millennia?

She slid along the wall toward some debris in a corner. Vases! A chair?

Her breath came out in a shudder. Could it be that this tomb wasn't completely robbed back in antiquity? That these were actual treasures from three thousand years ago?

The light from above blinked in and out. Her candle flickered in response. She looked up to see the silhouette of a man slowly descending on a rope. Resting her elbow against the wall to offset the weight on her ankle, she drew out a few pieces of paper and began to trace some of the carvings while waiting for Frederick. Who knew what might happen once the professor and his team came into the cave. With more air or daylight or breathing people, the walls may very well collapse. She had no idea.

A woman appeared prominently on the walls, and she was holding a baby. A male child, if Grace interpreted it correctly. And Akhenaten was placing a hand on the child in some sort of blessing. What letter was that one? The cup. But the rest of the symbols were marked out, like with Akhenaten. And in this tomb, the king's face was not desecrated.

Grace turned away from the wall in time to see Frederick land quite romantically before her, his hair in delicious disarray and those dark of eyes of his sweeping over her with a most tender concern. She grinned up at him as he neared, and he gently took her face in his hands, his gaze roaming over her face.

"Your cheek is bleeding," he growled, his brows creased with his frown.

"Is it?" She raised a hand to wipe at the spot, but he caught her fingers in his warm ones.

He looked down at her palm, and the flicker of light showed raw skin. "And your hand?"

Before she could prepare, he pressed a gentle kiss to her palm and then breathed out a long sigh against her skin. With his eyes closed and his profile so near, Grace could make out the worry lines at the corners of his eyes. The feel of his strength moved through her.

A tremble of something deep and sweet quivered in her chest, and her eyes stung. "I'm sorry I frightened you."

He looked up, holding her gaze. "You did."

She ran her thumb across his cheek before pressing a kiss there. "I must be very hard on your peace of mind, dear Frederick."

He lowered his forehead to hers and closed his eyes, almost as if he was trying to calm his emotions. Oh, how she loved him.

"Grace, darling, I've only begun learning to love you. I cannot bear the thought of losing you."

With those words, his lips found hers for a brief, but rather exciting kiss, before he drew back and looked up at the way he'd come. "Let's get you out of here so we can tend to your ankle."

"Oh wait, Frederick." She stopped him as he bent to sweep her into his arms. "Haven't you noticed where we are?"

Staring at her, his brows furrowed again as if she spoke a foreign language, and then he turned to take in the room.

"It's a tomb, I think. And there is still debris here. Possibly treasure. It's the same sort of symbols as in the other tomb, so this tomb must be during the reign of Akhenaten." Grace giggled. "What if the mummy is still here somewhere too? Can you imagine!"

"Is everyone all right down there?" someone called from above. It sounded like Richie. . .er. . .Trent.

"Should I go down and see to them?" Amelia's voice filtered into the space.

"We are fine. I'm only seeing to Lady Astley's wounds before sending her up." He stared back at Grace, holding her gaze as if trying to communicate something. "Can't be too careful."

Her senses lit to alert as he gently took the candle from her hand and gave the room another sweep of light.

A large, stone-shaped case stood on the far wall.

"Do you think this was the burial chamber?" she whispered, trying to see into the shadows.

He followed her gaze, and with her leaning against his arm, they moved across the space toward the adjoining room. Frederick shook his head and raised the candle higher. "Those are not centuries old, Grace."

Along the ceiling and walls, a line of wooden braces disappeared into the darkness of the corridor. "What. . .what are they?"

"It looks as though someone has recently been inside this tomb."

He stepped forward, his arm taking most of her weight. The adjoining corridor led through a small antechamber with similarly decorated walls and then stopped before a large opening. Daylight filtered around the edges of a rectangular stone which had been propped in front of the doorway.

"Why would they close up a perfectly good tomb?" She reached toward the stone, and the hot air from outside touched her palm.

Frederick looked back behind them and then to the doorway. "Didn't Trent tell us that antiquities that are excavated are taken by the government, and only a small percentage of the proceeds go to the archaeologists or donors of the dig?"

"Yes, but with a stash like an undiscovered tomb, even the smallest percentage would be worthwh—" Her bottom lip dropped in a gasp. "Do you think someone discovered this tomb and has been stealing the antiquities in order to sell them on their own?"

164

He looked at her. "And could the crate found by the police have been part of the discovery?"

He lowered the light to the ground, and she gasped. "Boot prints? Those aren't centuries' old either."

"Lord Astley!" Trent's voice called. "Grace?"

Frederick swooped Grace up into his arms and dashed back to the main room. "I'm attaching her to the rope now. Take care of her—" He lowered his voice and asked her, "Which ankle?"

"Left."

"Take care of her left ankle," he called, removing the candle from her hand and setting it at their feet. "And her hands will need tending as well."

He made the rope into a seat for her and fitted her in place. "Grace, I need you to disguise that intelligent mind of yours from the men above. Just for the present."

"Oh?" She met his gaze. "Do you mean to pretend I didn't understand what I saw here? Or didn't even notice?"

"Not as well as you did." His grin tipped, and she leaned forward to kiss it. "I think the less we seem to understand about this business, the safer we may be."

"And the more likely we'll find out even more about what's really going on."

His smile tightened, but he gave a quick nod. "Now hold tight." He tightened the knot in the rope once more and looked up. "She's ready."

This particular ride on a rope was much less chaotic than her last. Of course, it had been wonderfully memorable for the simple fact she was attempting to save her husband, but there was a hint of disappointment in her form. She'd swung down like a monkey gone mad.

"You are one for adventures, aren't you, Lady Astley?" Trent helped her to a standing position, careful to take the brunt of the weight of her left side.

"I don't believe a runaway camel is the adventure I was hoping for, Mr. Anderson." She smiled as he guided her to a seat on a nearby rock.

"It's a marvel you're still alive." Amelia walked past her and looked down into the hole. "That has to be a twelve-foot drop at least."

"What sort of cavern did you find, my lady?" Professor Andrews asked, as the men began to lower the rope down for Frederick. "Anything of interest besides bats and rocks?"

"I'm rather grateful I didn't see any bats." Grace quelled a shiver. "Though I am a little curious about them, since I've not seen them before and had hoped for a chance at the pyramids of Giza."

"You went inside the pyramids?" Professor Andrews turned, his eyes wide. "A lady like you?"

Grace sat up a bit straighter, not quite certain what Professor Andrews implied, but it didn't sound flattering at all. "How else was I supposed to see what was inside? I can assure you, Professor Andrews, I've found myself in many an unladylike place." Grace replayed her words and frowned. That didn't sound very flattering either.

"Suffice it to say, Professor, Lady Astley's upbringing is not exactly that of a typical countess." Trent sent Grace a wink, and she couldn't help but grin.

"I'm afraid it's true," Grace sighed. "I left my elder sister in despair more times than I care to recount."

"And you didn't see anything of importance while you were in the cavern, did you, Lady Astley?" This from Professor Andrews.

"It was much too dark to see very much, Professor, but I do wonder if you might ought to take some men for a search down there." Grace smiled up at him. "I thought I may have seen some artwork on the walls nearest me."

"Did you?" He studied her, his lips tilting into a smile that his gaze didn't match. "Anything else? Treasure? Mummies?"

She laughed and attempted to twist her hair back into a bun. "I'm not even certain what any of those would look like in their natural habitat. I'm sure they'd present as very different inside the museum or from whatever my imagination conjured up from a dime novel. But I'm very happy to report that no reanimated dead pharaoh emerged from the shadows and mistook me for his long-ago Egyptian bride."

Trent's laugh burst out as he grunted against the tug of the rope. "You haven't changed at all, have you? Reanimated dead pharaoh?" He chuckled again. "Though Professor, if she did see anything on the walls, it would be worth a look for the last few days you have."

"Yes." He turned his attention back to Trent. "I shall take some men down this afternoon to see if it's anything worth further investigation."

They were just pulling Frederick up to his feet when a shout rang out from the trail above. Frederick drew Grace up into his arms, a feat which always left her rather breathless and grinning like an idiot. She felt certain she could walk on her own, but having him take her up in his arms like that seemed so much better. And the anticipation of their shared discovery only made the moment sweeter. She loved sharing secrets with him. Especially of the mysterious sort.

They topped the hill back to the trail to find one of the English house servants rushing forward, his face as red as a fresh tomato. Some Egyptian servants ran behind him, holding the reins of a few donkeys, presumably their transportation from the house.

"Gray?" Professor Andrews stepped forward. "What on earth are you doing out here?"

"I was sent, sir." He leaned forward, palms on his knees to

catch his breath. "Mrs. Archibald, sir. She sent me straight away."

"What is the matter, Gray?" Trent moved to one side of the professor with Amelia to the other and Frederick and Grace close behind.

"I'm sorry to bear this news to you." The servant swallowed audibly and then blinked a few times. "But. . .but Mr. Archibald." Gray swallowed again. "Mr. Archibald is dead."

Chapter Thirteen

The morning moved along, quiet and slow. Elliott had only left for a brief sleep when the nurse came to relieve him, but then he returned, anxious to ensure Mr. Graham's safety. He encouraged the nurse to take breakfast and resumed his spot by the unconscious man. Unlike the night before, Mr. Graham shifted a little in his sleep, a good sign to Elliott's mind. It meant he wasn't as deep in a coma as before.

Zahra had kept near the door, waiting to run any errand he asked of her, and Elliott almost grinned. He understood the scrappiness, the need to show your worth, but he wondered what history could have placed her with the need at such a young age.

When she brought fresh bandages to him, he stopped her. "Do you know how to change bandages?"

Her curious eyes raised to his. "Not with such fine ones as you have."

He kept from reacting to the idea of what sorts of makeshift bandages she'd had to use in the past. "Then come on, help me."

Without hesitation, she bounded forward, watching him so intently, he could almost see her memorizing each move.

"Is he going to die?"

Elliott paused and pulled back the last of the old bandage,

which only held a little old blood on its folds. "It is good that he's survived so far."

"He will not have his wits if he wakes?"

Her expression held no malice or humor, only curiosity. What sort of past brought such a question? "I don't know, but we can hope for the best."

She frowned. "You sound like Sitt Haree."

"Do I?" Elliott almost grinned. "How so?"

"She paints sunshine with her words."

Elliot pinched his lips together. Of all the people in the world he'd imagined being compared to, Lady Astley was the last. "Her faith helps her see sunshine, I believe."

Zahra took the bandages he gave her and followed his gentle direction.

"Where are your parents?"

"They are both dead." She didn't seem upset by the question, merely continued her slow work with the bandages. "My father was an Englishman. He kept Mama as his Egyptian wife, but he had an English family also. He would spend time with Mama when he came to work in Cairo." She grinned up at him, her chin tipped high. "He taught me to read English words. Not many girls can read and very few read English words."

"That was very good of him." Elliott had heard of such things back in England. Women kept by men as their own, but never promised in marriage. No true commitment. His stomach curled at the thought. But at the very least, the man had appeared to care about his child. Elliott couldn't say the same for his own father. "How did you come to be at the English orphanage?"

"Mama died of sickness when I was seven, so until Papa found me, I was on the streets. He paid to keep me as a helper to the English lady who worked the orphanage. He would keep me with him sometimes when he would visit." She finished her work, a frown puckering her brow. "He died last year, and there was no more money for me, so the English lady said she would marry me off." Zahra raised her gaze to him. "That's why I ran. I can work, but I do not need to marry the old unkind man she chooses for me." She nodded. "I will work for Sitt Haree and Rabu Alasid."

"Rabu Alasid?"

Zahra shrugged a shoulder. "The Lion Lord."

Elliott felt his eyebrows rise with his grin. "The Lion Lord?" Lord Astley would find that amusing.

"He has lion eyes." She nodded, certain of her choice. "Gold, calm, but fighter beneath."

Elliott stared at her for a moment. The girl held an uncanny awareness at such a young age. Was it because of her difficult childhood or something native to this Egyptian world? To be honest, something different and unfamiliar had brewed across the air since they'd disembarked in Alexandria. An ancientness?

Just then Mr. Graham shifted in the bed, pulling at his shirt collar as if he was hot or thirsty. Elliott reached for the glass by the bed, supporting the man's head as he helped him take a sip. The action appeared to calm the man, for Mr. Graham sighed back into repose, but his sudden movements had shifted his clothing, revealing a small notebook in the shirt pocket.

With care, Elliott tugged the book from its precarious place, and the pages unfolded to a spot marked with a tiny pencil. On one side, a copy of some strange symbols marked the page, evidently some ancient markings of some sort, but a few notes scribbled across the other page:

> *Work happening at night on the north side of the mountain, but I was not made aware of it. Discovered it while out walking three nights past. Cave entrance noted at dusk yesterday. Possible stele, but was redirected back to camp. Unable to find cave entrance*

again this morning but found scarab of fine quality along the trail. Eighteenth Dynasty. Akhenaten. Unbelievable to find such a relic so carelessly left behind. Something isn't right. Will attempt another look later this evening. Who is digging on our site? What have they found?

Elliott looked up to find Zahra at his side, reading over his shoulder. He closed the book.

"What does it mean?" She pointed to the book. "He found something?"

Elliott drew in a deep breath. "I'm not exactly certain, but I believe it's time for you to collect some of that soup from the kitchen because Mr. Graham may be up for a bit of the broth."

She narrowed her eyes at him and stood when a scream sounded from somewhere outside the room. Elliott jumped to his feet and ran from the room, Zahra on his heels. The scream sounded again, followed by a sob, so Elliott followed it up the stairs. Mrs. Casper leaned against the wall just outside a room where the door stood ajar. She had her palm to her throat, her face pale.

When Elliott reached her, she shook her head. "The curse. We are all in danger."

He rounded her to find Mrs. Archibald standing by a bed, her shoulders quivering with sobs. She looked up when he entered, tears streaming down her pale cheeks. "I. . .I didn't know. I swear I didn't." Her curls swayed with a shake of her head. "I. . .I thought he was fine. That it was all an accident. I didn't. . ."

She turned away from the bed toward the window as Elliott rounded to the side, but it didn't take close inspection to see the problem.

Sydney Archibald lay on his back, hands at his sides, looking every bit the part of a man taking a kip, except for the unnatural pallor of his still face. He expected the chilled feel of the man's skin before he even touched him. With a step back, he scanned the room, taking in as much detail as possible. A broken vase lay on the floor by the washstand. An upturned chair tipped against the wall as if thrown there. The Persian rug by the bed crumpled at one corner, boasting a dark stain. Blood?

Elliott turned his attention back to the bed and noticed a similar stain beneath Mr. Archibald's head. Definitely blood.

"We should call the doctor, madam," Elliott offered. "And you need to sit down." He turned to Zahra, who was still staring at Mr. Archibald's body. "Zahra, help Mrs. Archibald to her room so she can—"

"I don't need help from the child." She pulled away from Zahra as if the girl might bite. "I've had enough jewelry disappear. I'd rather not invite temptation." She looked past Zahra to the doorway. "Mrs. Casper. Please?"

The older woman seemed to emerge from her stupor and came to the younger woman's side, but a small collection of servants stood nearby, peering in.

"No one should come into this room, Madam." Elliott took Zahra gently by the arm and pulled her toward the hallway. "Not until the doctor can see to Mr. Archibald. The authorities may wish to investigate further."

"Authorities?" She blinked up at him, her face paling. "But. . .but why? He was in his room by himself." She shook her head, color returning to her cheeks. "No, we only need the doctor."

Elliott didn't argue but pulled the door closed and turned the key in the lock, nonetheless.

Mrs. Archibald looked from Elliott to the key in the bedroom door. "Why would you lock it?"

"To prevent tampering, madam." He offered her the key, but she backed away, shaking her head.

"Tampering? Why would anyone tamper with a dead man's

room?" Her voice quivered as she leaned more heavily against Mrs. Casper.

The older woman, bright purple in her exotic robes, looked a bit dazed, and from the strong smell of whiskey coming from her, no wonder. With a sigh, he put the key in his pocket and followed the ladies as they walked ahead of him to the adjoining room, which must have been Mrs. Archibald's. She sent him another long look before sending her maid, who'd just arrived, for refreshments, and closed her door.

After giving directions for one man to fetch the doctor, Elliott sent Zahra to stand watch by Mr. Graham's room, while he considered his next steps. A man with a head injury from an archaeological accident? The financial benefactor of the dig dead in his bed from an apparent head wound? And some mysterious happenings at the site of the tombs?

Could these all be connected? And not at all accidents?

He looked out one of the nearby windows toward the rust-colored mountains in the distance and the first thought that came to mind dipped his shoulders from a sudden weight.

Someone had to tell Lord Astley.

And prepare him for the real task ahead: helping Lady Astley solve this mystery without getting one or both of them killed.

The doctor had arrived only a few minutes before the rest of the party came in from the tombs and without hesitation were led straight to Sydney Archibald's bedchamber. Trent had only glanced in the room before going directly to Georgia, who could be heard weeping from her nearby bedroom.

Grace had very little experience with dead bodies, so the lifeless appearance of Sydney must have been the reason she didn't take as much note of the surroundings at first.

A hollow sort of feeling swelled in her stomach. She'd always supposed a dead person would either look as if they were in sweet repose or be dismembered in some way or other, but the gray hue of Sydney's skin paired with his pale hair tempted a bout of nausea.

Life inside a person made a difference, of course, but she'd never considered how much of a difference.

How terribly sad. Even for an unfaithful brute of a man.

"He died in his sleep?"

Frederick's voice pulled her toward the bedside, where her husband and the doctor were in conversation. "Mrs. Archibald alluded to her husband's overindulgence in drink and some added stress he'd experienced financially and with his excavations. I feel it could be something as simple as him having a heart attack while alone in his room and then dropping to the bed."

"Dropping to the bed?" Frederick's tone laced with a bit more incredulity than she'd expected. "And proceeded to cover himself?"

The doctor's brows rose in synchrony. "Well, that could have easily been accomplished by Mrs. Archibald entering the room after he dropped to the bed. Thinking he was asleep, she covered him."

"He wasn't known for his sobriety, Lord Astley." This from Professor Andrews, who raised a brow and then turned back to stare at the body. "And he was quite furious with our lack of progress on the dig. Is it possible the combination was enough to stop his heart?"

Grace studied the professor. A swarthy, intelligent sort of man with deep-set eyes and a well-trimmed mustache. If she was going to write a murderer, Professor Andrews would certainly fit the bill. Though she wasn't too certain whether archaeologists made believable murderers. The fact they enjoyed discovering dead bodies could either throw someone off their scent, since they likely preferred very old dead bodies to recent ones, or prove their villainy, since they were so accustomed to dead bodies. Whichever one Professor Andrews was, Grace hadn't sorted out just yet.

"It is." The doctor nodded and stroked his graying beard. "Though he is younger than most who suffer from such a fate, but short of drawing blood, his symptoms all point to it."

When they'd first arrived, Dr. Craven had only begun his examination of Sydney's body, and he'd concluded cause of death was a heart attack within a few minutes. Grace knew very little about heart attacks or doctors, except for the family doctor she'd known growing up, but the speed at which Dr. Craven came to his conclusion bordered on fictional. And not in a good way.

Besides, her childhood doctor had always taken ages to come to a diagnosis, which she assumed meant he was either very thorough or extremely forgetful.

Grace supposed Dr. Craven was correct at the very basis of his diagnosis. Sydney Archibald's heart had stopped. Grace looked back at the body, her frown pulling with more force as his pale face came back into view. His hair curled in damp tendrils around his forehead.

Damp? Why would his hair be damp? The heat in the room was enough to dry anyone's hair within an hour, let alone a man like Sydney's, whose locks boasted a bit of thinning on the top.

"You have no concern for something more sinister at work, Dr. Craven?"

Grace turned back to Frederick, almost smiling at the way his mind had turned in the same direction as her own. She hadn't given him those detective books for Christmas in vain. Clearly he'd benefited from them, and paired with his natural intelligence, they'd contributed to making him a very clever detective.

She scanned over the room, searching for any other possible clues. It was an opulent room with a golden Egyptian statue of Ramses in one corner, massive wooden furnishings, and an impressive shelf in the corner filled with various antiquated knickknacks.

The only thing missing, to her mind, was a rug by the bed. The barren floor on the side of the washstand didn't match the rest of the room nor fit what she'd come to expect in their short time in Egypt. Rugs were aplenty, especially Persian ones.

"See here, Lord Astley." Dr. Craven lowered his voice and looked back toward the door. "Let us not create speculations where there are none. Surely if there had been something underhanded, other clues would make themselves available. But the room is in perfect order and no one has mentioned anything to the contrary. There is no evidence of poisoning or strangulation or any of the other such wild theories one might concoct of such a demise." He waved toward the hallway. "And poor Mrs. Archibald has been nigh inconsolable since your man mentioned the possibility of the authorities being involved."

Frederick's gaze met hers.

Elliott?

"I should never wish to make things more difficult for my cousin, Doctor." Frederick bowed his head and stepped back toward Grace. "I bid you good day."

He pulled Grace's arm through his and walked out the door.

They'd barely made it from the room when Elliott came bounding toward them from the courtyard stairs. "My lord." He dipped his head to Frederick and turned to Grace. "My lady. I only now learned you'd returned."

"Come, Elliott." Frederick gestured for him to follow before glancing over his shoulder from the way they'd come. "We need to talk."

Once in the solitude of their sitting room, Frederick relayed Dr. Craven's comments to Elliott.

"And you would be so proud of him, dear Elliott," Grace added. "He asked his questions as directly as any budding detective should."

She smiled back over at her husband, who, as he often did,

stared at her as if trying to sort out what expression his face ought to make. He finally gave his head a little shake. "I certainly hope my instincts are very wrong in this matter, Lady Astley."

"Did the doctor not note the blood? The pillow was stained."

Grace exchanged a look with Frederick before turning back to the valet.

"Stained?" Frederick repeated. "The pillow? With blood?"

"Indeed, sir. It was unmistakable. There was a spot on the rug by the bed as well."

Grace raised her hand to catch her gasp. "The rug by the window?"

"No, my lady." He leaned forward. "The rug by the washstand. Near Mr. Archibald's wardrobe."

"There was no rug there, Elliott." Her face went cold. "And. . .and the pillow had nothing on it."

"You noticed the pillow?" Frederick raised both his brows.

"Only because I noticed Sydney's wet hair."

Now both men leaned toward her, eyes sharp. "What do you mean?"

"I only thought it odd that, if Sydney had been dead for as long as the doctor thought, his hair had not dried. The room was shadowed, but not enough to keep the heat from doing its work."

"Was there an overturned chair?" Elliott asked. "Or a broken vase in the corner?"

"The room was in perfect order." Frederick stood and walked to the window. "Elliott, if you saw a disheveled room and blood-stained pillow, then between the time you left the room and the doctor arrived, someone entered it—"

"And changed things," Grace finished. She pulled her notebook from her pocket, tapping the tip of her pencil against the paper. "Cleaned up a head wound, removed any bloodstained items, and tidied the room."

"Early this morning, I heard an argument happening upstairs," Elliott began. "It seemed to come in the direction of Mr. Archibald's room. There was a crash of some sort, and soon after, the arguing stopped, but then a woman and man left through the courtyard."

"Who were they?" Frederick returned to his chair.

"I couldn't see them clearly, sir. And I'm not certain where they went."

"So we have the man funding the expedition suddenly come up dead just as he was planning to desert the expedition, much to the archaeologist's consternation. We have a room that was cleaned of all possible hints to a head wound in between the time the death was discovered and the doctor arrived. We have a mysterious tomb uncovered in secrecy."

"A mysterious tomb?" Elliott pulled a small notebook from his pocket and tossed it onto the table nearby. "I found this in Mr. Graham's pocket. It mentions his suspicions about some hidden tomb and nighttime excavations."

Frederick took up the notebook, skimming an open page. "He was planning to go in search of the tomb yesterday." Frederick handed Grace the notebook. "Because he was concerned about possible tomb robbing."

"Is it called tomb robbing if you're paid to excavate but don't tell the benefactor of your excavation that you'd discovered a tomb and plan to plunder it?"

Frederick and Elliott looked over at her, their expressions twinned with wide eyes.

"There's evidence of recent work in the tomb." Frederick turned back to Elliott. "Boot prints and some sort of small, square, peg-like print, which may have been some sort of tool they were using. And the scent of smoke, suggesting recent torches or lanterns."

"But why the cover-up of Mr. Archibald's wound?" Elliott spoke first. "And the door was supposedly locked between the time we discovered his death to the time the doctor arrived. Neither Professor Andrews nor Amelia could have accomplished that because they were with you."

"As was Mr. Smallwood," Grace added, and then she sat up a bit straighter. "Where is Mr. Smallwood? You would think he'd be invested in learning about his good friend's death."

"But this could all be speculation, you know?" Frederick sat back down on the chair with a sigh. "Mr. Graham's accident could have been just that, an accident. Sydney's death could have been one as well, except he could have fallen over in a drunken stupor, hit his head, and stumbled onto his bed."

"But what about the tidied room?"

Frederick shrugged and looked back at Grace. "A servant doing her job?"

"And the tomb?" Elliott offered.

"Worth killing over?" Frederick responded, shaking his head.

"And then there is the jewel thief," came a young voice in the corner.

Everyone turned toward the sound to find Zahra sitting almost concealed behind one of the translucent curtains by the window.

"Come here, girl." Frederick beckoned her forward. "You should have made yourself known at first."

She moved slowly toward him, her eyes down, but Grace could tell her response was more from shame than fear. She trusted them. "I would not interrupt you, Saiyid."

"Quite." Frederick's lips tipped ever so slightly, and something warm and sweet touched Grace's heart. He was such a gentle man.

"I expect you to keep all you've heard to yourself, Zahra. Do you understand?"

"Yes, Saiyid." She nodded, meeting his gaze, her expression sober. "You and Sitt Haree can trust me to protect you."

Grace leaned forward and took the girl's hands, pulling her

forward. "We appreciate your protection, but we mean to protect you as well, so you must be very careful."

"And what is this about a jewelry thief, Zahra?"

The girl turned to Frederick, her chin tipped. "The lady Archibald, her jewelry, I found one of her jewels on the floor upstairs outside the mad woman's room."

"Mad woman?" Grace repeated.

"Mrs. Casper?" Frederick guessed. "With the robes."

"It was a jewel for the ears." Zahra pointed to her own ears. "I did not touch it because the lady Archibald already sees me as a thief, but it was there."

Of all the people to steal jewelry in broad daylight, Grace wouldn't have imagined the intoxicated and eccentric Mrs. Casper. In fact, Grace had a difficult time imagining her doing anything covert or stealthy, since she seemed to stumble about in a stupor most days. She was a wisp of a woman, though, so she could move about quietly if she wasn't intoxicated.

"Do you think she's pretending to be intoxicated to throw us off her trail?"

"I think Mrs. Casper is as genuinely intoxicated as she regularly appears to be," Frederick said, turning to Elliott. "Mrs. Casper shares a room with Miss Sinclair, however."

"Miss Sinclair would make a good and proper thief, I'd say." Elliott raised a brow. "She has a certain look about her."

"What is this intoxicated word?" Zahra chimed in. "Does it mean glass-eyed from too much wine?"

"Actually, it does mean something like that." Grace turned to the valet. "What look do you mean about Miss Sinclair? And how do you know if she would make a good and proper thief or not?"

His lips crooked ever so slightly, but he glanced at Frederick.

"Because, my dear Lady Astley, Mr. Elliott used to be a rather adept thief in his early days."

"I thought you were a boxer in your early days?"

Elliott shrugged. "One led to another, I'm afraid, my lady."

"Oh my dear Mr. Elliott, you become more and more endearing with each passing day." Grace laughed. "I'm so glad we have you as a valet. Just imagine what an excellent sleuth you could become with all your prior experience with the criminal mind."

Elliott coughed slightly, but Grace wasn't fooled. She'd learned by now that he truly wanted to laugh, though she hadn't worked out exactly why. She was quite serious in her praise of him.

"So, we have a possible murderer, attempted murderer, and jewel thief all in one house," Frederick said.

"And some illicit tomb raiding," Grace added.

"But we only have proof of the tomb, at present." Frederick turned to Elliott. "Unless we can find the soiled garments from Sydney's room?"

"Or locate Georgia's jewels with the actual thief?" Grace offered.

Frederick stood from his chair, hands on his hips. "I think the best course of action is to go to the British authorities and seek their counsel. At the very least, we could wire Detective Miracle back in England for his guidance. Let us wait here for the evening and keep our eyes and ears open." Frederick looked from one person to the other, and Grace could almost picture him wearing his very own deerstalker in preparation for solving the mystery.

Of course she hoped he didn't take up pipe smoking, but she wouldn't mind witnessing him shoot a pistol once or twice. He would look ever so dapper with his frock coat flapping behind him in the breeze. Especially if he was wearing one of his embroidered waistcoats.

"I'll make some excuse to go to Cairo in the morning." Grace blinked out of her vision of her darling husband as he continued talking. "Perhaps to see to some business related to Havensbrook's renovations."

"And I could attempt to carefully question Amelia, Mrs. Casper, and Georgia." Grace squeezed her hands together. "I feel certain I can pull it off without giving too much away, Frederick." She looked over at Elliott. "With Elliott here helping with Mr. Graham, I feel we have a good chance at learning more."

The dinner gong resounded from belowstairs. Grace looked toward the sunlight streaming in the window. It was much too early for dinner.

They followed the sound to the courtyard, where the rest of the party had begun to gather. Georgia stood at the head of the table, supported by Trent at her side.

Trent. Grace hadn't considered him as a possible murderer. He seemed much too gregarious and welcoming for such a ruthless act. And he hadn't been there long enough to steal jewelry or dig up secret tombs. But could he still care so much for Georgia that his jealous fury had overtaken him during a heated argument with Sydney and he'd taken advantage of the moment? She shook off the thought.

Mrs. Casper sat in one of the dining chairs with Amelia standing nearby. Professor Andrews kept to the edge of the room, arms crossed and forehead crinkled in convincing introspection.

Once they'd reached the table, Georgia dabbed at her eyes with her handkerchief and then drew in a deep breath. "I. . .I have been hit with quite the blow today." Her voice trembled, but she raised her chin and steadied her gaze on those in the room. "Under the circumstances, I am even more determined to quit Egypt and plan to do so by tomorrow."

Professor Andrews took a step forward. Amelia looked from Mrs. Casper to the professor, an unreadable expression on her face.

"I know Sydney had given you until the end of the week, Professor, but I. . .I cannot offer you that. I must leave this place."

"I understand your desire to leave, Mrs. Archibald. Especially in your grief, but might I implore you to allow us to continue our excavation. In Sydney's honor, we may still discover something in which he—"

"I am sorry, Professor, but I mean for us to leave completely." Her voice firmed. "Sydney had intended to end the excavation early, and we would honor him by keeping to his plans."

"Mrs. Archibald, truly, please—"

"Where is Mr. Smallwood?" Georgia searched the room. "He will support my decision, I know it. And you need his funding to stay any longer."

But Charles Smallwood wasn't among them.

"If you wish, Mrs. Archibald, I will go and collect him from his room," Elliott offered.

"And I will inquire of the servants, if you like, Georgia." Grace stepped forward.

Georgia's porcelain brow crumbled, and she closed her eyes, nodding as if the effort took all her strength. "Yes, thank you."

Just then a sound brought everyone's attention to the entrance of the house, where Timothy marched through the archway into the courtyard. "No luck finding your baubles, sister-dear. I searched everywhere a person could possibly—" He took in the room and his smile faded by degrees.

Poor Timothy. What a horrible way to discover the events of the day.

"What is going on?" He looked from his sister to Trent and then Frederick. "Has something happened?"

"Timothy—" Trent started, but Georgia interrupted.

"Sydney died in his sleep last night."

The way she held her brother's gaze, the slow deliberate execution of her declaration must have been so painful.

Timothy froze, his face paling to a ghostly white. "Dead?"

"The doctor thinks the combination of his drinking and his

fury brought about an attack of his heart," she continued, her attention never leaving his face. "And I have just announced that I plan to leave Egypt tomorrow and take Sydney's body with me."

"I. . .I can't believe it." Timothy balanced himself against the table and slipped down into a chair.

Leave? Grace looked from Georgia to Trent. To escape grief or—Grace stifled a gasp—possible prosecution. Had the two of them planned Sydney's death in order to be together?

"We need to clear up the idea of the ongoing excavation, a fact only Charles can help clarify."

Georgia's statement urged Elliott and Grace to move off to their separate tasks. Grace took Zahra with her as an interpreter, but the same answer came with each inquiry. The cook declared Mr. Smallwood never took an afternoon meal. The maid confessed to having attended to his room in early afternoon but seeing the room had not been disturbed since she'd cleaned it after breakfast, she left it alone. And worst of all, the camel boy said that neither Mr. Smallwood nor his camel had returned to the stables.

Grace emerged into the courtyard, the reality sinking deeper. Mr. Smallwood was missing, and his disappearance could only be for two main reasons:

1. He had murdered Sydney Archibald and was escaping persecution.

2. Mr. Smallwood was another possible victim of a much larger plan related to the tombs of the heretic pharaoh, Akhenaten.

Chapter Fourteen

Elliott pulled his shirt over his shoulders, his thoughts turning to all the events of the day. Unfortunately, despite Mrs. Archibald's obvious wishes, the news of Mr. Archibald's death and Mr. Smallwood's disappearance had made it through the town in a matter of hours. A rumor-happy servant proved the most likely candidate, but in reality, she had to know it was the best course of action. A man was missing. Not only that, but an Englishman, which garnered much more attention by the authorities than one of the natives. On top of it all, the Englishman by all accounts had no reason to disappear.

With nightfall not too far off, the police, such as they were, issued the call for a search party to gather within the hour. Elliott, after speaking with Lord Astley and securing a nurse to remain with Mr. Graham, retired to his room to wash up and change into clothes befitting what he supposed would be appropriate for a search in the Egyptian desert.

He'd just begun buttoning his shirt when his bedroom door opened and Amelia Sinclair slipped in. His fingers paused on his buttons. Her gaze flickered from his hands to his face, but she only hesitated a moment before closing the door behind her. Elliott took a step back as a gust of heat swept from his stomach up into his face.

"How did you open my—"

She stepped forward. "I need your help."

Her request went in a direction he hadn't expected, especially given that she, a single, attractive woman, had entered his bedroom uninvited. "My help?"

She glanced around the room, as if nervous, revealing more of the woman he'd only caught glimpses of behind whatever facade she wore for the masses. "I saw Daniel today. He looked better. More color in his face."

"He appears to be making good progress."

"Yes." She dipped her chin in assent to this. "Which is why we need to remove him from this place as soon as possible." Her jaw tensed. "I would regularly manage this on my own, but I can't." Her gaze rose back to his. "And. . .and for good or ill, I trust you."

He hesitated, fumbling through the last few buttons of his shirt. "Why should we move Mr. Graham?" In truth, he wanted to know why she trusted him. . .a choice which she didn't seem to bestow generously.

Her attention flipped to the window, away from him, almost as if she was deciding what to share. . .or not. "Mr. Graham is one of the few truly good men I've ever met." She turned back to him. "And I fear he isn't safe here."

Elliott finished buttoning his shirt and spun around to finalize the tucking. When he turned back to her, a sliver of a smile played across her lips, and he wasn't certain why, but her entire body relaxed.

"I need you to explain, Miss Sinclair."

"I don't think what happened to him at the dig site was an accident." Her eyelids withered closed but when she reopened them, she did not look away. "And I fear that if he regains consciousness. . ."

"Someone will finish the job."

"I've gotten myself into quite the fix, Mr. Elliott." She released a long breath and slipped down into the chair nearby. "If I'd kept to the plan and frozen my heart to feeling, then leaving Daniel to die would be no hardship, but even after all I've done, I couldn't remain indifferent to his genuine kindness." She rubbed her brow, shaking her head. "I deserve my fate. He doesn't."

"And what fate is that?"

She remained silent for a long moment, so Elliott lowered himself to the edge of his bed, placing him closer to her eye level. "Who has a hold over you?"

Her gaze flashed to his, a question crinkling her brow.

"One wounded soul recognizes another, Miss Sinclair."

"Amelia," she corrected. "Our stations are not that much different, Mr. Elliott. You work for Lord and Lady Astley and I *work for* the professor." She spat out the words.

"And it's the professor who you fear?"

She studied him. "What is your Christian name?"

"The safest time to move Mr. Graham would be tonight, but where? Do you have trustworthy connections in the town?"

Her frown deepened. "No." She stood and stepped toward the door. "It was an impossible idea. You're right. Where could we move him to keep him safe?"

Despite the fact Amelia Sinclair exuded everything he should distrust in a woman, he couldn't quelch the desire to help her, the faith that maybe his help was exactly what she needed most of all. "I'll move him tonight."

She paused, her hand on the door. "Where?"

"Do you need to know?"

"No, Mr. Elliott." The slightest tilt curved her smile. "I don't."

With that, she slid into the corridor. Elliott took his first deep breath since Amelia Sinclair had entered his room. The faint scent of jasmine lingered in the air. He almost grinned. What was her story? Who had broken her?

He shook the questions from his head and sat down to pull on his boots.

The last thing Elliott needed on his mind was the beautiful face of Amelia Sinclair.

But that didn't stop her from revisiting his thoughts one too many times before he left his room to join the search for Mr. Smallwood.

Grace had promised her darling husband that she'd stay in the house until he returned. She'd given her word not to attempt a camel ride to the tombs, or confront Georgia about her possible involvement in her husband's death, or question the doctor about his lackluster examination of the body. She wasn't certain exactly why Frederick insisted on her promising not to do so many things, as if she would try to ride a camel to the tombs.

She glanced out the window toward the distant mountains and nibbled her bottom lip. Though she'd proven adept at camel riding, if one counted the fact that she'd been able to maintain her seat on a spooked camel and even calm him down by herself. She squinted the horizon into a clearer view. If the camel was at a run, she could possibly make it to the tombs and back before Frederick even knew she was missing.

But she'd promised.

And unless she thought Frederick's life was in danger somewhere near those tombs, she'd better keep her word. After all, she knew his requests were intended to keep her safe, and since she hadn't perfected her shooting skills just yet, her presence wouldn't likely benefit anyone a great deal.

She'd taken supper to Georgia, who retired much earlier than Grace wished. It was difficult to question or observe someone who wasn't present. So as to make wise use of her opportunities, Grace had completed a careful inspection of the courtyard for any clues related to any of the possible crimes happening among them, before looking in on Mr. Graham. The nurse agreed that Mr. Graham seemed much better and shared that he'd murmured in his sleep, which evidently was a good sign. He hadn't mentioned any names or possible weapons used as blunt-force objects, but Grace supposed she needed to wait until he was somewhat coherent for confessions.

The entire series of events had all transpired within an hour, and Grace was certain she had many more hours to wait for Frederick to return, so she needed to sort out what to do next. She returned to her room to make out a list of everything related to these mysteries taking place around her.

1. Possible Crimes

    a. Murder of Sydney Archibald

    b. Attempted murder of Daniel Graham

    c. Disappearance of Mr. Smallwood

    d. Mysterious tomb

    e. Missing jewelry

Yes, that seemed about everything. A few more crimes were involved than she was used to reading about in books, but she preferred rising to a challenge instead of being undervalued. Now for number two.

2. Possible Suspects and Motives

    a. Georgia Archibald—Sydney's philandering and overall unpleasant disposition. A lurid affair with Mr. Smallwood. (Highly unlikely. Georgia had much better taste than that, surely.) No idea about

Mr. Graham, unless he was going to oust the possible affair. And why would Georgia steal her own jewelry?

b. Professor Andrews—Sydney pulling his funding from the professor's dig. Mr. Smallwood pulling his funding from the tomb. (But why not just kill him off like Sydney?) Mr. Graham learned about the tomb when he wasn't supposed to. No idea about the jewelry.

She looked over the list and frowned. But Professor Andrews was with Frederick and Grace when Mr. Smallwood went missing, so how could he have contributed to the man's disappearance? And if the professor was looking for ancient treasure and dead people, why on earth would he care about stealing modern jewelry?

She sighed and continued.

c. Timothy—An overall dislike for how Sydney was treating Georgia, and Mr. Smallwood by association. No idea about the tomb or Mr. Graham, unless Timothy was somehow secretly involved with the professor's antics with the tomb?

She blinked and shook her head. But Timothy was in Cairo when Mr. Smallwood went missing. Maybe even when Sydney died. She sighed. And did he need money so badly that he'd steal his sister's jewelry?

d. Trent—Jealousy over his undying love for Georgia, but he couldn't have known about the tomb beforehand since he only arrived after Mr. Graham had been wounded. And he was rich enough not to necessarily need to steal jewelry.

e. Amelia—Sydney wouldn't choose her for his lover?

Grace grimaced. Perhaps she'd been reading too many melo-dramatic novels. She scratched that idea off the list and continued.

    e.   Amelia—paid by Professor Andrews to kill off Sydney to save the tomb search, and Mr. Smallwood got in the way.

Grace scribbled out that one as well. Amelia was with them at the tombs, so she couldn't have made Mr. Smallwood disappear. But she could have tried to kill Mr. Graham and stolen the jewelry. Hmm. . .

Grace looked at her list and tapped her pencil against her lips. There certainly were a lot of reasons to kill Sydney. And the most likely candidates for a large portion of the possible crimes were Amelia, Professor Andrews, and Georgia. Unless Mr. Smallwood had really killed Sydney, was secretly funding the mysterious tomb so needed to off Mr. Graham as well, and then disappeared with the antiquities.

Her eyes popped wide. That could be it! Everything except the jewelry!

She glanced out her window at the fading sunlight and stood. It didn't help anyone if she stayed in her room. The best detectives *did* something. And Grace knew the first thing she should try. . .and she wouldn't even need to leave a note.

Clues were annoyingly absent.

A local English Inspector Randolph had been assigned to look into Mr. Smallwood's disappearance, and though he took a great deal of interest in the situation, particularly since it was an Englishman missing in Egypt, his methods were not up to Frederick's standards. Despite the information Frederick and Elliott shared about the discrepancies between Sydney Archibald's room before and after the doctor arrived, Inspector Randolph sent his men toward the river to see if Mr. Smallwood had merely decided to leave Egypt.

And Professor Andrews, to Frederick's surprise, offered to accompany the inspector, stating that he felt "obligated to be of assistance since Sydney was not here to search for his friend."

"Everyone searching in the same location will help no one," Frederick finally said, ordering the stable boy to ready two horses. Gratefully horses. Frederick wasn't interested in another ride on a camel, despite his wife's adulations.

"Where are you going?" Trent emerged from the doorway of the stables, giving Frederick and Elliott an unveiled look of suspicion.

"I thought you were staying in the house to protect the women?" Frederick mounted his horse and peered down at the man.

"If there's a murderer on the loose, don't you think the women need our protection?"

"I think it's very good of you to stay." Frederick nodded toward Elliott, who'd mounted a fine black steed. "Elliott and I planned to retrace Mr. Smallwood's tracks and attempt to come up with some answers of what happened after he left the tombs."

"The tombs?" Trent rested his palms on his hips, his pale eyes narrowing. "We never discussed what you saw in that cave, and I don't like the way the professor was behaving while you were in there."

Frederick steadied his expression. "And how was that?"

"He was agitated—and not about the possible peril you and Grace were in but something else." He stepped forward. "Georgia seemed to think the professor was keeping something from Sydney. She'd even discovered a scarab from the Eighteenth Dynasty in Amelia's room one evening, and when Georgia asked her about it, Amelia had said it was a gift the professor gave her after one of their other digs." Trent shook his head. "But this is the first time

Professor Andrews has excavated during this time period. His other excavations have been either during the Ramesside period or later."

"And this. . .this scarab was certainly from the Eighteenth Dynasty?" Though Frederick only vaguely understood that significance since he'd toured Meryra's tomb the day before.

"With Nefertiti's name carved in the cartouche. The queen herself. A find like that. . ." Trent froze, his eyes widening. "The cave. You saw something, didn't you?"

Frederick looked over at Elliott, who only raised a brow in response. Could he trust Trent? It seemed highly unlikely the man had anything to do with the tomb, but Sidney's death? He wasn't certain.

"Are you coming with us, Mr. Anderson, or staying at the house?"

He studied Frederick for a few seconds and then ordered a horse to be readied, adding, "From what I hear, Lady Astley is adept at throwing knives, so perhaps the ladies here are much more protected than I thought."

Frederick wasn't certain whether to smile or not, because the very idea of Grace having to resort to throwing knives to protect herself didn't bode well. They were away from the house and riding across the sunset-soaked desert before Frederick spoke.

"It is a tomb, but someone has been excavating it recently."

"By night, you think?" Trent rode closer. "Andrews?"

"I'm not certain, but I can't imagine he is ignorant to the find." Frederick kept his face forward, watching for any movement ahead. "The ceiling and walls had wooden braces in place."

"Good night!" Trent's voice rose louder than Frederick liked, but they were still a good distance from the tombs. "Do you realize how long the process of digging out a tomb corridor takes? To remove the centuries of debris then put the beams in place? Weeks at the very best."

Then how on earth had Professor Andrews hidden the excavation from Sydney for so long? Surely Sydney had joined some of the digs and, between him and Mr. Smallwood, supervised a few, at the very least.

"He can't have done it on his own, and he must have more accomplices than the natives." Frederick nodded. "Miss Sinclair seems a likely candidate."

"Do you think?" This from Trent. "I mean, she's not your typical lady, with her trousers and readiness to dive into hard work and all." He paused. "But I suppose with a past like hers, she may be game for any way to make a living."

"Past like hers?" Elliott asked from behind.

"An orphan, you know," Trent answered, turning to look at Elliott. "Her parents were in some sort of boating accident on the Nile. It's a miracle she survived. Traumatized the poor thing to such a degree she could only remember her first name, but one of the bags they found near the child had the name Sinclair on it. So they gave her that surname." He shifted back to face forward. "Georgia heard the story. Said Andrews' wife, who had always been rather ill, had never been able to bear children and took the child in as her own. Andrews had just graduated and was often gone on excavations, so he thought the child would be a comfort to his wife. Unfortunately, Andrews' wife died a few years later, leaving Andrews with, at that time, an eleven- or twelve-year-old girl. So his aunt moved in to help care for the house and Miss Sinclair."

"Mrs. Casper is Andrews' aunt?" Frederick cast a look back at Elliott, who was staring off into the distance. The fact that his very quiet valet had even voiced his question said something about where his thoughts might be.

"From what Georgia and Timothy have said." Trent shrugged. "But I suppose a child with such a tragic history would be set up to do whatever was necessary to survive. Don't you think?"

"Or whatever necessary to remain in a safe place." Elliott's comment was so soft, Frederick barely heard it.

They rode along in silence a little longer, and the mountains grew closer, looming like jagged shadows against the fading sunlight. Frederick took a path going away from the trail to the royal tombs in the direction he guessed may lead to the entrance he and Grace had uncovered.

"On the far side of the mountain?" Trent lowered his voice, as if the darkening sky brought on a greater sense of caution. "A remote spot like this would be far out of the way of tourists."

"And easily hidden from curious investors," Frederick added, looking up at the rocky overhangs, now cast in shadow. A tingle moved over his scalp with the sudden awareness of being watched. He brought his horse to a stop and attempted to search those shadows, listening into the silence for any sound to alert him of a possible assailant.

Suddenly a gunshot sounded through the dusk, the bullet ricocheting off the rocky ground only a few feet in front of Frederick. His horse reared back in response, nearly dismounting Frederick, but he held on, attempting to control his mount.

Another shot rang out, this time landing closer to Elliott's horse. Frederick guided his horse back a few paces, away from the direction of the shots. This was ridiculous. Their assailant held the advantage of being hidden in the rocks above. The three of them were sitting targets. They could make no headway at this point.

"Back to the house," Frederick ordered, turning his steed back toward home just as another shot rang out.

Trent jolted in his saddle, releasing a grunt before he reached for his shoulder.

Another bullet pinged off the ground nearby, and Trent slumped forward in his saddle, slowly looking up to catch Frederick's gaze. Even in the setting sun, there was no mistaking the slow, dark stain spreading across the man's chest.

Blood.

He'd been shot.

Chapter Fifteen

"Now, Zahra, your job is to keep your eyes open." Grace bent down to the girl's level as they stood on the landing overlooking the courtyard. A small hallway fitted between two of the bedrooms provided a convenient hiding spot with both a view from the window toward the cliff tombs and an unhindered prospect of the courtyard below. "I'm going to take a quick look around Mrs. Casper and Miss Sinclair's rooms while they're having their late supper. All you need to do is alert me if you see them approaching while I'm in their rooms."

"Should I call for you?" Zahra's large greenish-gray gaze widened. "Or come to the door?"

"Either will work, but it would be very embarrassing to be caught." She shook her head. "After all, I've been at this detective business long enough to not make silly mistakes, and I'm counting on you to help."

The young girl tilted her head as if trying to decipher Grace's words, but then nodded too slowly for Grace to be sure she fully understood.

"And you think you will find the blood-stained things from Mr. Archibald's room in the mad woman's room?"

"I certainly hope not." Grace blinked at the question. "That would throw a horrible kink in my deductions." She patted the girl's shoulder reassuringly. "It would, however, give us some much-needed proof, so a very good find." She stood and smiled down at the girl. "I can tell you are going to be an excellent investigative assistant. Lord Astley will be so pleased."

Zahra's smile flared wide, and Grace placed a kiss on the girl's forehead. "Now, keep watch. This way, should I find myself in any trouble, you won't be in the thick of it."

With another quick grin and a set of her shoulders, Grace slipped down the hallway toward Mrs. Casper and Amelia's rooms. She cast a look back to Zahra, who stood pressed against the wall and peered toward the courtyard, before Grace quietly opened the door. The room glowed gold from the setting sunshine coming in through the western-facing windows, promising plenty of light for Grace's investigation. A set of two joined rooms, much like Grace and Frederick's, stretched before her, separated by a set of double doors that opened one room into the other.

The hint of a bitter scent filtered through the air mingled with a stronger sweet smell, creating a nauseating combination. Not enough to have Grace run from the room, but the whiffs of it invaded her senses. The pleasant aroma she'd recently learned was jasmine, but the bitter? She knew it. Experienced it when meeting with Detective Miracle last month when he'd been working a case back in Havensbrook and she'd. . .unexpectedly shown up. Not that she'd meant to surprise him. She'd thought for certain he'd known she was following him. After all, he was a detective.

She approached the nearest bed, its coverings of exotic colors, and the bitter odor grew stronger. A vial near the bed proved a source. Opium. Grace scanned the area with fresh eyes. A statue of Bastet stood on a dressing table nearby and an assortment of gaudy jewelry wrapped around the cat's neck, as if waiting for someone to make their fashionable choice of the day. This part of the room was clearly Mrs. Casper's.

With quiet movements, she sifted over some of the items on the dressing table and opened one drawer after another. Nothing of consequence. But as she opened a tiny drawer somewhat hidden behind a purple scarf, the light glinted off an item inside. Grace's breath caught. An emerald-and-diamond bracelet. She tugged the piece from its spot and found a ring underneath it. Mrs. Casper was the jewelry thief? That didn't fit with Grace's idea at all, although she hadn't put her mind to who the thief was yet, so if she had, she might not have been so surprised.

With a little gasp, her fingers found the familiar feel of her own bracelet that she'd thought had been lost. The lone sapphire twinkled up at her, and she quickly slipped it into her pocket before returning the other jewels to the drawer. Once she shared her find with Frederick, he'd know how best to reveal the truth to Georgia. Then the new widow could at the very least get her jewelry back.

Grace glanced out the window toward the mountains, the sun sinking deeper and causing a strange sort of effect on the dip between the mountains. The rays focused in on that indentation, splaying light in a strange halo format over the plain where Akhenaten's city once stood. She'd seen an artist's rendition of how the ancient city might have looked, all white stone and pillars to catch the beams from the almighty Aten, but to picture it in her mind haloed in dying daylight nearly took her breath. What must it have truly been like?

And what sort of treasure must have been housed among those tombs?

The money for antiquities must be worth the risk if someone killed for the tomb's secrets.

She moved on to the other room, which was much tidier and less extravagant than Mrs. Casper's. A simple bed veiled in mosquito netting stood to one side of the window with a dressing table to the other. A washstand waited in the corner beside a tiny writing desk, and a large wardrobe took up most of the opposite wall. The scents weren't as strong on this side of the room, proving Amelia Sinclair may not hold to the same addiction as Mrs. Casper, though if the elder woman was ensnared by the drug, it would help explain some of her odd behavior. The idea of someone purposefully being so odd felt incredibly inauthentic.

The dressing table offered nothing extraordinary, nor did the wardrobe, but as Grace approached the desk, several things caught her attention at once. A large piece of paper took up most of the desk space, featuring a hand-drawn map of sorts, but not the usual map of a land mass or directions. Instead, this map featured several varied-shape boxes that, as Grace studied it, she realized were rooms and corridors of a tomb.

Grace slipped down into the chair. This was the new tomb. The wall paintings Amelia had copied reflected some of the same scenes Grace had seen, and Grace wasn't adept at reading hieroglyphs, but she'd learned a few words. There was Aten, the sun god, and the only god according to Akhenaten. And the word *sister*, then. . .Grace gasped. She knew what those symbols resembling a guitar then a bump-like structure meant. Nefertiti?

The pictures, first a man and woman offering homage to the royal family, then the man and the royal family mourning a woman and a child. A male child, if Grace guessed correctly. The first name in the cartouche beside the couple looked too difficult to decipher, since some of the symbols were destroyed, but the other name in the cartouche displayed all the symbols. She sounded out the name. The arm which gave the *A* sound as in *amen* and beneath it the—Grace bit her lip. What was it? Looked like a bolt on a door— ah, yes! A hard *S*, then the two flag-like looking reeds which made an *ee* sound, another bolt, and then a vulture, the short *A*. Aziza.

Who was she? A wife of the king? A sister of the queen? And why wasn't she buried in Akhenaten's royal tomb with the rest of the family?

A list of items lined one side of the paper. Hapi funerary jar. Imsety funerary jar. Eight faience shabti dolls, golden scepter, bronze statue of Isis, a jeweled necklace (rubies?), chair, decorative table, silver statue of Horus. . . The list went on and on. Vases, cups, statues, beads, a wealth of objects taken from the tomb. Grace didn't know the cost of this list, but just a cursory and uneducated look promised a very handsome reward. And she'd read where the illicit selling of stolen antiquities happened much more often than it should because wealthy men and women were willing to pay a handsome penny to add these items to their private collections.

With Professor Andrews' experience, he must have met the perfect people willing to bypass legal means to gain these antiquities and make a fortune for the unknown archaeologist in the process. Had Sydney found out about the professor's nefarious actions?

Grace turned the map over to find a beautifully drawn replica of one of the tomb walls, colors of blue, red, green, and yellow vibrant in their depiction of a king, queen, four daughters, and another woman holding a child bowing to the sun disc, Aten. Smaller scenes in boxes surrounding the larger scene showed simple daily activities such as a ride in a chariot or a servant presenting a woman with a gift. A sentence beneath the drawing read: *A high priest's wife? Sister of Nefertiti? Who is Aziza?*

Grace's smile spread. She'd read the name right. That was definitely one benefit of not requiring a lot of sleep so she could spend more time reading. The other was that she could fix her hair against the pillow in a becoming way so that when Frederick woke up he might be encouraged to linger a little longer.

In the corner shadow of the desk, two objects that looked like stones propped up a water-stained photo. She reached for one of the stones, since they had some sort of carvings on them, and then, as the light hit the beetle-like replica, she realized what it was. She'd seen photos in books. It was a scarab. A golden scarab.

She turned the smooth item over in her palm to reveal larger hieroglyphs of a name she'd memorized before arriving in Egypt. Akhenaten. A golden scarab over three thousand years old in beautiful condition? How much would something like this cost? She took the other scarab, this one in bronze with faint teal, as if painted. The name Nefertiti inscribed on the back.

How remarkable!

The photo had fallen over at Grace's disruption, so she placed the scarabs back in their spot and drew the photo close. It had been a photo of four, from what Grace could make out with the water stain. Only two faces stared back clearly; the other two had been damaged enough to make them unrecognizable, except one was a man and the other a little girl. The other two faces showed a beautiful young woman with a bright smile on her face, and behind her stood an older gentleman, some of their matching features pairing them as family. Father and daughter, perhaps?

Grace turned the photo over. The smudged note only revealed a partial description.

Father, Bobbie, . . .little Amelia.

Amelia? The child? Grace looked back at the face of the older gentleman, drawn to him with a strange sense of familiarity.

"I am done with it all." A voice sounded from the doorway. "This has gone too far."

Grace gasped and searched the room. What had happened to her warning from Zahra?

"You can't get out," Mrs. Casper responded with a small laugh, a creak at the door alerting Grace of their nearness. "You're too entrenched."

Grace's attention landed on the wardrobe, and she dashed for it, crawling inside as quickly as possible and pulling the door closed enough for a tiny slit of light to wink through.

"Not after this. I already told John I want to leave"—Amelia came into view in the other room—"to be on my own, and I plan to go through with it."

"Where are you going to go?" Mrs. Casper moved to her dressing table, her robe-like gown floating around her. "You have no skills except for what you've learned here in Egypt." The woman's voice lathered with sarcasm, and Grace's frown deepened at the sound. "No money, no connections. Nothing. What could you possibly do except sell yourself?"

"I've been doing that for much too long already." Amelia turned from Mrs. Casper and walked into her own room. "You saw what he became after Lillian died. Nothing mattered. No one mattered except his reputation and his archaeology. I don't want this for my future. I want something more."

Grace's heart pinched at the quiver in Amelia's voice. Had she been wrong about the woman all along?

"Oh, you mean marry?" Mrs. Casper laughed too loudly. "You won't settle for a bad man, I'm sure, and there are no good men." Her tone suddenly hardened. "Only those who are useful and those who are not."

Amelia had walked out of Grace's sight. Mrs. Casper sat at her dressing table, fumbling through some vials. Where was Amelia? Grace's stomach tensed. Quiet spread through the room, and to Grace's utter horror, a tickle started in her throat. She bit down on her bottom lip. No, no, no! This was not quality sleuth behavior! Sherlock Holmes or Lady Molly of Scotland Yard never felt the urge to laugh when they were nervous. Why was it her lot in life?

"You don't agree?" Mrs. Casper turned at her dressing table. "Oh, have you met someone who has given you false hope about the state of men? That valet, perhaps?"

The tickling sensation faded. Valet?

"Don't think I haven't noticed your attention being drawn to him." Her laugh emerged again. "A valet? Yes, that seems appropriate for someone like you."

"Like me?" Amelia came back into view, much closer than Grace realized.

"A thief." Mrs. Casper stood, taking a long drink from one of the vials. "A liar." She took an unsteady step forward. "A seducer?"

"I am what you and John have made me." She spat out the words. "But I will remake myself. I have to. This thieving and lying and moving from one set of horrible circles to the other cannot be what life is about. Lillian would have hated this. And I don't remember much about my mother, but I remember enough to know she believed in better things. Lovelier things than this."

Grace's stance softened, and she had the strongest urge to take Amelia, mostly likely against her will, into her arms for a long hug. Grace felt certain the woman could do with a few. Her mind flitted back to Mrs. Casper's words. Could the valet be. . . ?

"As if any decent man, your valet included, would have you."

Elliott? Elliott and Miss Sinclair?

Grace raised her hand to cover her mouth but realized too late that she still held the photo. It slapped against her chin. The noise couldn't have been large, but it felt as if it filled the entire wardrobe. Amelia flinched and looked over her shoulder toward the wardrobe.

If the woman could see Grace through the slit in the doors, she didn't react except to take a step nearer. Grace froze, holding her breath, her mind spinning through various ways to respond to Amelia should she be found out. She was looking for a lost shoe? Grace crinkled her nose in rejection. Not only was that a lie, but it was also completely unbelievable. A rogue assailant determined to find the map to the mysterious tomb had locked her in? Again, a lie, but much more exciting.

And it would give away the fact that she knew about the tomb. What about sleepwalking?

A loud bang sounded from the distance, pulling Amelia and Mrs. Casper's attention toward the door. Raised voices followed. Male and agitated. Amelia rushed from the room, followed much more slowly by Mrs. Casper. Grace waited a second before pushing open the wardrobe door and stepping back into the room. The voices below grew clearer as she neared the door. Frederick was back.

Just before she reached the threshold, the bedroom door flew open, giving her only time enough to press her body against the wall. Mrs. Casper rushed past, completely ignoring Grace's position, which was barely concealed by a table. Grace backed toward the door and was almost out when she met Mrs. Casper's eyes through her dressing-table mirror.

All heat fled Grace's face, and she slowly slipped the photo in her hand behind her back.

"Did you need something, Lady Astley?" Some of the previous edge in the woman's voice had dimmed, likely from her self-medication.

Grace forced a smile. "Mrs. Archibald had mentioned how good you were at palm reading, and I'd always been curious about it." The voices rose again, and Grace gestured toward the hallway. "But it seems my request will have to wait for another time, if you're willing."

The woman's tense expression softened. "Oh, I should very much like to read your future, Lady Astley." Grace sighed at the successful distraction. "I feel certain it would be most interesting."

Mrs. Casper walked up to Grace, her gaze roaming with dull curiosity. "But I'm afraid we must tend to the future of Mr. Anderson at the moment."

Georgia's cry came from below. "Oh dear God, what's happened?"

"Mr. Anderson?" Grace started moving more quickly down the hallway toward the stairs, with Mrs. Casper following more slowly.

"I predict he won't live through the night."

Trent Anderson had lost a lot of blood. Frederick had mounted Trent's horse to keep the man from falling as he'd fought losing consciousness, a battle he'd lost as they'd brought the horses into the stables. A few other shots had followed them on their flight from the tombs. Elliott took the reins for Frederick's horse and kept nearby as they rode in silence back to the house.

Whoever shot from the ridge had some skill with a gun. It couldn't have been easy to fire on moving targets in the fading light, especially with the shadow of the mountain falling over Frederick, Elliott, and Trent. Did Andrews have experience with rifles? Who else could have been hidden among the tombs in the evening, as if protecting his secret hoard? It had to be him! Andrews must have gotten away from Timothy and the police and made his way to the tombs.

The idea didn't sit well. Even though Andrews had left with the police a good half hour before Frederick left the stables, Andrews would have had to come back to the house, gotten a horse, and then remained ahead of them without being seen along the plain in order to take position.

What about one of the ladies? The only one among the bunch who might have the ability to ride ahead and then fire a gun, besides Grace, might be Amelia Sinclair, so if she'd been missing from the house, she might be the one sent to protect the treasure.

True suspects were down to a definite duo. And what had they done to Mr. Smallwood?

With Elliott's help, they'd carried Trent into the house, shouting an alarm before placing him on the cleared dining table in the middle of the courtyard.

Amelia came into view first, from atop the balcony. "What happened?"

"Mr. Anderson has been shot."

Even in the fading light, he could make out the pained expression on her face. She rushed down the stairs to Elliott's side, staring down at Trent's pale face. "How?"

"Someone was waiting at the tombs," Frederick answered, ripping back Trent's bloodstained shirt.

Amelia winced and looked up at Elliott. Their gazes caught for a second, before Elliott turned back to helping remove Trent's shirt and proceeded to use it as a sponge for the wound. Amelia looked up at him, her expression slipping to neutral, but a slight darkening of her cheeks had Frederick making all sorts of assumptions related to the two. Especially now knowing some of Amelia's history. And Elliott wasn't easily tempted in his affection.

"Could you go for cloths?" Frederick asked, and Amelia straightened to attention.

"And whisky?" she asked, raising a brow.

"Thank you."

She'd barely slipped from view when a soft cry came from the top of the stairs. Georgia stood wearing her pale blue gown, moonlight shining down on her like a specter of the night. "Oh dear God, what happened?"

"He was shot." Frederick turned back to Trent as Elliott pulled back the cloth. "It looks as though the bullet made a clean entrance and exit."

Elliott nodded. "And the bleeding is slowing, but we'd do well to clean the wound."

Georgia wilted into a chair on the other side of the table. "I must leave this place."

"I had some acriflavine in my bag."

Frederick turned to find Grace at his side, offering him a small bottle as if it was the most natural thing in the world. And he didn't even know what acriflavine was. As if in answer, she continued, "It's an antiseptic. I bought some for my medicine bag after asking Dr. Peters back home what he'd recommend for our trip. I have some dried lemongrass too. It's antibacterial. And a few other things, although I don't remember what all of them are for."

In the middle of this madness, he almost smiled. "Thank you, Lady Astley."

"I would offer to suture the wound, but I'm no good at sewing," Grace whispered. "Once I even sewed the glove I was wearing onto a handkerchief I was trying to repair and then into my skirt. It was quite the debacle."

She looked down at Trent. "Did the shooting happen near the tombs?"

Georgia's head came up. "How on earth could you know that?"

"They were retracing Mr. Smallwood's steps," Grace explained. "And I can only imagine what a terrific place it would be to hide from approaching people without their noticing. After all, if anyone was hiding on the mountains, they'd have long-range views of someone riding across the plain. It's a very good idea for anyone with nefarious plans."

Georgia stared and blinked, but any response, if she had one, was interrupted by Amelia returning with one of the servants, the latter carrying a pot of steaming water.

"Good thinking, Miss Sinclair," Elliott said, taking a cloth from her and nodding to the pot. "That will be helpful."

He and Frederick began using the whiskey and water to clean the wound.

"But who would be up at the tombs at night and shoot you?" Georgia stood. "What is happening here? First poor Mr. Graham, then Mr. Smallwood's disappearance, and now this?"

Did she realize she'd left Sydney's name from the list? Frederick caught Grace's gaze and realized she'd noticed the omission as well, and if he was reading the look in her eyes correctly, she had an idea why. Is it possible that Georgia lumped the other three circumstances together, but not Sydney's? Why? Unless, as he feared, she knew on a quite personal level how Sydney had died.

"Someone could be trying to protect something," Grace offered.

Amelia sent a sharp look from Grace to Frederick and then away.

Grace raised a brow as she handed Frederick the vial of antiseptic.

"Protect something?" Georgia asked, her confusion apparently genuine, which made her involvement in the whole secret tomb less likely. Though Frederick hadn't placed her among the possible suspects related to the tomb, her response confirmed her innocence.

The door to the courtyard swung open, and in walked Timothy, Andrews, and two other men—a policeman and the lead inspector, Randolph. Andrews paused as he took in the room, but Timothy ran forward, his gaze fastened on the body on the table. "What. . .what's happened?"

"Trent's been shot," Georgia answered. "And it's just another reason we need to leave this place as soon as possible. I am finished here."

"Shot?" Inspector Randolph fastened his dark gaze on Frederick. "Where? By whom?"

As he held Trent's body for Elliott to wrap the wound, Frederick gave a brief account of what had happened, answering questions from the inspector and Timothy as he did so.

"I would wager my life it was some tomb robbers," Andrews announced, slamming his palm against the table. "They're a notorious lot for showing up under cloak of darkness."

"You are right, Professor, but there is nothing to find at the north tombs, is there?" This from Inspector Randolph.

Andrews' eyes widened and Frederick caught him glance at Amelia before he began shaking his head and backing away. "They've found an undiscovered tomb. The one the natives had been telling me about." He took a few more steps away. "And I will not have them steal those artifacts for something I've worked much too hard to find."

"Andrews, it's not safe," Frederick shouted after the man. "You can't go up there without some support."

But Andrews ignored them all, and Frederick looked at the inspector as if waiting for the man to chase after Andrews to stop him, but the man sat down in one of the chairs.

"Peters, follow the professor to ensure he does not get himself killed." Inspector Randolph waved toward the policeman, who gave a curt nod and left the room.

Timothy slid down into a chair, his gaze fastened on Trent. "What on earth is happening? This is a madhouse."

"I am finished here," Georgia repeated, her voice breaking with a sob. "I think we should take Sydney's body and Trent back to Cairo tomorrow and be rid of this place for good."

"I can't have you do that, Madam Archibald." Inspector Randolph lit a cigarette, the pale light flickering against his eyes. "After what Professor Andrews and Mr. Withersby shared about what has happened here over the past few days, I'm afraid no one will be leaving for Cairo until we've resolved Mr. Graham's accident, Mr. Archibald's death, and Mr. Anderson's attack."

"But"—Georgia shook her head—"Sydney's death was from . . .from natural causes, and Mr. Graham's was an accident."

"Were they?" The inspector raised a brow. "I am not so certain. So many unfortunate events happening with only the people of this house in a matter of days?" He shook his head and scanned the room. "Oh no, I feel there are far too many coincidences,

Mrs. Archibald, for this to be a series of accidents. Mr. Anderson's incident may be the most obvious, but the rest are too coincidental to keep us from taking very careful note of all of you. So I believe you all need to settle in for the night."

"You can't keep us here against our wills," Georgia announced, but she had lost some of the fire in her voice.

He shrugged a shoulder, clearly unconcerned. "The doctor has been called to see to Mr. Anderson and, I would suggest, give another examination of Mr. Graham. In the meantime, I will look forward to questioning each of you on all the events, and then we can discuss the findings together at breakfast." He waved toward Mr. Anderson. "And perhaps Mr. Anderson will live through the night and give us some of his own information."

Chapter Sixteen

The doctor arrived half an hour later and inspected Elliott and Frederick's care of Trent's wound. With the doctor's approval, Trent was moved to his own room, where Timothy and Georgia offered to take turns keeping watch over him, with strict instructions to alert the house when Trent regained consciousness.

The inspector didn't seem in a hurry and began his inquiries with the staff, encouraging everyone else to go about their usual business, as if there weren't two wounded men in a house where a possible murder had happened only a day before. It was the strangest turn of events Elliott had ever imagined, even after listening to some of Lady Astley's more creative stories.

Elliott had been so certain the rifleman at the tombs must have been Professor Andrews. With the list of clues against him, along with some of the information Lord Astley had shared, it seemed only fitting Andrews would attempt to protect his illicit find, but Timothy Withersby confirmed that Andrews had been with their group until they'd returned to the house.

Could the gunman have been one of the tomb robbers so endemic to this part of the world? He shot with skill. Was that typical of the tomb robbers? Perhaps Lord Astley would ask the inspector when he came to question them. He'd wanted Elliott to join Lord and Lady

Astley during their turn.

As for Mr. Smallwood? Elliott had listened to Lord Astley question Mr. Withersby, who said their search near the docks and in town revealed nothing of Mr. Smallwood's whereabouts except rumors, of which the natives seemed to have plenty. One stated they'd heard of an Englishman being sent down the Nile in ropes. Another shared the tale of an Englishman years ago who'd disappeared from the same area, and folks attributed his disappearance to the man's disrespect for the tombs and Egyptian gods.

Elliott was following Lord Astley up the stairs to prepare for their meeting with the inspector when a sudden commotion came from Mr. Graham's room. Heat fled Elliott's body. Had what he feared come to pass?

"He's awake." The nurse appeared in the doorway, her eyes wide. "And he is speaking."

Lord Astley caught Elliott's attention, and they both rushed into the small room. Dr. Craven hovered over the bed, pressing a stethoscope to Mr. Graham's chest, but just above the doctor's hands Elliott caught a glimpse of pale blue eyes. Awake. Somewhat alert.

A very good sign. There was definite clarity in the man's eyes.

"Looks like Mr. Graham is beyond the worst of it." Dr. Craven nodded and pulled the light blanket up to cover Mr. Graham's chest. "Some foggy-headedness, I should think, but he was able to answer some questions quite coherently."

"That's good news, Doctor." Lord Astley moved farther into the room. "We have all been anxious for your well-being, Mr. Graham."

Mr. Graham looked up at them, his brow creasing as he searched their faces. "I'm sorry?"

"We've not met, Mr. Graham." Frederick stepped nearer. "I am Lord Astley and this is my man, Elliott. We only arrived on the day you had your. . .accident."

"Lord Astley?" The man blinked a few times, and his expression cleared. "Yes, I remember Mrs. Archibald mentioning your impending arrival." His words came slowly. "She was quite keen on meeting your new wife, as I recall."

Elliott almost grinned. Lady Astley's reputation preceded her.

"The feeling was mutual, I assure you." Lord Astley sent an amused glance his way before turning back to Mr. Graham.

Despite their unconventional meeting and unexpected marriage, the two had become an admirable pair. An example for Elliott in how two unique individuals could become even better when sharing life with the right person.

"I don't think I should have recalled much at all last night, when I first woke. My thoughts were jumbled, slipping in and out." He took a deep breath. "But Nurse. . .what was her name?"

"Nurse Beaumont?" Elliott offered.

"Yes." Mr. Graham nodded his thanks. "Nurse Beaumont talked me through the confusion, and I feel a bit more myself now."

"That's good." Lord Astley gestured toward the head wound. "You took quite the bump on the head."

Mr. Graham frowned. "I'll have to take your word for it, because I don't specifically remember how I ended up here."

Lord Astley met Elliott's gaze. Well, that lack of information wouldn't help in finding the culprit.

"But I think. . .I think it might have been about the tomb," Mr. Graham continued.

"The tomb?"

"I saw them. The antiquities. From the new tomb." Mr. Graham sat up straighter in the bed, his breathing coming fast. "Someone was stealing them. I'm sure of it."

"Come now, Mr. Graham." The doctor placed a palm on the man's shoulder. "Let's not get overexcited or you may very well relapse."

Mr. Graham released a long breath and relaxed back against the pillows. There were more reasons than the danger of relapse to keep the man from sharing too much information in an unsecure place. If he remembered too much, which appeared to be the case, his life was likely in as much danger now as it had been a few days ago.

"Daniel?" Amelia rushed into the room, an unfurled smile transforming her previously cautious countenance. With her hair loose and golden around her shoulders, she looked like a younger, more carefree woman.

Elliott couldn't help but stare as she made her way to the man's bedside. She usually wore her hair up and dressed in clothes of a less feminine flair, but seeing her in this simple rose day dress with her hair haloing her face, his heart lurched forward completely free of his control. Learning of her orphaned past only bound him to her more deeply. He understood that sense of being lost. The craving to find one's place, no matter the consequences.

She took Mr. Graham's hand into her own, and pain slid into Elliott's foggy fascination. Of course. No wonder she held such a desire to protect the man. She was in love with him.

"You're awake," Amelia released a quiet laugh. "I had thought. . .well, the worst may happen."

"It almost did, miss." Dr. Craven gave a sad shake to his head. "He's a fortunate young man." The doctor reached into his vest pocket and removed a watch, studying it before stepping toward the door. "Now, I have a patient to see in the village and will need Nurse Beaumont to come with me to interpret. The man is a Frenchman." He took his black bag from the table and walked to the door, where he nodded to Mrs. Casper standing at the threshold. "The visit shouldn't take long, and I shall return here to check on Mr. Anderson's progress and ensure Mr. Graham is continuing his improvement." He gave the group another long look. "Let's make certain Mr. Graham isn't overtaxed, shall we?"

The doctor exited with Nurse Beaumont close behind.

"What do you remember, Daniel?" Amelia rose to sit on the nearby chair. "Do you recall how you were injured?"

Would she be the one to ask him? Wouldn't his confession incriminate her as well? Elliott released his held breath, some of the pain easing in his chest. Perhaps she was who he wanted to believe she was. A woman attempting to escape her past.

"I can't remember," Mr. Graham responded, staring off into the distance as if attempting to locate the memories. "But. . .but it was near nightfall, and I'd followed a trail around the north side of the mountain."

North side. The place where Lord Astley thought the opening of the secret tomb must be. The same direction from which the gunshots had been fired last night.

"I had sent Akeem for the camels to meet me so we could return home."

"Yes, I remember walking with Akeem back to the place where you were," Amelia added. "That's when we found you unconscious on the ground." Her attention flickered up to Elliott, her gaze softening into something akin to an apology. Had she felt the draw between them too? Her focus returned to Mr. Graham. "Do you remember anything else? Why you went to such a remote part of the site?"

"I. . .I had suspicions about something happening there. Something unlawful, mocking all of our hard work over the past two years. But you didn't know, did you, Amelia?" He focused on her. "Not you."

A watery film filled her eyes as she stared back at him, and her gaze faltered.

"I see." Mr. Graham's jaw tightened and he looked away, drawing back from her.

Her eyes closed for a moment, and she stood, gripping the chair back as if for support.

"I'm sorry I cannot be more helpful right now." Mr. Graham straightened and looked up at Lord Astley. "But I would like to rest, if I may. I feel I may be better fit for further conversation later."

"Of course." Lord Astley dipped his head and moved toward the door, lowering his voice toward Elliott as they met on the threshold together. "We should lock this door until the nurse returns."

Elliott nodded.

"Meet me upstairs."

"Yes, my lord." Elliott waited for Amelia to slip past him in the doorway before he closed the door. He turned to seek out Mrs. Archibald for the key but found Amelia waiting for him, her face upturned.

Despite his best efforts, his heart softened to the entreaty in her eyes.

"Miss Sinclair?"

"I'm sorry, Mr. Elliott." She stepped forward slowly, her dark gaze fastened on his. "I wish I was what you thought, but I'm not."

"Mr. Graham seems to be a good sort." Elliott cleared his throat. "I'm glad he is well for your sake and your future together."

"What?" She tilted her head, examining his face with such open curiosity, his fingers itched to brush a thumb across her puckered chin. Then her expression suddenly lit. "Oh no, it is not like you think. Daniel. . .he was always so kind to me, unlike so many of the. . ." She sighed. "No, I care for Daniel more like a brother, I suppose. Though I don't know how it would be to have a brother. Yet there was a comfort with him that I rarely experienced with others of John Andrews' company."

She wasn't with Mr. Graham? He looked away, attempting to sort through a host of emotions ranging from relief to caution to a powerful need to rescue this woman's heart in any way he could. What was wrong with him? She had as much as admitted to her villainy and may very well have contributed to Mr. Archibald's death, though he doubted it. Yet he wanted to prove to her that life and people could be very different than what she'd known. He took a step back, distancing himself for his own sake. "Not all men are scoundrels."

Her lips curled as if preparing a retort, but then their gazes locked. Her expression stilled, and by slow degrees, her entire countenance softened into the smallest of smiles. Heat swirled around them, tugging him toward those eyes, toward the woman peeking from behind her protective facade to offer him a look at her real self.

"I wish we'd had the chance to meet in another life." Those same tears swelled back into her eyes. "In a world where I could, perhaps, match you in goodness. I think we could have been very good together."

Her fatalistic response pierced afresh. "I don't believe in accidental meetings."

"No?" She raised a brow. "Then what a cruel hand of fate to offer something I can never have."

"Never? Do you believe you are so lost?" He tilted his head, studying her and fighting the urge to take her by the shoulders and give her a little shake. "I know what it is to climb out of a broken life, Amelia." Her name slipped through his lips with such ease. "I understand better than you think."

She bowed her head and wiped a hand over her cheek. "Then you know what I have to do to climb out of *my* broken life." Her gaze found his again. "I must confess to the inspector what I know. It's the only way to protect anyone else from suffering Daniel's fate, or worse. And there isn't much time to do so."

"Do you know what's become of Mr. Smallwood?"

She shook her head. "I have no idea where he might be, truly. John Andrews doesn't share his plans until I need to know them." Her lips curled into a sneer. "Or when he needs to use my particular skills."

Elliott didn't want clarification on that score. His fist tightened at his side.

"I must go." Her voice shook, and she paused in her turn, offering him a sad smile. "Thank you, Mr. Elliott, for showing me that a good man like you can learn some of the worst about me and still. . ." She drew in a shaky breath. "Still look at me as if I am not beyond compassion."

"Jason."

"What?"

He cleared his throat. "My Christian name."

"Of course." Her eyes widened and a laugh burst from her. "You would be named after a Greek hero, wouldn't you?"

"My mother was a teacher." Heat swarmed up his neck and settled in his face as he tried to explain. "Father chose the name of the firstborn and mother chose the name of the second."

"And what was your elder sibling's name?" Humor danced in her eyes, and for some reason it made the embarrassment more bearable.

He shrugged a shoulder. "Wilfred."

Her smile split wide. "I feel certain you received the better choice of the two, Jason."

It had been so long since he'd heard anyone refer to him by his Christian name, he couldn't immediately respond. There was an intimacy to it he hadn't expected. A sweetness. To the whole world for a decade or longer, he'd been Elliott or Mr. Elliott. But Jason? Jason seemed like another person. A man who existed in another time, who had dreamed of a family of his own one day. Or perhaps that man had been waiting to be found again.

"I must go." She stepped back, her gaze searching his. "But it was such a pleasure to meet you, Jason."

And she left. He stood there like a stump and watched her go. What could he do? Once she confessed to the inspector, she'd likely be arrested for dealing in stolen antiquities. He was a valet with nothing much to offer her except a solid amount of savings and a polished reputation. Besides, what on earth could he even propose to her? "Come back to England with the Astleys and. . . ?" And what? Lady Astley was notorious for collecting castaways, but a grown woman with a criminal past? He felt certain Lord Astley would have a few things to say about that. And where would she stay?

Elliott shook his head. He couldn't stop the woman from confessing. It was the right thing to do. He groaned and stared at her retreating silhouette, his chest pinching again.

No. He couldn't do anything. . .but let her go.

Grace was not in their room.

Neither was Zahra.

Grace had not left a note, either, which Frederick hoped meant she was somewhere nearby. She *had* promised to leave a note should she decide to dash off somewhere unexpected. And she'd always been faithful to her promises, so far—though at times distracted. But surely she understood the importance of keeping him informed, especially with all the chaos happening around them.

He shot a look heavenward. Hopefully.

He'd checked with Elliott and Timothy, but they hadn't seen her. Georgia looked positively distraught when he checked with her. She'd even started packing her trunk with the evident hope of Inspector Randolph changing his mind about the party leaving soon. No one answered the door of Mrs. Casper and Amelia's room, though Frederick had noticed Elliott speaking with the latter as he left Mr. Graham's room.

Frederick couldn't quite shake the memory of Amelia when she'd entered Mr. Graham's room, her hair down and wearing a simple dress of older fashion. Something about her appearance dug into his thoughts and contrasted with the idea he'd built of her. She reminded him of someone, but he wasn't quite certain who. A faded memory. Almost but not quite.

But he couldn't turn his thoughts to it at present. There were too many immediate concerns. Mr. Graham's admission. Trent's welfare. And if Frederick guessed right, his cousin Georgia could very well have murdered her husband.

Of slightly lesser concern were these feelings Elliott seemed to have for Amelia Sinclair.

That idea solidified all the more when Frederick observed Elliott and Amelia's exchanges during their discussion with Mr. Graham. The attention appeared reciprocal, despite Amelia's open affection for Mr. Graham. Was she using her wiles as a way to distract Elliott? Lure him into a trap? Frederick knew that sort of woman all too well from his past, but even at the thought, doubt wiggled into his conscience. She'd gotten a public confession from Mr. Graham that incriminated herself—an act not usually attributed to the colder hearted.

Still. . .Frederick felt a certain protectiveness over Elliott. He knew the man's past—the dark path from which the man had come—and despite Frederick's firm confidence in Elliott's upstanding personality, women had a strange way of disrupting the most resolute.

Frederick shook his head at the idea. His sensible, no-nonsense valet! With a thief and possible murderer?

He looked heavenward again. Surely God knew exactly what was going on, but was there a particular something in the Egyptian air that led to a preponderance of odd and mysterious things happening? He sighed. Perhaps it was just a by-product of being married to Grace Ferguson Percy.

Odd and mysterious things seemed to follow her.

After searching the whole of the common rooms downstairs,

Frederick moved toward the servants' quarters and nearly ran directly into his wife as she was leaving the kitchens.

"Oh, Frederick! I am so glad to see you." Her smile was alarmingly absent, and her brow puckered with the worry she usually reserved for her fictional friends.

"Whatever are you doing back here in the kitchens?"

"I met Inspector Randolph on his way to question the cook and mentioned that I couldn't find someone, and he offered to help me look." She stepped around him and peeked into a nearby closet, evidently unsatisfied with the contents. "He was very pleasant about it. I got the feeling his life had been fairly boring of late, and he's rather pleased to be a part of our murder, tomb robber, missing persons investigation."

Her words caught up with his comprehension. "*You* can't find someone?"

"Didn't I mention it?" She turned back toward him, as if he was the confusing one. "Zahra is missing."

"What?"

"I know she's rather catlike in the way she can move about unexpectedly." Grace shrugged. "I caught her scaling up a tree outside this afternoon to attempt to peek inside Georgia's window to see if she could find any clues about Mr. Archibald's death." A little smile played across her lips. "I did admire her ingenuity for that one. However, while I searched Mrs. Casper and Amelia's rooms, she was supposed to—"

"You searched Mrs. Casper and Amelia's rooms?"

"Well of course I did." She looked up at him, azure eyes wide. "You didn't expect me to just do nothing. That wouldn't have been very sleuthing of me, would it?"

Nor very fitting to his wife's overall personality. Idleness never seemed to be a problem for her. "And that's where you lost Zahra?"

"Yes, though I did find my bracelet there, interestingly enough."

"You found your bracelet in Mrs. Casper and Amelia's rooms?"

"You see? A thief is among us." Grace paused in her search and looked up at him. "I misplace things sometimes, but not a gift as dear to me as one you gave me." She sighed. "Zahra was supposed to keep watch for me as I searched the room, but she must have disappeared right before Mrs. Casper and Amelia arrived because she never warned me of their coming." Grace turned and continued down the hallway. "I thought of checking Amelia's room again to see if she or Mrs. Casper had taken the girl, but after what I overheard between the two of them, I don't think Amelia is our real villain. I get the feeling she has a sad sort of past, which would make sense. In books, some of the most interesting characters have sad pasts."

"Amelia spoke of her past?" Frederick followed after Grace, scanning the room as they went. "Did she happen to mention anything about where she was born? Or her family?"

"Since I was hiding in the wardrobe when I heard the conversation, I didn't feel it the best time to ask questions. And Amelia and I are not exactly on pleasant speaking terms as of yet, though I'm not averse to being acquainted with tomb robbers and possible murderers." She dropped to her knees and looked beneath a table. "Grandfather had a whole host of reformed and unreformed rascals he'd introduced me to when I was a child, and we all got along quite well."

He mentally stumbled through her response, but then she came to a blinding halt in front of him.

"Oh wait. I did find something related to Amelia's past, I think." He helped her up from the floor, and she reached into her pocket. "I didn't mean to take it, I promise. It's just that I heard Mrs. Casper and Amelia coming into the room and had to hide and this was still in my hand." She shrugged a shoulder. "It was an honest mistake."

Frederick took the proffered photo but barely had a chance to look at it when the back door slammed open, revealing Inspector Randolph pulling a dirty-faced Zahra behind him. An unexpectedly powerful wave of relief poured through Frederick when he saw the girl whole and well.

"You found her!" Grace rushed forward, kneeling down to take the girl by the shoulders. "Are you hurt? You don't look hurt. What happened?"

"She's thirsty, I should think, but seems well enough." The inspector answered, gesturing with his chin toward the door. "Someone locked her in a building out back."

"Locked her in a building?" Grace repeated, looking from Randolph to him and back to Zahra. "Whatever for?"

"Evidently the girl had made an incriminating discovery." Inspector Randolph gestured toward her. "She found a blood-covered pillow sham with the initials S. A. on it."

"Oh no," Grace sighed, reaching for a glass and pouring some lemonade into it before handing the glass to Zahra. "It's as we thought."

The poor girl, sweat pearling across her forehead, drained the contents within seconds. Who would have placed a young girl into one of the hot outbuildings?

S. A. The initials on the pillow sham. Frederick's eyes pressed closed. Sydney Archibald. And putting all the pieces together, he was fairly certain who the culprit was. Especially since the killer didn't hurt Zahra, even though Zahra had information that would incriminate her. She only wanted to get Zahra out of the way.

"I told the inspector all the things I knew," Zahra said, wiping her mouth with the back of her hand. "What I heard you and Rabu Alasid speak about. Inspector was very interested. Especially when I told him the Sitt Archibald is the one who locked me in the building."

Rabu Alasid? Was Zahra referring to him? Had she given him

one of her special names?

"I plan to visit with Mrs. Archibald straight away," Inspector Randolph added, doffing his hat, a glimmer in his eyes. "Assuming she hasn't made a run for it."

The inspector made the statement almost as if he wished she had.

"I doubt my cousin would try to escape, Inspector. I'm sure her hope was to leave here before anyone put all the pieces together." Frederick shook his head. His poor cousin. What had she gotten herself into? "There are a few things you should know, however, in order to help you understand." Perhaps what little they'd learned, paired with Elliott's observations, might give some clarity to Georgia's actions.

Frederick gave a brief summary, with Grace adding a few thoughts, both hopefully painting a picture of a woman in a painful marriage whose typical disposition was not one of a murderer.

"Few murders are committed by those with a disposition for it," Inspector Randolph said, holding the kitchen door open for them to enter the courtyard. "But your information will certainly help me encourage Mrs. Archibald to share the truth. There's nothing quite as perfect at inducing a confession as having evidence."

"Well, I do hope you'll come question us soon, Inspector." Grace said, as she started for the stairs. "I'm headed to our room to help Zahra get cleaned up, but we have many more crimes in which you might take great interest. I feel certain we could keep you busy for days and days." Grace paused and stared ahead. "Good heavens, Mr. Elliott. What is the matter?"

Frederick looked toward the stairs to find a very pale Elliott just outside Mr. Graham's open door, a key fisted in hand. One glance at his expression and a sinking feeling pooled through Frederick with unwelcome foreboding.

"Mr. Graham." Elliott's gaze finally focused on Frederick's. "He's. . .he's dead."

Chapter Seventeen

"He's been poisoned." The doctor's gray brows rose in abject astonishment. The movement reminded Grace of a shocked owl. In fact, Dr. Craven offered a very owl-like visage in many ways, from his wild white hair to matching mustache, topped with a pair of circular spectacles.

Everyone crammed into the little room except Professor Andrews, who'd failed to return from his flight to the tombs. A very curious bit of behavior that left all Grace's grand detective theories in a quandary. If the professor had been with Timothy and the inspector for the entire time, he couldn't have shot at Trent. And if he was shocked by the shooting and angry that someone else had discovered the undiscovered tomb he'd been searching for all these months, then who had truly discovered the tomb in the first place? Unless Professor Andrews had blamed tomb robbers to confuse Grace, and if so, he'd done an excellent job. She was very confused.

She desperately needed to consult Detective Miracle's sleuthing book to review which techniques to employ when confused during an investigation.

"How?" Frederick asked, stepping forward, his hair a bit disheveled from his many adventures of the day, she supposed.

The inspector raised a glass poised on the table by the bed and gave it a sniff before running his finger along the inside. "Laudanum, Doctor?"

"Were his eyes dilated?" Grace asked.

Dr. Craven's brows took an upswing. Inspector Randolph's did the very opposite.

"They were."

"I'd read that's a sign of poisoning, but he doesn't have the pained look of someone who died in an excruciating way." Grace frowned, staring down at the still body of the young man. Her heart pinched at the sight. How horrible could someone be to do this? "Wouldn't someone have heard him if he'd been struggling to breathe or seizing or something like that?"

Dr. Craven looked at the inspector and turned back to Grace. "If the dose was high enough and the patient's body was unaccustomed to such a drug, the death could be fairly swift and rather painless. It is likely Mr. Graham fell asleep and eventually just forgot to breathe."

Grace placed a palm to her chest, the idea of Mr. Graham planning to wake up and. . .

"It must have been someone in the house." Frederick stepped close to her and placed his palm at her back.

How had he known the sudden sadness pressing through her? She wasn't even sniffling. But she caught a glimpse of Amelia Sinclair and silent tears streamed down her cheeks. Perhaps she wasn't a part of Mr. Graham's accident. Had she been in love with the man?

The memory of seeing Frederick tied up and beaten by the villainess Cecelia Blackmore Percy pinched pain through her chest. She leaned in against him ever so slightly. She couldn't imagine losing him. Well, she could. She'd done it a few times when her imagination took off and she'd ended up crying until she'd talked some sense into herself, but she didn't like the idea at all. And now poor Amelia felt the sting.

"Didn't your valet have the key?" Timothy offered. "Perhaps he knows."

Elliott lifted his face and scanned the room, awareness dawning on his face that the group was waiting for his response. "I had the key with me the entire time."

"Then perhaps we already have our answer on who is to blame." This from Mrs. Casper, who stood just outside the threshold of the door. "I told you all what would happen if the tomb was disrespected, and now we are seeing the fruit of such tampering. The curse is taking hold of those easiest to persuade."

"Don't be ridiculous." Grace stared at the woman, attempting to understand her nonsensical talk. "Elliott didn't kill Mr. Graham."

"He has the key, and the door was locked the entire time Dr. Craven was gone," she continued. "Mr. Elliott said so himself."

"Except for when I first closed it," Elliott added. "I had to retrieve the key from Mrs. Archibald, but I couldn't have been gone more than a few minutes."

"And he has no access to laudanum." Grace stared hard at Mrs. Casper.

Something about the woman set Grace's scalp to tingling with a fury.

"Laudanum is easily accessible here, Lady Astley," came Inspector Randolph's quick reply.

What was he doing, implying Elliott had something to do with Mr. Graham's death? She frowned at him. And he'd just been so nice to help find Zahra.

"Are you sincerely implying my valet had anything to do with this murder?" Frederick stood taller, taking his time looking from Inspector Randolph to Dr. Craven and finally ending with Mrs. Casper.

The latter merely narrowed her eyes at him. "He's the most

likely candidate from my view."

"Most likely?" Grace laughed out her words. "Of course he's not. He doesn't come close to meeting the MAP criteria of a crime at all."

"The what?" Inspector Randolph burst, the air wiggling his mustache.

"The three requirements to prove someone guilty of a crime." She raised her first finger. "Method. Ability. And Purpose." She stepped forward, continuing her explanation. "The method used in this case is the laudanum, which I am certain you would not find a hint of if you searched Mr. Elliott's room, so let's remove that one. Ability, which appears the most convicting, but I would suggest that if we ask individuals in the house, such as Mrs. Archibald and the household staff, they would be able to give hints to Elliott's whereabouts."

"And purpose?" Inspector Randolph folded his arms across his chest, his mustache twitching.

"The rationale. Mr. Elliott has no feasible reason to kill Mr. Graham."

"And since you appear to have some knowledge in these sorts of things, Lady Astley"—the inspector's gesture encompassed the room—"who would you suggest the murderer could be?"

"I don't care who the murderer is at this moment." Georgia wiped at her eyes with her handkerchief. "I just want to leave this place."

"As I said, Mrs. Archibald"—Inspector Randolph stood taller—"no one is leaving the house until these crimes are resolved." He turned toward Elliott. "And MAP or no, you were the last to see Mr. Graham alive and the first to notice his death, so Mr. Elliott, I would like you to come with me for questioning."

Elliott's attention shot to the man, his posture straightening all the more. He looked so very dashing at that moment. Brave and affronted. Her gaze slipped to the room and stopped on Amelia Sinclair. The woman stared at Elliott, their gazes locked in some kind of unspoken conversation.

Oh dear. Surely Elliott hadn't been drawn by the wiles of Amelia Sinclair into killing poor Mr. Graham, had he? She'd been so sure about the MAP for her dear valet. Certainly he was made of sterner stuff than to fall prey to a beautiful and clever woman. Though they were incredibly powerful, if fiction could be believed at all.

"He didn't kill Mr. Graham." Amelia's whispered words barely made it across the room.

"Amelia," Elliott responded with a tightening of his jaw, and Grace's bottom lip dropped.

Mr. Elliott referred to Amelia Sinclair by her Christian name? Oh no! She had seduced him into villainy! Grace had to do something to protect Elliott from himself, but Frederick's palm increased pressure on her back. She looked up at him, and he gave a little shake of his head. What did her dashing hero know? And why hadn't he shared that knowledge with her?

"Mr. Elliott did not kill Mr. Graham, Inspector." She stepped forward, her voice shaking. "There is someone here with method, opportunity, and purpose. And I have no doubt of her guilt."

"What?" The inspector stood to attention.

"Method?" Amelia paused as if second-guessing her confession, but then she looked back at Elliott and appeared to gain courage. It was a very romantic moment, and Grace began to wonder if Amelia might be more under Elliott's spell than Elliott was under hers. How very clever of him.

"There is ample supply of laudanum in my room, enough to kill quite a few men if someone had the mind to do it." Her gaze flickered to the doorway, but she continued. "Ability? This woman taught me how to pick locks, so something simple like a locked door would not stop her. And purpose?" Amelia swallowed, hesitant.

"She would do anything to protect her nephew, including murder."

A movement at the doorway caught Grace's attention. Mrs. Casper, pale face flushed a horrid shade of red, opened her mouth as if to protest and then. . .she turned and ran. Without a moment's hesitation, Frederick dashed after her, Elliott on his heels. The woman barely made it to the dining table in the courtyard when Frederick caught her. She writhed against his hold, brandishing a knife, but Grace's heroic husband easily maneuvered out of harm's way, pinning her hands behind her.

The woman's pale eyes bulged as the inspector took control of her. "He'll take care of me. I'm not afraid." She screeched out the words, her attention moving to Amelia. "I know where my protection comes from. It seems you've forgotten."

"Or maybe I've just finally become brave enough to want something much more." Amelia kept her head down, her chin tightened to such an extent it trembled. "Something better."

"Better?" Mrs. Casper's laugh burst, ruthless. "You ungrateful child. This is how you repay us, after all we've done for you—"

"Done for me?" Amelia faced Mrs. Casper. "Neither you nor John Andrews have ever done much *for* me, but you've certainly done enough *to* me to keep me trapped in this life for too long. And taking poor Daniel's life? For what? Your greed? Nothing is worth that."

"Do you think you're free?" Mrs. Casper's eyes glinted with an evil light. Grace knew the look. Besides imagining it dozens of times in her fiction, she'd witnessed it firsthand just before Christmas.

"You're a part of it. All of it. There is no freedom for someone like you."

The words appeared to hit Amelia like a blow, because her hand flew to her stomach and she looked away, clenching her fist. Grace moved to her side, hoping the woman felt her care, but Grace wasn't quite sure what else to do. The last murderer and thief she'd known wasn't nearly as agreeable.

"That's enough, Mrs. Casper." Inspector Randolph tugged her toward the door where two of his deputies waited on guard to ensure no one left the house. "Take her to the station and lock her up. I will follow shortly. I have one last inquiry for the night. Would you send Patterson in as you leave."

The deputies followed his command, leaving out the door with a squirming Mrs. Casper in tow, her robes wrapping around her writhing body. A massive man entered, his face devoid of emotion, but for some reason he reminded Grace of a human version of the fierce ape, Kerchak, from *Tarzan of the Apes*. Perhaps it was the frown.

"Mr. Elliott, would you be willing to assist the doctor in preparing Mr. Graham's body for transport?" The inspector nodded toward the valet. "I feel as though you would be quite capable of the task."

Elliott looked to Frederick, his brow raised.

"If you wish, Elliott."

"I do, sir." Elliott nodded.

"Might I be of assistance, as well?" Amelia asked, another look passing between her and Mr. Elliott. There truly was some sort of connection going on between them. That "knowing" look Grace had read about in romance novels. Did she and Frederick share knowing looks?

She glanced over at him, and he caught her gaze, searching her face as if, she guessed, to ensure her well-being. She offered him a slight smile, and his expression softened.

Yes, that felt very knowing.

"If you are able, Miss Sinclair, but"—Inspector Randolph approached her—"I would like to speak to you after I finish my inquiry with Mrs. Archibald. So please, don't make any unexpected trips elsewhere."

"Inquiry?" Georgia stood from the place she'd been sitting at the dining table. "Why should we need an inquiry, sir? We had no hand in Mr. Graham's death."

"There are other matters to discuss."

"Inspector, with all due respect. . ." Timothy moved as a barrier between his sister and the inspector. "We've had a most harrowing day already, and it's nearly nine o'clock as it is. Can't any further inquiries wait until the morning?"

"It is *because* of the events of the day that we should answer as many questions related to any deaths or disappearances as soon as possible." Inspector Randolph waved toward the dining table and looked at Georgia. "Would you be so kind as to suggest a room with seats enough for Lord and Lady Astley, myself, you, and your brother?"

"Lord and Lady Astley?" Her dark gaze shot across the room to Grace and Frederick, and she seemed to suddenly become aware of Zahra at Grace's side. Her face paled, and Grace felt a sudden pang at the next scene in Georgia's story.

"The sitting room upstairs?" Timothy offered, turning his attention to Georgia, but her gaze was transfixed on Zahra. Timothy offered a sad smile to the inspector. "I think that would be the best choice, sir."

"Very good. I shall be up straight away." Inspector Randolph gave some sort of instruction to his deputy, so Grace touched Amelia's arm.

"You were very brave," Grace whispered. "Your actions were truly those of a heroine at heart. I am sure of it. And the kindness will not go wasted."

Amelia looked over at her, her eyes narrowing, despite the slight tilt in her lips. "You are a very unusual woman, Lady Astley."

"Yes, I keep hearing that, but I'd like to think that unusual for all the right reasons is still a good thing."

Her smile broadened ever so slightly. "In your case, Lady Astley, I believe it must be true."

The sitting room connecting Mr. and Mrs. Archibald's room was only slightly larger than the one in Grace and Frederick's room, yet much more ornately adorned with rich rugs, Egyptian artifacts of the inauthentic variety, and colorful curtains that blew slightly from the evening breeze.

"I think you know why I've asked to meet with you in private, Mrs. Archibald." Inspector Randolph paced in front of the door of the room, a cigarette between his fingers. He wasn't as debonair as Detective Miracle, but his actions certainly met with Grace's expectations for an inspector. His relaxed steps almost mocked the intensity in his gaze, and something about the way he scanned the room reflected a lion waiting to pounce on its prey.

"I'm sure I don't know," she countered, but Grace heard little conviction in her voice.

The inspector stopped his pacing and steadied his severe attention on her. Grace had seen a great many severe expressions, especially from her wealth of governesses, but this one may have withered even the most dour in her experience.

"We found Zahra today, Georgia," Frederick offered, his voice soft. "She told us about you locking her in the shed when she'd located some soiled cloths, including Sydney's stained pillow case."

"And you'd believe a street child over me?" Her voice quaked.

"Georgia." This from Timothy. "There's no point in pretending anymore." He stood from his chair, his shoulders drooping as if he carried a much heavier weight than someone of his young age should bear. "But it isn't Georgia's doing, Inspector. It's mine."

"Yours?" The word slipped out before Grace could stop it. Hadn't Timothy been in Cairo when Sydney died?

"Timothy, don't." Georgia snatched his hand.

"I won't let you take the blame." He looked back at the inspector.

"I didn't know he was dead." Timothy's expression pleaded with them. "I swear, when I left, he was still breathing."

"I think you ought to explain, Mr. Withersby." Inspector Randolph ceased his pacing and leaned against the wall.

"It is no secret that Sydney was a philanderer and a rather poor manager of finances, but he wouldn't allow my sister the same freedom of romance or money, despite the fact that all his money came from her." He growled out the words, his fingers still entwined with his sister's as she stood beside her chair. "He treated her horribly." He waved toward Frederick. "I know you got a glimpse of the truth during your short visit."

"Mr. Archibald's debt and propensity for affairs was known, Mr. Withersby, and though grievous, does not justify murder."

"Murder?" Georgia barked out the word. "It was not murder." Her voice faltered and she drew in a breath. "Despite how it looks, I suppose. It was an accident. Timothy would never willfully take someone's life, despite his protectiveness of me. He wouldn't."

"I was done with him, Inspector," Timothy continued. "And that's the truth. When I overheard him soliciting Amelia to join him in his room, I saw red. That's all there was to it." Timothy crumbled back down in the chair, placing his head in his hands. "I confronted him, and we argued."

"Which our valet overheard from Mr. Graham's room below," Frederick added, and the look he sent to his cousins held such compassion Grace wanted to reach out and take his hand as a show of support.

"I didn't think about that," Timothy sighed. "Though I should have. The argument quickly turned into an outbreak of fisticuffs, which brought Georgia from her room. She attempted to get in between us, but Sydney shoved her back, and that's when I hit him square in the nose."

"The impact sent him stumbling," Georgia continued. "And

then he tripped on the carpet, hitting the back of his head on the washstand as he fell, which shook the bowl from the stand and sent it crashing to the floor."

"At that point, we knew someone must have been disturbed, but since Sydney had lost consciousness, the argument was over."

"He was murmuring when we placed him in the bed." Georgia nodded, her gaze desperately searching theirs. "I couldn't tell what it was, but he was so drunk, I just thought. . .well to be honest, I thought he'd sleep if off as he'd done every other time he'd taken a fall in such a state." She looked over at her brother. "I sent Timothy off to Cairo straightaway to create distance between him and Sydney, because I didn't want the situation to escalate the next day, but then when his servant said that he couldn't rouse Sydney, I went into the room and saw what had happened."

"So between your discovery and the doctor's arrival, you tidied the room to protect your brother," Grace stated.

"Yes." Her chin tilted. "And I will not apologize for it. We will do a great many things, good or bad, for the people we love."

Grace knew the strength of that love and the power of such a decision. She'd not had to hide an unexpected murder, but to protect her father and sister's reputations, she'd taken her sister's place to leave her home forever, redirect her dreams, and marry a man she barely knew. Her attention shifted to Frederick. But it had been a sweet choice. The right choice.

She looked back at Georgia. And though she understood Georgia's decision, it had still been the wrong one. One which would put them both in jeopardy for now. Georgia had assisted in covering a murder. That was quite different than marrying an earl for the sake of one's family.

"As you can imagine, Mrs. Archibald and Mr. Withersby, I will need to take you with me to Cairo." Inspector Randolph lowered himself into a chair, leaning forward with his fingers braided together. The intensity had left his expression. "If you had not tried to hide what happened, the law would have been more lenient, but, since you are both British citizens and, I expect, will do everything in your power to do what I ask you to from this point on, I have hopes the law will show compassion on your case."

Georgia raised a handkerchief to her face and began weeping. Timothy wrapped an arm around her shoulders.

"I will be happy to do all I can to help them, Inspector," Frederick said. "They are my family, and I know too well what it is like to live with the consequences of regretful choices."

"I would appreciate you and your valet assisting me in removing Mr. Graham's body as well as helping me escort Mrs. Archibald and Mr. Withersby to the train station." He nodded. "Perhaps you and Lady Astley can pack your things and join us in Cairo within the next few days. I feel certain your presence and character references for your cousins will benefit them."

Frederick turned to Grace, as if to gauge her response, and nodded. "Of course."

"Do you think it would be a good idea to take Mr. Anderson to Cairo as well?" Grace offered. "Would the medical care prove superior?"

The inspector's brows rose. "Indeed, Lady Astley. He would have faster access should his healing not go as smoothly as we hope. Yes, we shall take Mr. Anderson with us." He stood. "I will return tomorrow to continue the investigation regarding the tombs, and hopefully end all this nasty business. In the meantime, I will leave two of my best deputies here to look out for the house." He tossed a look over his shoulder as he walked to the door. "Surely, we've had enough villainy for one evening."

Grace squeezed her eyes closed with a groan. Didn't he read his fiction? What a horrible thing to say! For in doing so, he practically confirmed that there was certainly a lot more villainy yet to come.

Frederick drew her into their room after speaking with Elliott regarding their plans to assist Inspector Randolph in getting everyone to the station. "Do you feel as though you could start some of the packing so we can leave for Cairo tomorrow? I'd feel better being near Georgia and Timothy if they should need us."

"Of course." Grace smiled. "I have Zahra to help me, and what I can't do, I'll leave for Elliott."

"Excellent." He ran a palm down her arm. "And I shouldn't be gone above an hour, so you should be perfectly fine here during that time. Especially with the deputies outside."

"Of course"—she smiled up at him—"I have my pistol and knife should I need them."

His smile faltered, but he pinched his lips together and nodded. "I believe the worst is over for tonight. If there are tomb robbers or Andrews wants to protect his treasure, then keeping away from the tombs is our best option." He pressed a kiss to her cheek. "And let the police sort out whatever nefarious business is happening there."

"I do so like it when you use words like *nefarious*." She tugged on his jacket lapel.

He chuckled and rested a palm against her cheek. "I'd rather that the word *nefarious* be the only dangerous thing for the rest of the night."

Not if Inspector Randolph's villainy statement took on a fictional premonition.

"Though my heart aches for your cousins, I do hope there will be understanding and leniency as the facts emerge."

"As do I."

"Lord Astley?" The call came from the courtyard. "We are ready for your assistance."

"I must go." He gave her a quick kiss and backed to the door. "Enlist the guards if you need them."

She nodded and watched him disappear out the door. Zahra

emerged from her place by the window, still as dirty as she'd been when they pulled her from the shed.

"Well, I think the first thing we are going to do is get you a bath."

It didn't take long until the little girl shone fresh and fragrant like an exotic flower, and then she and Grace began making plans for packing. Their trunks had been stored in a room downstairs, so Grace instructed Zahra to begin folding some clothes while she went in search of a servant to assist her in locating the trunks.

Grace had barely left her room when a commotion at the end of the hallway pulled her attention. A crash? From Amelia's room? Grace started to move in the direction when a dark figure filled Amelia's doorway. A man cloaked in black from head to toe.

Grace stepped back into her bedroom and motioned for Zahra to keep quiet, as they both peered around the doorframe down the hall. The man carried something. Grace gasped. *Someone.* Amelia Sinclair. And two men held her. One had her lower body and the other her upper, and they looked to be natives. Was he one of Andrews' right-hand man? Akeem?

Heaven and earth, was someone kidnapping Amelia? Grace shook her head. Though if she was going to be consistent with her idea of "kid"napping being solely related to children, she supposed woman-napping would have to describe the event she was currently witnessing.

With a twist of her hand, she reached into her skirt pocket, but she didn't have her pistol. She looked back in the room. Where had she placed it? At least she had her knife, but by the time she raised the skirt far enough to reach the weapon, the men had made it to the courtyard.

Surely, the guards would stop the woman-nappers.

Grace rushed to the edge of the balcony to view the daring rescue, but a collapsed shadowy figure on each side of the door proved the guards had been incapacitated.

Good heavens! Grace had to do something! She rushed back to the room and took a piece of paper from the table by the bedroom door, scrawling out a quick message that she handed to Zahra.

"Give this to Lord Astley when he returns, Zahra. I have to go help Miss Sinclair."

Grace grabbed her coat and dashed down the stairs.

Chapter Eighteen

Grace had imagined chasing after a captured person on several occasions. What mystery-loving reader hadn't? But the actual reality of the moment hit with a bit more uncertainty than her daydreams. The cool of the Egyptian night smoothed over her heated cheeks as she slipped behind a building here or a tree there, following the men through the streets to the far end of the village. A ramshackle building, even by the standards of these Egyptian villages, stood near the Nile, an impressive boat docked nearby.

How strange. Why would such a fine boat be this far from the others docked along the Nile much closer to the main part of the village? She paused as Amelia disappeared through the door of the building. Then Grace ducked behind a bush when one of the men looked out the door one last time before closing it.

A rustling noise sounded behind her and she turned, but only the vacant street and the vast desert greeted her. She should go for help, but who could she ask? The house was empty except for the servants and the incapacitated guards. She had no idea when Frederick and Elliott might return, which meant it could be too late for Amelia. What would a true detective do? Sherlock wouldn't likely barge into the building. Lady Molly certainly wouldn't. But. . .they might listen for more clues. Yes. She could certainly do that. Besides, she might overhear news about the whereabouts of Mr. Smallwood.

The lone sound of a jackal calling from the desert startled her back to the present, and with another look around, she rushed from her hiding spot to crouch beneath one of the building's windows. Ill-fitting shutters had been pulled closed, but they didn't impede light leaking around the edges of the window or the sound of voices, and one voice in particular.

Andrews.

"Do you realize what sort of damage you've caused?" A smack sounded. "You were supposed to buy time in whatever way necessary. Not send my aunt to jail."

"Her actions sent her. Not mine."

Another smack. "You realize what I've had to do, don't you?" His voice rose. "I've had to use Lane to get rid of her. My own aunt, all because of you."

"So Lane is your policeman?" Amelia's response remained calm. "I should have known you had an insider ensuring no one asked questions about your nightly deliveries to the boat."

"You're missing the point, my dear." The edge in his voice sent a chill down Grace's spine. "With the little stunt you pulled at the house, turning on my aunt as you did, I can't trust you to keep all the information you have in that pretty little head of yours to yourself. So I'm afraid I will have to break my promise to my dear wife."

"You broke your promise ages ago, so don't be melodramatic."

Another slap and this time a grunt followed. Grace winced.

"I had thought to kill you quickly, but after your rather tiresome behavior, I believe a more torturous end will have to do. Besides, it will allow me the opportunity to destroy any evidence from this place."

"I'm surprised you've kept me alive as long as you have." Her response held little emotion. "If I hadn't proved useful all these years, I imagine you would have either married me off to some sheikh or disposed of me."

"You've been clever, I'll give you that," he growled. The sound of pouring—water? Liquid of some sort?—followed his words. "My aunt could have never stolen as many antiquities as you, despite her penchant for jewelry. So you will be missed for that reason, at least."

"And look where that particular talent has gotten me." Sadness filled her voice. "I wish I'd realized long ago that I would have been better off in an orphanage or perhaps even married to a sheikh, than to have spent my life being a slave to you. After your wife's death, I knew that all you had left to offer anyone was a callous heart. And I'd believed that brand of so-called kindness you showed me was all I could ever have."

"So you see, Amelia"—his voice edged with humor—"I'm doing you a favor. Putting you out of your misery so to speak, before your tender heart is broken."

Grace's chest constricted. Poor Amelia. Grace had been so wrong about her. She'd been trapped in a life she didn't know how to escape. All her confidence and allure had been a smoke screen for a broken heart, for an imprisoned life. Now Grace understood the tone in Amelia's voice. Resignation. Sadness. Perhaps she thought she deserved death or craved an end to her prison. Or maybe she already grieved the loss of a life she knew she'd never have.

Grace's eyes began to sting, but she wiped away the blurriness. This was no time for such emotions. She had to *do* something. But being as this was only the second attempted human rescue of her life (if she didn't count the one time she thought her sister was being attacked by someone when—well, they were actually kissing under a magnolia tree), Grace wasn't exactly certain how best to go about it. The last time, she'd had a rope and the advantage of a taller hiding spot.

Perhaps there was another entrance?

She slid against the wall toward the back of the building. The full moon shone down in all its glory, giving a wobbly reflection in the expansive Nile. Surely there was a way to rescue Amelia, but she needed to be prepared. She raised her skirt ever so slightly to reach for the knife tucked in her boot when a twig snapped nearby.

"Well, well." A voice emerged from behind her. "What do we have here?"

She spun around. A policeman approached, his dark eyes narrowing. Was this Lane? "What would a lady be doing out this late at night?"

Just over the policeman's shoulder, movement caught her attention. A little flutter of blue and a face peeking from behind a tree. Zahra!

"I had lost my servant and was desperately afraid she'd gotten herself into trouble."

"Out at night for a servant?" His brow rose, and he tsked. "What do you say we see what the professor thinks of your reasoning? I'm sure he'll find it entertaining." He grabbed her by the arm before she could run and nearly dragged her to the door. The last thing Grace saw before the door closed behind her was Zahra running back through the night.

What a wretched turn of events! Frederick peered out of the hansom cab window into the evening sky, rife with stars. The moon shone down, illuminating the town's box-shaped houses and flat roofs, giving the narrow streets and dusty surroundings a soft look. The charge of manslaughter offered some relief, but the stigma and emotional consequences remained. Society would not be kind. And Sydney had nearly extinguished most of Georgia's funds from her father. Timothy still had some, but not a great deal.

He could help them, would help them, once he confirmed Grace's support of the idea. He had little doubt she'd disagree, but despite her significant dowry, renovations to Havensbrook would take a considerable amount. They would need to be smart, regardless of how much financial support his cousins required.

"The inspector's assistant said that he would send your telegram as soon as he reached the station." Elliott's comment broke into Frederick's thoughts, and he looked over at his valet.

"Good."

"Are you certain about her?" Something in Elliott's voice had Frederick studying his valet more closely.

"If you'd seen her mother, you would have no doubts either." The man looked away.

"Elliott, you're at a prime age to consider your future, your. . .heart."

"Valets don't marry earls' daughters." The words emerged in a hardened whisper. He cleared his throat. "At any rate, after all this, who is to know what will happen to either of us."

"She may not wish to know her real family," Frederick offered, though part of him knew that once Amelia's grandfather learned she was alive, the older man would give anything to have his lost heiress back in his life. The lone child of his lone child.

Elliott looked over at Frederick and offered a sad smile. "She needs to know who she is, my lord. She needs to know her current situation is not where she must stay, nor how she must see herself."

"Indeed."

"And I'd never wish to sully the Astley name with such a relationship, for there are certain to be legal ramifications for her involvement in all this."

Frederick's chuckle pulled Elliott's eyes back to him. "Could she truly do any worse than my own past sins or the most recent attempted murder by the former lady of the house just before Christmas?"

The tension in Elliott's face relaxed a little.

"And now I have two cousins who will likely make front-page news with their involvement in Sydney Archibald's death," Frederick sighed. The way God kept killing Frederick's idol of his family's legacy was almost humorous. "It has been a hard lesson, and one I'm still learning, but God is slowly teaching me that I am not to be defined by my past, my relations, or my station, but by Him. Life's consequences do not always make that choice or outlook easy, and many times we do not and will not get what we want, even though we hold the proper perspective. But keeping to the view that my identity is in Christ helps place the proper importance in the proper places, I think."

"There is no understanding between me and Miss Sinclair." Elliott paused. "What would her true title be? Not Sinclair?"

"Well, she's the granddaughter of Thomas Kingston, Lord of Kerth, so I believe she would be referred to as Lady Kerth or Amelia Kingston."

"Lady Kerth." Elliott sighed. "What a turn of events."

"That is an understatement, my friend." Frederick laughed. "To think I'd hoped this would be a relaxing and enjoyable honeymoon trip to make up for Grace's loss of one when we were first wed."

"I do not mean to contradict you, sir, but there is a high probability that Lady Astley may be enjoying this adventure with as much delight as she ever would should the situation be more. . .relaxing."

"Elliott, I do believe you may be right." He patted his valet on the shoulder as the cab stopped in front of the house. "I know that this situation between you and Miss—Lady Kerth, is uncertain and may very well end before it begins, but don't negate it on my account. I have known you for years, and you are the sort of person who can do great and right things."

"Thank you, sir." Elliott nodded. "Your opinion means a great deal to me."

They exited the cab, and Elliott paid the driver as Frederick walked to the entrance. His first attempt at opening the door failed. It seemed something was blocking the way. His pulse began a faster beat. He pushed harder and made enough room to slip into the house. The dark entry gave slow clarity to the heavy mound on the floor.

Heat left Frederick's face. One of the police guards? He stepped forward only to see a similar body to his left. Both guards. Frederick knelt to examine the nearest body as Elliott entered, pausing in the doorway.

"This one is alive." Frederick moved to the other guard. "But not this one."

His breathing grew ragged, and he rushed through the courtyard and up the stairs. "Grace?"

The silence left a resounding answer. He burst into their bedroom. The empty room confirmed it. He drew in a deep breath and searched the space for any clue to her whereabouts.

"Sir." Frederick turned to find Elliott holding out a slip of paper. "I found this on the floor by the door."

Frederick took the paper with a note written in familiar hand.

> *Amelia has been woman-napped. The guards are incapacitated. I have to help, if I can.*
>
> *Grace*

Frederick turned the paper over, searching for anything else, but there was no other clue. No direction or information. He ran a palm down his face and shoved the paper in his pocket. Perhaps she didn't know the direction at the time? An empty feeling swelled in his stomach. Likely these men had much worse plans than merely kidnapping, especially if they learned how much Grace knew.

A sudden sound from the courtyard drew Elliott and Frederick to the door. Elliott's hand rested on top of the pistol he had secured after Mr. Graham's death. Frederick had done the same.

"Rabu Alasid?" The call echoed through the courtyard.

Zahra came into view, her large eyes frantically searching the space until she found him. "Lord Astley, sir."

"Zahra." Frederick rounded Elliott and dashed down the stairs to meet the girl at the bottom. "Do you know where Lady Astley is?"

She nodded, her breaths pumping her chest. "She has been taken, sir. A policeman took her."

A policeman? Did they have one of the authorities working in the stolen antiquities business too? Frederick looked over at Elliott and then back to Zahra. "Can you take us there?"

She nodded, turned, and ran for the door.

How many brides have died on their honeymoon?

It seemed a horrible spin on all the fairytales Grace loved so much. Dying on one's honeymoon. What a waste of a perfectly romantic adventure! And poor Frederick would have to live with the horrible fact. The idea nearly brought tears to Grace's eyes. Her poor Frederick. He didn't deserve that at all.

Even as Lane pulled her roughly into the house, she determined that she could not die on this trip. For Frederick's sake. Her death would just have to wait for another time. Now how to ensure that resolution was an entirely different story.

The vast, dark room was lit by a few dim lamps, and at the center sat Amelia. A rope wrapped around her chest, strapping her to the chair, with her hands tied behind her.

At Grace's entry, Amelia and Andrews turned, both pausing in their dialogue. A trickle of blood darkened the side of Amelia's lips, and even in the shadow, Grace could see swelling around Amelia's left eye. Heat twisted through Grace's chest, and she shot the professor a glare she wished had much more power than his response suggested.

Clearly, since she'd never been a governess or a mother, she'd failed to hone her glaring skills to a powerful enough level. Perhaps Aunt Lavenia could teach her. Grace had witnessed a few excellent glares when Aunt Lavenia scolded her gardener on occasion.

"I found her sneaking around outside." Lane pinched her arm more tightly.

Andrews tugged the cigarette from his mouth and frowned. "This muddies the water." He stepped toward her, his dark gaze roaming over her face. "You're rather a nuisance, aren't you?"

"Usually only for people who are engaging in nefarious business." Which wasn't actually true, because Grace was certain she'd been a nuisance for quite a few very good people in her life, but she'd always supposed it was because of her active imagination. . .or her talking.

"I'm afraid, Lady Astley, you've gotten yourself into business much too nefarious for the likes of the genteel sort." He took another draw from his cigarette and continued to examine her. "Which begs the question, what are we to do with you?"

"I have no doubt her husband is close behind, Andrews, and I doubt he'll take kindly to you mistreating his wife."

Amelia cast a look Grace's way, her expression softening as their eyes met.

The woman was trying to help Grace while Grace was trying to rescue her! Oh, how brave and magnanimous they both were, certainly heroine worthy.

"Is that so, your ladyship?" Andrews' brows rose. "Well, we must be on our way then." He turned back to Amelia. "We only needed one more day, Amelia. One more day and we could have all left this place with our pockets full of treasure and a plan for a new life, but you had to go and ruin everything."

"Daniel didn't have to die," she whispered, a sudden sheen showing in her dark eyes. "No one has had to die."

"That's the unfortunate bit about this line of work, pet. You can't leave loose ends." The professor turned back to Grace as he slowly twirled the cigarette in his hands. "Let's take her with us, Lane. We may need to use her as leverage should her husband or the police show up." He tsked and stepped closer to Grace. "And then, once all is clear, we can dispatch her."

Grace pulled against Lane's grip to no avail. If she could just hold off long enough for Frederick and Elliott to arrive, then everyone could be saved and the treasure rescued.

"You won't get away with this, Professor Andrews." Grace stood taller, but her head barely made it to the professor's cheekbone. Not intimidating at all. "The police know of your scheme, and they'll be here as soon as they return from the station."

"Ah, the station?" His smile spread. "Not on the way to the tomb? I'm afraid, Lady Astley, it is not becoming for a lady to lie." He shook his head. "If the police knew we were raiding the tomb, do you think they'd really come here first? And if they're all the way at the station on the far side of town, I feel we have ample time to finish removing the last antiquities to the boat and disappear off into the sunrise."

If Grace had expert fighting skills and secret gadgets, she'd easily overcome two men and free Amelia from her bonds. With the amount of fury currently boiling beneath her skin, she might possibly produce a few excellent glares too.

Andrews looked to Lane. "Did you take the last few crates to the boat?"

"They're secure."

Andrews turned and walked back to Amelia. "I did attempt

to keep my promise to my dear Lillian, but you were too apt to misbehave." He ran a finger down her cheek. "And I do hate to lose such a good thief."

"You never deserved her." Amelia glared up at him with such malice, Grace felt a deep appreciation for the woman's skills. "And if she could see what you've become, it would break her hea—"

His backhand stopped Amelia's response, and Grace attempted to rush forward to Amelia's defense, only to have Lane tighten his hold until it pinched.

"I thought I'd feel some regret at killing you." He raised a brow. "But I feel nothing."

With that, he flicked his cigarette to the floor and a flame burst alive, taking a path set by the liquid he'd poured earlier. Fire brightened the room, creating a growing wall of heat.

"Let's go," Andrews said, snatching his jacket from a nearby chair and leading the way as Lane pulled Grace behind him. She pulled against him, causing him to stumble. Grace had to get free. She couldn't allow Amelia to die such a horrific death. She jerked one arm free from Lane and brought her fist up to land against his cheek. The impact wasn't as satisfying as she thought it might be. Of course, it was the first time she'd ever tried to punch someone and her lack of practice proved her downfall, because Lane merely grunted and caught her arm, twisting it so tightly against her back that pain shot up her shoulder to her neck.

Her knees weakened as he pulled her a few more steps, and then a flare of anger took over. She slammed the heel of her boot firmly down on his foot. Lane cursed and pulled Grace close so that his fish-laden breath coated the inches between them. "I don't care if you're a lady. I won't let you keep me from getting my part of the treasure, so don't try me."

"Then let me go and I won't slow you down." Grace shot back.

He growled and shoved her forward.

The last thing Grace saw as the door closed behind her was Amelia looking at her, golden flames and fear reflected in her eyes.

Dear God, help us!

Chapter Nineteen

Lord Astley's expression remained impassive, but Elliott knew his master too well to question his concern. If the people who had taken Amelia had no qualms with killing a policeman and possessed the physical ability to do so, they were not dealing with amateurs. The gunman from the tomb had proved his skill as well.

This group of thieves wasn't to be underestimated.

Greed moved many a heart to disastrous ends, and an entire tomb of treasure? Elliott could only imagine the power such a find would wield.

He attempted to keep his mind from Amelia's part in all this as they raced through the streets of the village following Zahra. His suspicions rose despite himself. He knew the tug of an old life. The power of the habitual and easy path. Had she truly been a victim of the kidnapping, or was she playing a part to draw Lady Astley from the house? He prayed the former proved her character as much as she'd shown when she stepped in to name Mrs. Casper as the murderer of Mr. Graham.

Even if there was no chance to contemplate a future together, he would not wish her to remain a prisoner in her current life. Oh no! He only wanted the very best for her. To learn the pleasure of honest work and the pride of earning one's own way. To experience care and healing. To know love.

Amelia. His mind breathed her name, but he shook his head. Lady Kerth.

An earl's granddaughter.

Not a simple, unknown thief.

A plume of smoke rose into the night, and Lord Astley sent Elliott a look, the fear in the man's eyes unmistakable. Lord Astley broke out into a faster run, bypassing Zahra and charging directly for a small building with smoke billowing from one of the small windows. Elliott followed, a growing dread gaining weight in his stomach. Elliott nearly slammed into Lord Astley's back as he burst through the house door, the heat and smoke pausing them. The mudbrick exterior created an almost oven-like interior with no escape for the fire except the wooden rafters of the roof.

Elliott's attention fastened on an object in the center of the room. A woman tied to a chair, her head dropped forward.

Amelia.

Elliott started forward, but Lord Astley's arm came out to stop him.

"The rafters over there are not stable." Lord Astley gestured to the right where the fire burned strongest. "We'll have to go around. Stay near that wall. Follow me."

Frederick held his shirt up to cover his nose and mouth and Elliott followed suit, but it didn't fully protect from the smoke-filled air.

The sweltering atmosphere stung Elliott's eyes and dried his skin. Tears formed to combat the heat, blurring his vision momentarily until the heat dried them up. The fire had caught on Amelia's skirt and started an ascent, but Lord Astley quickly dropped to his knees at her side and used the surrounding cloth to blot out the fire.

"Do you have your knife?" he yelled over the sound of the flames.

In answer, Elliott pulled the tool from his pocket and handed it over.

"I'll cut the ropes"—Lord Astley flipped the knife open—"and you catch her."

Elliott nodded as the man moved behind Amelia and began slicing through the ropes holding her in place. The air grew thicker, harder to breathe. Lord Astley coughed but continued his work until Amelia's body slid toward Elliott and he caught her up in his arms. She weighed less than he thought she would, and her forehead dropped against his chin, causing her soft hair to tickle his cheek. But she didn't wake up.

Without direction, he ran back toward the open door and breathed in the cool night air, continuing a rain of coughs. Frederick followed and bent forward, palms on his knees, coughing as well.

Elliott placed Amelia down on the ground and loosed the top button of her blouse. "Come on, Amelia. Wake up. Breathe."

"I have this." Zahra ran forward, holding a small bucket at her side. "Water."

Elliott took the bucket from the girl and dipped his hand inside, bringing the cool water to Amelia's face. Nothing happened. He repeated the process, rubbing a thumb across her lips.

"Sir, could you support her head?" Elliott attempted to keep his voice calm. "I will try to get some water into her mouth."

Lord Astley supported Amelia from behind, keeping her in an almost-sitting position, and Elliott slowly tilted the bucket up enough to allow a small amount of water into her mouth. She immediately started coughing. Elliott sent a smile up to Lord Astley. "That's a good sign."

"It is."

Elliott waited until the coughing subsided and then offered another drink.

This time she didn't cough as much, and those caramel brown

eyes of hers finally flickered open. She looked up at him, brow creasing, and then recognition dawned.

"Jason?" Her voice rasped out his name.

Heat climbed up Elliott's neck, and he refused to look over at Lord Astley. What would his employer think to have this woman refer to him by his Christian name?

"Take another drink," he said, bringing the bucket up to gently allow a little more water between her lips.

She searched his face with such openness he almost brushed his thumb against her cheek to let her know he understood, but this was not the time for such tender sentiments. In fact, he shouldn't have those thoughts about Lady Kerth as it was.

"Have you seen Lady Astley?"

Amelia's eyes closed for a second, and he wondered if she'd lost consciousness again, but then she spoke. "The tomb. The professor took her."

Elliott met Lord Astley's gaze before the latter spoke. "I must get to her."

"Yes," Elliott replied, adjusting to take Amelia back in his arms. "You'll need one of the horses."

They made it back to the house. A servant stood near the table, serving the surviving policeman a drink. The man held his head in his hands, a red stain near one temple.

"What's happened?" he asked, his words slow.

"Professor Andrews attempted to kill Miss Sinclair," Lord Astley answered, gesturing toward the other policeman's body, who had been laid out on the floor nearby. "And I suspect he may have been behind your injury and your colleague's death."

The man stood but lost his balance and returned to the chair. "I must alert the inspector."

Lord Astley looked about the room in an almost desperate search, when his gaze landed on Zahra. "Zahra, you have proven your skills. I must ask you to be brave yet again."

She smiled up at him, her willingness evident in her quick response. "I am brave, my lord."

"I need you to take a note to the police station." He knelt down to meet her eye to eye. "Do you think you can do that?"

"It is near the docks?" Her brow wrinkled a little as she appeared to search her memory. "With the cross flag flying."

"That's right." He nodded, placing his palm on the child's shoulder. "They usually have the British flag on display since men from my country are stationed here."

"I know where it is, Rabu Alasid."

Frederick shot Elliott a questioning look but didn't inquire further. "Then return to the house without delay, so that you can help Elliott attend to Miss Sinclair. Do you understand?"

"Yes, sir."

"I will catch you up, my Lord." Elliott held Lord Astley's gaze, hoping his friend understood the urgency behind his words. "You can't do this alone."

"If I can wait for you, I will." Lord Astley's shoulder dropped ever so slightly. His face firmed with purpose. "But I have to find her."

Without another word, Lord Astley wrote his note and sent Zahra on her way, then left for the stables. Elliott requested some water and wine be brought to Miss Sinclair's room. She'd gained enough strength to walk with his aid, so he guided her to her room and helped adjust her pillows as she lay back.

He walked to the washstand and brought a damp cloth back, at first planning to hand it to her, but her eyes had drifted closed again. He hesitated, studying the way her golden hair fell around her in something of a halo. With gentle movements, he sat on the edge of her bed and ran the cloth over her forehead, wiping away the gray soot. Her small smile encouraged him to continue. He slid the cloth over her right cheek to her ear and then down along her jaw, the movement slow, gentle, allowing him to touch her in ways he wouldn't allow his skin to do.

She opened her eyes, looking up at him with watery vision.

"I have to leave, Jason," she whispered. "I have to finally be free and find where I truly belong."

He cleared his throat, the words "Could you belong with me?" clogging his throat. "You have family."

Her eyes narrowed, and she pushed to a sitting position. "What did you say?"

"Lord Astley knows your grandfather."

"I. . .I have a grandfather?"

He looked down at the cloth in his hands. "Lady Astley. . .came upon your photograph in your room and thought she recognized the man in the photo."

"She came upon?" Amelia's lips crooked the lightest bit, and he had the sudden urge to lean forward and taste those crooked lips. He focused back on the cloth.

"At any rate, when she showed the photograph to Lord Astley, he recognized your grandfather and wishes to speak to you about him."

"Who is he?'

"I am not at liberty to say. I believe Lord Astley should be the one to tell you." Elliott looked back at her, holding her gaze. "But he's a good man and will provide you with a life much better than the one you've known."

Her eyelids wilted closed. "What have I to offer a good man?" She looked back at him and then away. "Any good man?"

"Don't say that," His hand covered hers against the bedclothes. "Everyone needs a second chance. You are no exception."

"I wish I had met you years ago." She released a sad chuckle. "When I had a whole heart and some semblance of a future to give you."

"We've met *now* for a reason, and I am certain there is as much heart in you as ever there was."

"It feels true when I'm with you." Her gaze faltered. "I want it to be true, but I am a thief and a liar, Jason."

"Is that where you want to stay?"

She blinked up at him, as if the question surprised her. "No. No, I don't."

"I believe in you." He gave her fingers a squeeze. "Lord Astley believes in you, or he wouldn't attempt to connect you with your grandfather, but the bottom line is what do you believe?"

She searched his face as if trying to find the answer.

"Are you brave enough to try? To face your past head-on but then hold on to hope for your future?" He lowered his head again. "Lord Astley rescued me from a life of thievery and brokenness. I didn't believe there was anyone in the world who cared about me, but he did. He taught me what faith was like. Not just faith in myself and other people, but faith in God, and without that faith, I wouldn't have had the courage to believe there was hope for me." He met her gaze, hoping to infuse some of his own faith into her. "He will help you to start over. He'll give you strength if you ask Him, Amelia."

She stared at him, her large brown eyes tearing. Without warning, she leaned forward and grabbed him by the front of the shirt, pulling him toward her. His breath caught just as her warm lips found his. She pressed in, taking charge of the kiss until his senses caught up with his desire. He couldn't remember the last time he'd been kissed, and never like this. From someone. . .well, he cared for her, didn't he? There was no denying it, and if he only had this moment to show her, then he'd make it count.

He brought his palms up to cradle her jaw, his fingers slipping to her ears, and she gasped, tightening her grip. So he took his time, tasting those lips, allowing his fingers to learn the texture of her hair, the softness of her cheeks. His care seemed to temper her need, because she gentled her approach too, exploring. One of her hands slipped to the back of his neck, fingers weaving into his hair.

And then his thumb brushed along her jaw to her cheek and felt dampness there. He pulled back, and she stared at him, a single tear escaping to trail down to his thumb again.

He didn't ask.

She didn't explain.

But they both knew.

"You are a very good man, Jason Elliott." She brushed back his hair from his forehead before returning her gaze to his.

"Amelia—" She pressed her finger against his lips and shook her head.

"Lord Astley needs you, Jason." She replaced her finger with her lips to give him a gentle kiss. "Be careful."

With those words, he knew she'd made her choice. And he'd never see her again.

Chapter Twenty

If Lane hadn't seated Grace in front of him on his horse and hugged her arms to her body, she'd have found a way to retrieve her knife, jabbed it into his leg, pushed him off the horse, and taken over the mount. But he must have already recognized her cleverness, so he took extra precautions.

She smiled to herself. It was nice to know he had to take precautions because of her cleverness. Then she frowned, or at least she tried. Lane had muzzled her with her own scarf, but she wasn't exactly sure why. Perhaps Lane wasn't an admirer of H. Rider Haggard's books, but Grace couldn't help telling him about how her current experience reminded her of one.

Maybe that had been the trouble.

Lane wasn't a reader. She sighed. What a shame.

And it was a lovely scarf. One she'd purchased in Cairo. Long, thick, and multicolored, though it tasted of perfume and horse hair at the moment.

Grace looked back behind her, sending another prayer that Frederick and Elliott would find Amelia before it was too late. There was no knowing when they'd receive her note, or if Zahra could even find her way back to the buildings. The girl was clever in her own right, so surely she thought of some way, because Grace couldn't bear the idea of Amelia burning to death.

"It's going to take much too long for anyone to find you, Lady Astley." Lane lowered his mouth to her ear.

If she'd been able to talk, she would have said quite a few things about heroes and miracles and faith in love, but as it was, her attempts failed to erupt much more than an unintelligible combination of syllables.

Andrews led the way through a narrow pathway between the mountains, and quite unexpectedly, in a turn in the rocks, a horse-drawn wagon waited by a cave entrance faintly aglow. Well, not a cave exactly, but a tomb. Like the ones she'd visited a few days earlier. A rectangular frame built into the rock.

"I'll go tell him the news," Andrews said, sliding from his mount. "Allow me a few moments before you bring her inside. He'll be put out when he discovers what's happened with my aunt, not to mention Amelia and"—he looked over at Grace—"our current guest."

He? Professor Andrews wasn't the mastermind behind all of this?

Lane took his time helping her off the horse and even more time removing the cloth from her mouth and tossing the piece to the ground.

Grace swallowed through her dry throat and studied their surroundings. The rocks blocked a quick view of the entrance so that a rider passing by might easily overlook the direction that led to the entrance of the tomb.

She leaned down and retrieved her scarf.

"If I were you, I'd place the horse near the entrance of the tomb instead of out here." Grace gestured with her hands to where they stood. "Anyone could come along and steal it, and then where would you be if you needed to make a quick escape?"

Lane growled his response but grabbed the horse's reins, turning away from her long enough for her to wrap her scarf around a pointy rock at the entrance of the path. It fluttered a little in the wind and might not be eye catching, but at least it was something.

Lane was at least twenty feet in front of her, she suddenly realized, and paying much more attention to his horse and the tomb than her. With a sudden gasp, she burst into a run back the way they'd come, refusing to look behind her. Her skirts slowed her pace, but she pushed forward. This was definitely one of those moments where trousers would have proved much more practical than skirts.

The cliff hemmed her in on both sides, creating shadows across her path. She'd read about the prevalence of snakes in Egypt, not to mention the jackals, but a death to one of those seemed much preferential to whatever nasty thing Lane, Andrews, or "he" might do.

The sound of boots on dirt came from behind, closing in. She'd never outrun him, so she stopped, raked up some rocks, and then turned and started throwing them. He released a long stream of curses, arms raised to block her onslaught as she continued backing up, dropping to gather more. A rather large-sized rock hit him quite solidly in the shoulder, clear evidence of her grandfather's instructions in baseball.

When he got closer, she took off at another run but didn't get far before he caught her, shoving her to the ground. She released a scream, which just made her mad. She hated screaming. It made her sound scared, and even if she was somewhat afraid, she didn't want Lane to know it.

The jagged rocks bit into the flesh of her palms. Even her cheek scratched against the rough ground. Her eyes watered. Lane jerked her up by her arm and part of her hair, which had come loose throughout the ride and run. She bit back another cry, instead focusing her full attention on his dirt-stained face as he tied her hands at the wrists.

"If I had my way right now, your ladyship"—he gripped her arm tighter and drew her so close to his face, there was no escape from his breath or the spittle coming from his mouth—"I would tie you up out here and let the jackals finish you off."

"Well, at least that would be a creative way to kill me," she shot back. "There's no sense in wasting a perfectly good imagination on expected ways like shooting someone or burning up a building. Poison even has its predictability."

His grimace slacked, so she continued. His silence was rather refreshing.

"At least tying me up for the jackals shows some semblance of imagination."

"Did you understand me, woman?" He shook his head and pulled her back toward the tomb. "We're going to kill you. There's no way you're making it out of this alive, even if you have your precious Lord Astley coming for you. You're going to die. Do you hear me?"

"It's difficult not to with the way you're carrying on about it." She sighed. "I imagine you've scared away any possible jackals."

He stopped and looked down at her. "You're mad! I tell you that you're going to die, and you're chastising me about scaring away the jackals when you should be pleading for your life."

"I'm not afraid of dying, Mr. Lane."

"Not afraid of dying," he repeated, pulling her back into a fast walk. "That's unlikely, your ladyship."

"Actually, I know where I'm going when I die."

He stopped again, his expression morphing as comprehension dawned.

"What about you?" She raised a brow, and the smallest hint of fear flashed across his features.

The sudden explosion of a gunshot met them as they reached the tomb's entrance. Lane looked back down at Grace, his eyes wide as if her statement somehow brought about the gunfire. Gunfire, though not as creative, certainly meant something unsavory.

Lane drew Grace through the entrance, and like in the pyramid of Khafre, a corridor descended toward the antechamber. A few pieces of board had been placed as a bridge over a gaping hole between the corridor and the entrance into the antechamber, a device used as a trap so potential grave robbers would fall to their deaths. A chamber opened to one side. It looked half-finished and plain; however, the hieroglyphics and brilliantly colored wall art lined the corridor similar to the other north tomb she'd seen. Red, green, black, yellow, and of course, the brilliant blue.

Lane didn't give her time to study them, but she noticed more of the sun disc, Aten, and caught a glimpse of the royal family. The wooden braces she'd seen with Frederick framed the corridor and blocked some of the scenes, but supported the corridor all the way down to the bottom of the steps, where they entered a large room.

Crates stood to the left in various stages of packing, but otherwise this particular room was empty. The next room, however, was larger and more ornate and held a small group of men. The first people Grace noticed were the robe-clad person of Lateef, one of the professor's most important workers, and Ali Hassan, the servant who had taught her how to ride a camel. She narrowed her eyes. Perhaps he'd set the camel against her all along. Then there was another servant who helped supervise the native diggers. What had his name been? Omar? But her attention followed the men's gazes.

In the center of the room, lying in a heap by a square hole dug into the floor, was the lifeless body of Professor Andrews. A red stain pooled against his dirty white button-up, and his dark eyes stared into space. Lane came to a stop, with Grace by his side, her attention fixed on the body.

"Finish loading the last crates. We need to leave as soon as possible." The voice shook her from her stare, and she followed the sound, but a sinking feeling fell through her. She knew the voice.

The man turned, stuffing his pistol back into his waistband as he did, his gaze coming up to meet hers. Standing before her, alive and well, was Mr. Charles Smallwood.

Grace stood as dumb as a statue for a full five seconds, attempting to align her expectations with reality. Mr. Smallwood? But that couldn't be. "No, no, no," she finally said. "Not you, Mr. Smallwood. We got on so well, and you were ever so interested in fiction."

The man's white brows rose, and then, as if he'd come to some conclusion, he tilted his head, examining her. "I assure you, Lady Astley, none of this is personal. Indeed, you weren't even a factor in this part of the affair until this very moment, my dear."

She shuffled forward, bringing Lane with her. "But Professor Andrews wanted to find the tomb and you. . .you disappeared."

His lips softened beneath his Santa Claus beard. Oh dear, she'd never see Santa Claus the same way again. She would have to start referring to him as Father Christmas in her mind just to keep the Christmas magic untainted.

"Disappearing was brought on by your little mishap with the camel." He shook his head, his voice quiet, almost gentle. Grace cringed. Especially since the body of Professor Andrews lay close behind him in such a horrid state of deadness. "If you hadn't stumbled upon the tomb, I wouldn't have gone missing in order to draw attention away from the dig site."

"Because you were still removing artifacts?"

"Precisely, and I dare say you wouldn't have been involved at all."

"Oh!" Grace's bottom lip dropped. "A diversion. Very clever." She shook her head, still trying to piece it all together. "Why didn't I ever take you as the mastermind sort? Perhaps it was your general appearance as a Santa Claus sort of person. And of course, who could love Charles Dickens so much and at the same time be so devious? It just doesn't fit at all, Mr. Smallwood."

She felt Lane's eyes on her, so she looked over at him. He shook his head, squinted, and then shook his head again before looking away. Clearly as a nonreader, he didn't understand Grace's dilemma.

"Devious?" He chuckled, gesturing for the men to continue their work. Grace counted two more, which brought the total working for him to six, not including Professor Andrews, of course. "An opportunist is actually what I am, Lady Astley." He placed his hands behind his back, cane twitching behind him like a stiff tail, and paced the distance between them. "Last autumn, when Sydney and I crossed paths again in London, I'd been in the stolen antiquities business for a while—ever since taking it over from my brother. He'd developed quite the systems and contacts but had never made a discovery worthy of his hard work. Then I over-heard Sydney, quite irresponsibly, speaking about his archaeologist and the possibility of an undiscovered tomb in Amarna. At this time, Sydney had already procured archaeological rights to the site, so—"

"You renewed your friendship," she finished, the pieces clicking together. "And enticed grieving and desperate Professor Andrews with the chance of a real find and lucrative outcome."

"You are quite clever yourself." He tapped his cane on the ground and smiled. "Quite clever, indeed."

"But why kill poor Mr. Graham?" She would have folded her arms across her chest if the ropes had allowed. It was one of her favorite thinking postures, and the inability to do so created a true nuisance. "Did he know of your involvement? And why kill Andrews? He would have kept your secret, surely."

"Believe it or not, I had no designs to kill Mr. Graham." Mr. Smallwood's gaze caught on something just over Grace's shoulder. "Lateef, you cannot toss dynamite around like it's a football. Good night, man!"

Grace turned to find Lateef, turban head bowed and a collection of dynamite sticks in his hand, carefully tied together with a black rope. She'd never seen dynamite in real life before. Only in books, and it really wasn't as large and bright red as she thought it would be.

Mr. Smallwood shook his head and lowered his voice. "I shall be happy to get rid of these natives, once the boat is finally loaded. They're hard workers if the pay is right, but not the most careful sort when it comes to antiquities."

"Or explosives, I gather," Grace added, an annoying shake in her voice.

"Precisely. But they're all in the business, so they, at least, understand discretion." He turned back to Lateef. "Yes, place it by the corridor entrance and I'll sort out what to do with it from there, since we haven't needed it."

He cleared his throat and looked back at her. "Where were we?" He tapped his cane and glanced at Lane. "Do let go of the woman, Lane, and untie her. There's no way out of here except through the tomb entrance, and she'd have to get past all of us to do so." He waved Lane away. "The last few crates are left. Help Ali Hassan so we can be on our way. I'd like to set sail within the hour."

Lane gave Grace another narrow-eyed glare before slicing through her bonds and joining the other men by the last eight or so crates. Eight. With six men working, that didn't give her much more time, did it?

"So the professor became nervous when Mr. Graham discovered the tomb?" Grace took a few steps to the right, trying to get a better view of her surroundings. The men carried the crates from the left of the room through the corridor behind her. A lovely, decorated wall stood immediately to her right, and just beyond the present room, she could see the room she'd fallen into earlier. The burial chamber. Not as large as what she'd read of Akhenaten's tomb, but similar in size to Meryra's, except for the long corridor from the outside to the antechamber. So antechamber, treasure room, and burial room. She glanced back behind her. The corridor caused all sorts of trouble. How on earth could she escape all the way up those stairs without getting fired upon?

"Yes. It was a poor decision, really." Mr. Smallwood resumed his walk. "Mr. Graham wouldn't have located the tomb in time to discover our plans. We were near the end of removing the artifacts as it was. All Andrews did was create great suspicion by embroiling his half-wit aunt in the whole scheme." He nodded. "Thankfully she had no idea of my involvement in the affair, so once Andrews unfortunately had to silence Miss Sinclair, then my silencing Andrews ended any possible connection in that regard."

Poor Amelia. Grace's eyes pinched closed. And now Mr. Smallwood would have to silence her too.

Surely Frederick had to be close, unless in an attempt to rescue Amelia from death, he'd gotten caught up in the fire, the ceiling collapsed, and he'd already gotten to heaven before her! She squeezed her eyes closed. No. Elliott would never let that happen.

Well, she had to escape, or at least die trying. It was ridiculous to just wait around to be killed off. That wasn't heroic at all.

She glanced back to the men who were moving the last few crates. She only counted five now, apart from Mr. Smallwood. Where had the others gone? No matter, she needed to do something to buy time. One thing she recalled from both Detective Miracle's book as well as some of her favorite fiction was to get the villain talking. Talking created a possible distraction, which might make an opportunity for escape.

"I wish the artifacts weren't already crated," she sighed, taking a few more small steps back. "I imagine they're magnificent."

"Indeed, they are." His smile resurrected. "Some of the best I've ever seen. My buyer in Germany has promised a pretty price for them, which will allow me a respite for a while." He reached down into his pocket, and Grace braced herself, but he merely drew out a necklace. "Taking a reprieve from Egypt for a few years should clear up any suspicion surrounding me." The beaded chain led to a blue central amulet with carvings marked in gold.

Mr. Smallwood took her hand and placed the necklace in her palm. "Do you see the amulet? Look how they've shaped a phoenix of gold into the front. It's remarkable."

He smiled at her as if they were having a typical conversation, and it was the strangest thing. She knew she had a tendency to detour from reality at times, but Mr. Smallwood proved much better at it than she. Of course his real reason could be that he was so certain of victory he had no concern that his plan wouldn't come to fruition.

"Lapis lazuli and gold," he added, smoothing his fingers across it, then looking up at her. "The blue holds an uncanny resemblance to your eye color. Very nice."

She met his gaze, and the same internal tremor as before moved over her skin. There was something unnerving about a man who could kill someone in one moment and speak of the beauty of a necklace in the other without so much as a flicker of change. A devilishness. An almost Professor Moriarty likeness.

Yes. That was it. The villains who lost control and splayed their emotions across the page carried something predictable in their responses. Something expected. But Mr. Smallwood's coolness, his unaffectedness bordered on a darker type of evil. One that moved beyond feeling or remorse.

"Everything is ready, sir," Lane announced. "And if I might say, sir, Carter just came from the village and says the police found Mrs. Casper dead in her jail cell earlier than I'd hoped and are keen to locate the culprits. They're organizing a posse set to come here directly."

"Well, that's unfortunate." He took a step back and pointed

his cane toward Omar. "I suppose we will need to enact our plan a little early. Too bad. I had wanted to take a few photographs of the reliefs before we destroyed it all."

"Destroy?"

He offered his arm as if they were going to take a stroll through the park. She hesitated before slipping her arm through his. "It's a shame, I know, with the wealth of knowledge held inside this tomb, but destroying the tomb will serve two purposes. It will cover the bodies of those we don't wish to have found too soon, and in an attempt to save anyone who may be trapped inside, the police will spend their time here while we escape."

Heat left her face. "Anyone trapped inside?"

If she read the situation right, *anyone* meant her.

•

Chapter Twenty-One

One sound chilled Frederick's blood as he neared the mountains housing the tombs. The distant and familiar crack of gunfire. He refused to let his thoughts follow the possibilities. Grace was not only brave but smart as well. She had to use her cleverness to stay alive until he could get to her.

He swallowed the gathering lump in his throat.

She had to.

As the path split between the mountains, Frederick slid from the horse and guided it behind him a little farther. Dark shadows jutted in various directions, confusing the path. He didn't have time to search them all.

Something fluttered in his periphery, and he pulled his pistol from his waistband, leaving the horse behind while he investigated the movement. A scarf? His breath pulsed from its hold, and he brought the scarf to his nose. Mint. Grace's.

The moonlight highlighted a narrow path along the edge of the rock where the scarf had been wrapped. He almost smiled. His clever wife was pointing the way for him. Then he heard another sound. Voices and the thud of wood on wood? He moved among the shadows toward the noises as they grew clearer. Men's voices. A mixture of English and Arabic.

From behind a boulder, he watched as men ascended from the tomb entrance, their arms laden with crates. Seven? Was that right? He slid nearer. One of the men stayed behind, one of the native workers, his pale robes glowing in the moonlight. The other men returned to the cave, but this man separated himself, moving behind some of the taller stones nearby. Perhaps to relieve himself?

Frederick took the opportunity presented and crept in that direction. The man had just returned toward the wagon when Frederick grabbed him around the neck and pulled him behind a nearby rock, arm fixed against the man's throat. The man struggled to no avail. Most of the workers were smaller in height, though scrappy, and within only a few moments, the struggling ceased. Frederick kept his hold a few seconds longer, ensuring the man had lost consciousness, and then he placed him against the boulder and well out of sight of the tomb.

The other men delivered a few more crates to the wagon and then walked back into the tomb. Frederick rounded the wagon and pressed himself against the rock wall of the mountain, his position protected by shadow and stone. Then he heard it. A sound that nearly brought him to tears.

His wife's voice.

He couldn't make out what she was saying, but he knew the cadence and rhythm. She was alive and well, from what he could tell.

"There are only a few more, and then we'll be ready to go," a man spoke as he came up the tomb's corridor. He knew the voice.

Sergeant Lane, one of the police who'd greeted them upon arrival here and was one of the first officers to respond to Mr. Graham's death, emerged from over the threshold on one side of a crate with the dig's foreman, Lateef, holding the other.

"And what of the woman?"

"He'll get rid of her," Lane answered. "He only kept her on to ensure we could finish loading all the antiquities. Andrews kept her as insurance."

"A lot of good it did for Andrews," came another man's response as he and two of the workmen navigated another crate to the wagon. Carter. "But I suppose the professor gets what he wants in the end. Becoming a mummy himself."

The men laughed and turned back through the tomb entrance. That had been five. Frederick had removed one from the list, but where was the sixth?

"You?" came the harsh word as if in answer.

Frederick turned just in time to dodge a knife aimed for his chest. Frederick grabbed the man's wrist as the knife bypassed him and jerked the man's arm around to his back, but they both stumbled back against the rocks. The knife pierced the man's back, plunging deep as they fell. Within seconds, his body slumped lifeless to the ground.

Frederick's shoulders sank, and he knelt to wipe the blood from the knife, now in his hand. A casualty of the attack, but he'd hoped to keep as many of these men alive as possible so they could face legal justice. Not justice at his own hands.

Voices echoed up from the tomb, so Frederick pulled the body back against the rock wall into the shadows. This time, the five remaining men worked together to carry a large, rectangular crate, shaped much like a coffin. Frederick shook off any curiosity of what lay inside and took advantage of the men's absence from the corridor, quickly making his way down the stone steps and nearer to Grace.

The antechamber boasted a set of alabaster columns, much like they'd seen in Meryra's tomb on the hill above them. And just on the other side of the columns stood his wife, her arm through the arm of. . .Charles Smallwood? Frederick rolled his gaze to the ceiling.

Of course! It made perfect sense, didn't it? The man who had business connections in various parts of the world. A rifleman in the Boer War who'd have no trouble hitting a moving target like Trent on his horse. An Egyptian enthusiast with the right amount of knowledge and charisma to design such a plan.

He'd never gone missing at all.

He'd premeditated the entire affair, likely to draw attention away from his work on the tomb.

And if Smallwood held the ingenuity and intelligence to enact this scheme, he was not a man to be trifled with. At all.

To prove that point, the matter-of-fact manner in which the man gently told Grace how he was going to leave her in the tomb to an uncertain outcome chilled Frederick's skin. Frederick hadn't known many men with such controlled malice, but the ones he had known were only gracious in their revenge.

There would be no deviation to Smallwood's plan nor any mercy granted. Frederick would have to kill him.

He braced himself, moving to the first pillar and retrieving his pistol from his waistband. The men would return any minute. He couldn't waste time. He moved to the next pillar, his attention on Grace. Her chin tipped toward him, attention darting in his direction, as if she'd become aware of his presence. Good. She would work with him, if she could.

"I suppose you wouldn't change your mind if I promised to come along quietly?" she said, causing Smallwood to relax his stance, likely charmed by her seemingly innocent statement.

Frederick almost smiled. His brave darling, likely trying to keep Smallwood's attention fully diverted. Frederick slipped to the last pillar, close enough to take a fatal shot.

"I suppose that's not believable at all, is it? I rarely go anywhere quietly." Her voice remained strong, even tinged with humor. She was simply remarkable.

Frederick shifted his position, bringing his pistol up, when a call from the corridor erupted into the silence.

"Smallwood, behind you."

With almost panther-like speed, Smallwood turned, pulling Grace against him and placing his own gun to her head. "Ah, Lord Astley, so good of you to join us." The man's expression gave nothing away, his smile unnerving, though a slight bit of perspiration at his wrinkled brow may have offered some insight that his calm only rested at the surface.

Frederick took a step forward, but the man pressed his gun so tightly to Grace's head that she winced. Frederick froze in place, his attention focused on Grace's pale face.

"I see all the players have arrived." Lane and Carter came up behind Frederick and took him by the arms, twisting his pistol from his hold.

"Excellent. I do hate loose ends, and we have a schedule to keep."

Grace searched his face, her expression offering an apology she didn't owe him. If she and Zahra hadn't followed Amelia, Amelia would be dead. Who knew what other people may have suffered from Smallwood's plans?

"I have a perfect idea for our Lord Astley." Smallwood turned toward an inner room, large and ornate with brightly colored reliefs on every wall and the ceiling splayed in a diamond pattern of blue and gold. Some sort of treasure room, was it? With the additional lantern light not available to Grace and him when they'd first visited this room, Frederick almost didn't recognize the space. The body of Professor Andrews lay in the center of the room next to some sort of pit about five feet wide by seven feet long.

"What do you mean by loose ends?" Grace's voice echoed in the large room. "You said that you didn't plan on killing us all along."

"Once Andrews brought you here, it forced me to rework the plan, my dear. If you knew about the tomb, then I felt certain your husband would be aware as well." He sighed. "I had hoped to keep my presence free of common knowledge so that everything would fall back on Andrews, you see. He was an easy and perfect scapegoat." With a shove of his foot, Smallwood pushed Andrews' body the few inches it needed to slip into the pit, making a thud as it hit the bottom.

The pit couldn't have been more than six feet deep, and a series of square holes ran along the top quarter of it in what looked to be two-foot intervals. Frederick looked over at Grace, who stared down at Andrews' body with a frown pulling at her lips. How on earth his wife could find a way to feel sorry for everything and everyone was beyond him.

Another noise erupted. A strange "click" followed by the sound of rock sliding against rock.

"Ah, I had hoped to find one of these in my travels. I'd read about them but didn't believe they truly existed," came Smallwood's almost giddy response. "These ancient Egyptians never fail to fascinate and surprise me."

A hollow feeling started growing in Frederick's stomach.

Suddenly, a burst of sand shot from one of the square holes in the pit. Then another. Spraying the granules down over Andrews' body. What was it? Some sort of sand trap?

Frederick looked over at his wife only to find her in the strangest pose. With Smallwood still holding his pistol against her temple, she poised on one foot with her other leg bent at the knee, so her boot tilted upward. Her fingers slid down her skirt toward her boot as if she was reaching to untie it or scratch her leg or. . . He caught his smile.

While everyone focused on the sand pit, Grace was reaching for her knife.

Likely his beloved had already imagined sand traps before and it held little fascination.

"Clever, isn't it?" Smallwood grinned over at Frederick. "There must have been a pressure point in the bottom of the pit. These pharaohs went to great lengths to keep tomb robbers from stealing their precious items for the afterlife, but clearly, we're the first to activate this one."

Frederick counted the position of the men. Lane and Carter held him, but only one of the workmen had joined them in the tomb. Were the others on watch? He was already horribly outnumbered, but he had to try something. For Grace's sake.

"You said you wouldn't kill me unless forced," Grace announced, slipping her hand back to her side. "I must say, Mr. Smallwood, it would be very ungentlemanly of you to go back on your word. Leaving me in a tomb is one thing. Tossing me in a sand pit is quite another."

Carter's hold had loosened slightly, likely due to the theatrics Smallwood was bringing to the room, and Lane's pistol jutted just above his waistband, an easy grab if Frederick could get his arm free of Carter.

"Oh my dear Lady Astley, I don't plan to toss you in the sand pit." Smallwood turned toward Frederick. "I mean to have Lane and Carter escort your husband to the edge of the pit and push him into it."

Grace's gaze met his, and her eyes grew wide. "No." She struggled against Smallwood's hold, giving quite the show of her own theatrics.

"Then while you're attempting to rescue him, we will make our leave and close off the passage. It's rather ingenious, isn't it?"

"No, no, please." She pulled against him. "Just leave us here. Please. We won't follow you."

Her violent struggling and overly dramatic response forced Smallwood to return his gun to his waist in order to get a firmer grip on Grace, which proved the perfect opportunity for two things to happen in synchrony. Grace met Frederick's gaze and, almost as if she'd gotten the answer she wanted, dropped to her knees and dug her knife into Smallwood's hip.

One thing, Frederick felt certain, was *not* a part of Smallwood's plans.

At the same time, Frederick jerked free of Carter, bringing his elbow up to the man's nose and immediately reaching for Lane's pistol. He'd barely gotten his hand on the grip when Lane brought his fist into direct contact with Frederick's cheek, sending him back a few steps, but Frederick hadn't lost his hold on the gun.

Carter regained his footing and lunged back toward Frederick, attempting to take the gun. Frederick shot a glance back toward Grace, who was playing tug-of-war with Smallwood's pistol, the front pointed upward. A discharge erupted from the gun, sending debris raining down on them from the ceiling.

"Are you insane?" Smallwood shouted. "You could bring the whole place down on us."

A fist landed into Frederick's side from Carter, nearly doubling him over, just as Frederick pulled the trigger of the gun. Carter's eyes grew wide, and he stumbled back, seizing his shoulder as blood oozed through his shirt.

Another shot from somewhere behind him had Lane dropping to the ground.

Frederick turned in time to see Elliott jump behind a stone cistern as he opened fire from the nearby pillars, a workman named, Omar, in pursuit. A bullet must have ricocheted to the ceiling because another dusting fell down on them, adding smoke-like haze to the room.

Lane stumbled back to his feet and reached out to grab the gun from Frederick, but Frederick sidestepped the man, pistol slapping him in the cheek as he passed, dashing toward Grace.

Almost as if in slow motion, Smallwood tore the pistol free from Grace's hold with such force it sent her staggering back, and before Smallwood could fire on her, she teetered and fell over into the sand pit.

Pain shot up Grace's hip as she landed on a mixture of sand and. . .Professor Andrews. Sand rained down on her from various holes above, and she quickly pushed to a sitting position, strategically angling herself between the sand bursts. Her palm pressed down on what felt like the professor's head, and she quickly pulled back.

She shouldn't feel sorry for squishing the dead man—after all, he'd put her in the predicament to begin with—but there was something pathetic about a man being betrayed, killed in a tomb, and then thrown into a sand pit, only to have a person land on top of him. That being said, she took a little comfort in knowing he was already dead. Especially since she was sitting quite firmly on his back.

Another gunshot sounded from above, and Grace looked around her. She'd dropped her knife after stabbing Mr. Smallwood, so currently, she was weaponless. Sand hit her on the back and nearly covered the professor, but she dug around his body until her fingers came in contact with his pistol. Perfect. At least she could still help in the fight. She pushed the pistol into her pocket so her hands could be free to help her stand.

At her first attempt, thinking this sand would be very similar to the packed type at the coast, her boots sank down into the loose grains all the way to the top of the laces. Soft, absorbing her weight and sending her off-balance, the granules created a heaviness on her legs. She looked at each sand hole and attempted to calculate her time. Not long, at this rate. And if she couldn't stand on top of the sand. . . Well, the unhappy outcome of being stuck in the pit for a prolonged period of time didn't bode well for her or her boots.

She looked over at Professor Andrews' almost-covered body and grimaced. "I'm sorry about this, but I take comfort in the fact that you can't feel a thing." She stepped onto his legs and cringed. "I can't imagine what these heels would feel like if you were alive. If I had time, I'd remove them."

She braced her arms on either side of the pit in order to keep her balance. The professor's body gave her just enough height to see over the rim of the pit, and she braced her fingers over the lip in order to hold steady. She couldn't keep this stance for long. Not at the rate of the pouring sand and the uneven. . .foundation.

Frederick was struggling with Mr. Smallwood, blood on his face and arm. Omar lay motionless by the antechamber entryway, and Carter stumbled toward the fight between Lateef and Elliott. Elliott had the upper hand, for certain, and with his boxing history, no wonder. Lateef's face had taken the brunt of the force so far, but the man knew how to wield a knife, which Elliott had to keep dodging as Lateef sliced in Elliott's direction. If Carter joined the fray, even wounded as he was, could Elliott manage?

Lane must have been knocked down by someone, but he stumbled to a stand, his shirt bloodstained. His focus moved directly to the struggle between Frederick and Mr. Smallwood. Frederick had the advantage over his older peer, but both men's military experience appeared to be at play. Frederick even rolled out of the way of Mr. Smallwood's attempt to bludgeon him with a piece of stone.

What an excellent move! And much easier to do in trousers, clearly.

As Lane neared Frederick, he made a flipping motion with his hand, revealing a knife. She grappled to pull herself farther up, but couldn't.

With his focus on Mr. Smallwood, her dear husband wasn't at all prepared to take on a second assailant.

"Frederick, behind you," she called, scraping her finger for a hold within the rocks, but she lost her footing and crashed back down into a sitting position. The sand quickly took advantage of her reduced height and covered her nearly to her chest, weighing her down much more than she imagined sand could do.

With great effort, she used the walls of the pit to regain her footing and unfortunately had to move a little farther up Professor Andrews' body to advance an inch or two in height.

She pinched her eyes closed at the thought of where her heels might be at the moment. The sand's weight pushed against her, nearly causing her to lose her footing, but she had gained enough elevation on tiptoe to hook an elbow over the rim of the pit.

Frederick slowly struggled to a stand, a dark stain showing at his side. Had Lane succeeded in stabbing him? But before Frederick could fully regain his fight, Lane punched him in the stomach and grabbed Frederick by the arms.

"He's mine," Mr. Smallwood growled, rising from the ground himself and reaching for a knife on the ground nearby.

Grace gasped. Her very own knife. She grappled for a better hold, pulling herself up a little more. Almost enough to get her other elbow secure.

"I'm finished playing this game." Mr. Smallwood stepped closer, breathing hard.

Grace looked over to where Elliott had been, but though Carter had been incapacitated, Lateef continued to wrestle with him, even as Elliott pushed to get to Frederick. Elliott knew what was going to happen next also. And neither could do anything but watch.

The sand pushed harder, pressing in on her waist now. She had to do something. Anything. She blinked. The gun!

She balanced as best she could against the wall on her secure elbow and reached beneath the sand to her pocket, carefully drawing the pistol into view. With every bit of her energy, she braced the pistol against the rim.

Her position placed her directly in Frederick's line of vision.

He met her gaze, just as Mr. Smallwood advanced. Her arm shook from the tension of attempting to hold her balance. She only had one chance. Both Lane and Mr. Smallwood were in her line of vision. At least she could hit one of them.

Her foot started to slip, so with a prayer, she pulled the trigger. There was no chance to see the results, because the action knocked her off balance. With one last look and a deep breath, Grace slipped beneath the sand.

Chapter Twenty-Two

Frederick lunged forward just as Grace fired. Smallwood flinched, and Lane released his hold on Frederick, but Frederick only had eyes for his wife.

Who lost her grip and slipped back out of view.

Frederick rushed toward the sand pit, dodging Smallwood and heading to the side of the pit that bordered the wall, where no one could attack him from behind. Smallwood made no attempt to follow. He limped toward the antechamber, with Lane as his support.

Smallwood leaned down to take the gun from Carter's body.

"Elliott," Frederick warned as the two men drew close to him.

Elliott jerked to attention, having Lateef trapped by his throat against the ground, and jumped from their path just as Smallwood fired a shot. Elliott rolled behind the stone cistern just as another shot bounced off the stone, the sound echoing in the room.

Released from Elliott's hold, Lateef scrambled to a sluggish run behind Smallwood and Lane, rushing toward the exit tunnel. It didn't matter where they went.

Frederick scanned the sand pit, not one sign of Grace in sight. His stomach tightened as an ache reverberated through him, and he plunged his hand into the sand.

"You're going to leave them alive?" Lane's voice rose from the antechamber room. "They'll follow us."

"No, they won't follow us," Charles Smallwood rasped, his breathing labored.

Frederick looked up in time to see Mr. Smallwood at the edge of the corridor pointing his pistol toward a spot on the floor.

Elliott pushed up from his place behind the stone cistern and turned wide eyes to Frederick, then started at a run toward him, just as Mr. Smallwood fired.

An explosion shook the place, nearly sending Frederick into the pit with Grace, but Elliott caught him. The wall between the antechamber and their room collapsed, rock after massive rock, walls peeling down like crumpling paper. Omar and Carter's bodies disappeared beneath the gathering debris, and one by one the lanterns crashed over or disappeared beneath the rocks, leaving Elliott and Frederick in the vast silence and pitch dark.

"God, help me." Frederick forced his hands deeper into the sand, ignoring the increasing ache at his side from the knife wound. He couldn't lose Grace. Not when he'd just learned by meeting her what it was like to love and be loved, freely and truly.

And she'd risked her life to save him by firing the gun. If she hadn't, perhaps she could have crawled out of the sand.

He slid to his stomach, his arms in the sand nearly to his shoulders. Where was she? Frederick's fingers caught hold of something soft within the sand. His breath burst out, and he fisted the cloth, pulling with all his might.

"Steady me, Elliott," he called, hoping his friend still crouched nearby. "I think I have her."

A strong hand pressed over Frederick's back and steadied him at his shoulders, giving him additional stability. With a tug, Frederick grabbed another part of his wife with his other hand. A shoulder? Her limp weight and the heavy sand made it difficult to navigate, and the dark didn't help, but Elliott shifted his hold to wrap around Frederick's chest.

"Pull," Frederick called, and with a final tug, he held Grace against him.

She lay still and unmoving in his arms. He couldn't see her face, only feel across her skin, dusting sand off her face, her neck.

Only silence. Too much silence.

God, please help her. Please keep her with me.

He rolled her on her side, patting her back, hoping she hadn't breathed the sand too deeply, that he hadn't been too late.

Every breath paused. Each passing second, too quiet.

And then, she convulsed against him in a long strain of coughs. His throat tightened with emotion, and he squeezed his eyes closed. Grateful for the dark, he buried his damp face into Grace's hair, patting her back as she continued to cough against him. Elliott moved away, his steps crunching against the dirt of the tomb, but Frederick just sat, cradling Grace close. His hands moved over her disheveled hair, her face, her coughing slowly subsiding.

She buried her face into his neck, her arms finally moving to wrap around him. "I. . .I knew you'd find me."

Her rasped words broke something in him and stole any response except to squeeze her more closely. She buried deeper against his chest, continuing to cough a little. Sounds of Elliott moving about, a stumble here and a crunch there, filled the darkness. Suddenly a flash of light glinted nearby and went out. Elliott made some sort of groan. The light glimmered again, and this time held. Elliott's face came into view as he raised one of the lanterns that had toppled but not broken. The golden glow brought their current situation into painful clarity.

The explosion had closed off the path to the antechamber and the subsequent exit, and created a rocky debris field that reached so far into their current room that some of the smaller stones had fallen into the sand pit. A few rocks still broke free from the ceiling, hinting of more instability.

"We should move into the next room, sir," Elliott said, shining the light in the final room of the tomb. The burial chamber. "The ceiling out here isn't secure."

Frederick nodded and lowered his lips to Grace's ear. "I'm going to carry you, darling."

He grunted as he stood, the movement and her weight pulling against his side.

"I can walk," she whispered, her voice raw.

He merely continued with her in his arms, following Elliott over the threshold into the vast room. They'd hardly settled down on the ground before another crash resounded from the next room, sending a cloud of dirt into the burial chamber.

"The dynamite certainly did its work, but I don't think the damage made it this far back into the tomb," Elliott said, setting the lantern down in front of them and bracing his palms on his hips to study the room.

"Dynamite?" Frederick brushed at the sand on Grace's back and shoulders.

"It was on the ground, sir." Elliott's upper lip boasted a cut, and one of his eyes was swollen and bruised.

Frederick didn't even want to know what he must look like.

"I heard Mr. Smallwood speak of it." Grace wiped at her eyes, adding another cough. "They had it on hand in case they needed it for excavation, I think."

"I feel certain Professor Andrews would have argued against any such means of destruction," Frederick added, his hands moving to her tangled hair as he continued brushing back the sand.

More rocks fell in the next room, and Elliott walked back to the doorway, disappearing into the next room.

Grace rested her head against Frederick's shoulder, smoothing a palm over his chest. "I'm so glad you're alive."

He nuzzled his nose against her head, still unable to trust his voice in regards to what had almost happened. Her fingers worried one of his shirt buttons, pausing at the *V* where his collar lay open. "When you stepped from behind the pillar, pistol raised, you looked incredibly dashing." She coughed. "I thought for a moment I was in a wonderful dream. I do love dreaming about you."

He captured her hand with his and brought her fingers to his lips. He released a long breath, as if he'd been holding it since he entered the tomb, and dropped his head back against the rock wall.

Then Grace seemed to realize something, and she pushed off his lap, her fingers slipping down his shirt to his side. Her hair stood in all directions, her eyebrows and lashes coated with sand, but he couldn't stop looking at her. Thanking God she was alive and talking.

"Frederick!" She coughed, tugging at the damp cloth of his shirt. "You're bleeding."

He followed her gaze down to the dark stain on his shirt.

"Lane did this, didn't he?" She tipped back so the light shone on the wound. Not as deep as he'd thought, but highly uncomfortable nonetheless.

"He might have done worse if you hadn't warned me, darling." He took the opportunity with her lovely face turned upward to brush at her sand-covered eyebrows. She shook away his touch and scooted back from him. With pinched lips, she pushed back her outer skirt and took her petticoat in both hands.

"What are you doing?"

She pulled at the white cloth as if. . .she was trying to tear it?

"Attempting to make cloths for your wound." Her nose wrinkled and her lips pinched more tightly as she pulled harder. "Women do this in books all the time. It's supposed to be simple."

She gritted her teeth and pulled again, then dropped the skirt with a sigh. "Perhaps the petticoats in books aren't made as well as Madame Rousell's."

He chuckled and took the opportunity of their momentary privacy to draw his bride back toward him for a lengthy kiss.

She pushed back and looked up at him. "That was a very nice try, but I'm not distracted enough from tending your wound." She studied his clothes and then went back to her own, a sudden light coming to her eyes. "My trousers!"

"What?"

With a look to the doorway, she stood and began reaching under her skirt.

"Grace?"

"I wore my trousers beneath my gown." She smiled as she worked and coughed.

"Your trousers?" He pushed himself up to a stand, then moved to block any view of her from the doorway.

"They're simple cotton things, but I had high hopes of wearing them out in the wilds of the desert, free of all skirts." She braced her hand against his shoulder to balance herself as she slipped the simple trousers from beneath her skirts. "Aha!" She stepped back and then studied his side. "Just as I thought. You are still bleeding, and now we can apply fresh cloth and pressure."

Elliott paused as he reentered, most likely witnessing Grace with her arms wrapped around Frederick's waist as she attempted to tie the legs of her "trousers" into a knot to hold the cloth tightly against his wound.

"She's binding my wound, Elliott." Frederick met Elliott's gaze, and his friend offered a swollen-lipped smile.

"It's good to see everyone is back to normal, sir."

Frederick released a much-needed chuckle, despite the pain it sent through his center.

"I know that the two of you are amused at my expense." She

raised a brow as she looked up at him. "But since we all could do with some amusement right now, I will try very hard not to be offended."

Frederick brushed a thumb against her cheek. "I think it may be utterly impossible to offend you, Lady Astley."

Her smile flashed wide. If she hadn't caught herself, Frederick felt certain she was going to kiss him full on the mouth with Elliott watching. Part of him didn't mind a whit. It was difficult to care for decorum after a near-death experience in a tomb.

"There are many more productive things to do than finding offense in everything, don't you think?" Grace asked. "Like, sorting out how in the world we're going to get out of here."

"The rocks have covered most of the room." Elliott stepped closer, holding Frederick's gaze, the answer clearly written on his face. There was no way out. "But I noticed this when I lit the lantern. It must have been dropped by one of Smallwood's men."

Frederick took the bag and opened it. A few slices of beef jerky and a canteen came as welcome sights, and there were some papers. Nothing more than that. Frederick took out the canteen and handed it to Grace. "This may help clear your throat."

She took the canteen with a smile and walked to the doorway.

"The police will come," Elliott lowered his voice. "The officer back at the house would send them."

"But how long could it take to clear the way?" Frederick shook his head. "Days? A week?"

"What about the way we first discovered this room?" Grace walked back to them and peered upward, clearly having overheard them.

It was no use trying to protect her from the reality of their situation. She always rose to the challenge in situations that would cause many women of his acquaintance to dissolve into hysterics.

"Andrews had that entry covered, as I recall, to keep others from suffering your fate." Frederick followed her gaze to the arched ceiling, which, over time, must have eroded through from the surface. The designs and artwork from the previous rooms, like other tombs, had dissolved into the cavernous vault of the mountain.

"More likely to keep people from locating the tomb," she added. "Apart from the police and the villains who conveniently left us here, does anyone else know we're here?"

Frederick shared a glance with Elliott and turned his attention back to Grace. "Zahra?"

"And Ame—Miss Sinclair." Elliott added.

Grace spun toward him. "Oh, you were able to save her?"

"Barely," Frederick answered. "We were just in time thanks to you sending Zahra back."

"Oh, I'm so glad." Grace shook her head, dusting at her skirt. "It was horrible leaving her there and knowing. . .well, hoping you'd find her in time." Her face brightened. "Maybe she'll help the police find us. She knows where the tomb entrance is, which will bring them faster."

"I think we may have seen the last of Miss Sinclair." Elliott cleared his throat. "I mean, Lady Kerth."

"Lady Kerth?" Grace focused on Frederick. "Do you mean like Lord Kerth? Thomas?" Her mouth opened into a wide *O*. "Yes, the portrait in the front of Kerth Hall. The large one. Of him, his wife, and his daughter. Amelia looks just like that woman. But how?"

"Her parents died in a boating accident on the Nile about fifteen years ago. I suppose everyone thought their little daughter died with them. Lord Kerth was beyond himself with grief."

"Won't he be thrilled to discover the truth?" Grace walked up to him and took his hand. "And she's perfectly reformable. You should have heard her take on Professor Andrews. And she stood up for Elliott when it was suggested he poisoned Mr. Graham.

She'd been wanting out of the stolen antiquities business for a long time."

"Yes," was all Frederick managed to say before she continued.

"A reformed thief is much better than an unreformed one, and I dare say, she may make an even better lady because of her reformation." Grace nodded toward Elliott. "And we can have her come back to England along with us."

"I'm afraid that won't be possible, my lady." Elliott drew in a breath. "I feel as though Lady Kerth has chosen to disappear. To start afresh somewhere else and. . .as someone else."

Grace's brow pinched and she studied him. "Well, that's exactly what she can do as Lady Kerth, isn't it?"

"She would have had to turn herself in to the authorities for whatever punishment might be given, and I don't think she would have felt worthy of taking on such a title."

"Worthy or not, it's hers." Grace frowned. "And if the authorities heard her story and learned what good she was trying to do, I think it might matter to everyone, even her grandfather."

"Her grandfather would have taken her back without question, regardless of her past," Frederick added. "I am sure of it. In fact, I had Inspector Randolph wire Cairo to send the information on to England."

"But now he'll lose her all over again? Poor man." Grace sighed and turned back to the room. "We could have been neighbors of sorts. With her varied life opportunities and experiences, I imagine she could teach all sorts of interesting skills. Friends who know how to do special things are the best sorts, you know? There's always something to learn."

Perhaps there was a small silver lining in Amelia's choice to run away. Silver for Frederick's peace of mind, at any rate. Though he couldn't imagine anyone proving a better influence to a broken person than his wife. She had a way of accepting someone as they were and proceeding to lavish the very best faith upon them, as if she saw them as they could be instead of as they were.

"I must say that here is another perfectly good example of the value in having a rope along with you at all times."

A cough erupted from Elliott which then turned into a laugh.

Grace shot him a look. "Ah, you laugh, but what sort of predicament would we have found ourselves in with the dangerous Cecelia Percy if we hadn't had a rope, dear Elliott?"

"Quite right, my lady."

She sent Frederick a wink, and his grin spread. Sunshine even in the darkest places.

"Though I'm afraid a rope from this direction wouldn't do us much good." She placed her hands on her hips and looked at both of them. "And it will take days for anyone to remove all those stones to reach us, so I suggest we ration the water. Of course there's always the possibility we suffocate first."

Frederick refused to look in Elliott's direction, because he already knew his friend's amused response. One minute Frederick's dear wife was being brave and ingenious, and the next, her imagination delved into unusual and sometimes terrifying discoveries. "Suffocate?"

"You know? Run out of air." She looked around the room again. "We *are* basically in a tomb. I've not studied how long it would take to suffocate from a space this large, though. Most of my projections involve European or American tombs. Coffins, even less, of course."

"Well, it's a good thing we have such a vast spot," Frederick stated as matter-of-factly as he could.

"Though there are three of us breathing the air, so that would change the numbers."

At this point, he did make the mistake of glancing at Elliott, and the man had covered his mouth and turned his back to them, his shoulders shaking. Well, Frederick supposed it was much better to have his wife calm, collected, with a somewhat dramatic view of things, instead of breaking down into hysterics and sucking up who knows how much air.

He grinned. If this was to be their final day together, he'd rather have them face it strong and as relatively positive as possible. He closed his eyes. But he wouldn't mind at all if God chose to make a much better plan, since the Almighty had already proven over and over again that His plans were superior to any of Frederick's.

Another crumble of rocks sounded from the other room, with a few larger stones rolling into view of their doorway.

"Perhaps they'll shift enough to make another hole through which we can climb out?" Grace offered, her eyes brightening.

Something knocked Frederick in the shoulder, and he turned toward Elliott, but the man had his focus on Grace as she paced back to the doorway of the other room and peered within, most likely trying to gauge her theory.

Then something, like dust, landed on his head. He looked up at the rock ceiling and another rock dropped.

"Get back," he called. "I fear this ceiling is readying to collapse as well."

Frederick marched to Grace's side and tugged her into the threshold between the two rooms. Elliott joined them, lantern in hand.

"I suppose the reverberations from the explosion loosened other parts of the mountain." Frederick looked from their current room into the one that had caved in. If they survived the roof collapsing in the burial chamber, there was a good chance it could lead them out.

Another rock tumbled from above, bouncing across the burial chamber and hitting the stone casing that must have, at one time, held the sarcophagus.

"Wait. Look." Elliott held the lantern higher. Up in the ceiling of the burial chamber, the faintest hint of starlight sparkled in the distance.

Frederick blinked. Was he imagining it? He shuffled a step forward, peering upward. No, it was starlight, and the slightest edge of the moon.

Two dark silhouettes came into view, blocking some of the starlight.

"I'm rather hopeful that someone is still alive down there, since I see lantern light." Inspector Randolph's voice echoed down to them, and Grace's laugh responded. "Unless the mummies have been about with some mischief or other."

"We're here" Frederick rushed to the center of the room, looking up toward the entrance Grace had fallen through almost a week earlier. "How did you find us? No one alive or. . .on our side knew where that entrance was."

"Someone did," came a female voice, the second silhouette.

Frederick caught Elliott's gaze. Amelia.

"That's right," Randolph continued, his tone jovial. "It's been a night for the books, gentlemen. Miss Sinclair met us on our way to the station and told us everything. Then when we noticed the collapsed tunnel in the tomb entrance, she led me and a few of my men here."

"What about Mr. Smallwood?" Grace called.

"Not to worry, my lady," Inspector Randolph responded. "I think he was met with quite the welcoming committee when he arrived at his boat. It's just a shame that two of my own were among the nasty lot, but that's enough chatter. Let's get you lot out of there."

Epilogue

Wind blew the white curtains as Grace and Frederick sat by the window of their room in Shepheard's Hotel, the rose and amber hues of sunset playing across the azure sky and the scents of jasmine and roasted meat filling the air.

This was their first evening of leisure since arriving back in Cairo three days ago. Between providing testimony to the police in both El Minya and Cairo, navigating support for Georgia and Timothy, as well as speaking with the police about Amelia's future, moments of quiet reflection when they both weren't exhausted or recovering from wounds had been few. Already a full week had passed since the events in the tomb, and Grace's minor cuts and bruises had faded to minor scars.

"I'm glad the authorities agreed to allow Georgia and Timothy to move their trial to England, for their sakes." Grace smiled up at Elliott, who refreshed the lemonade in her glass, his eye still slightly swollen, but the scar on his lip reduced significantly. "I've read that Egyptian jails aren't pleasant places."

"I feel most jails would garner the same description, my lady." Elliott smiled down at her with his usual mixture of amusement and kindness. He really would be a wonderful catch for some woman. Handsome, kind, excellent in a fist fight, loyal, and the perfect server.

"You are right, of course, Mr. Elliott." She returned his grin. "But Egyptian jails are particularly nasty, if fiction can be believed."

"I feel as though I've been living through one of your books since meeting you, my lady, so it would be rather irresponsible of me to disregard the wisdom of fiction."

"You are very smart, Mr. Elliott." Grace looked across the table at her husband. "Which demonstrates all the more why both of you could benefit greatly from detective books, especially if our lives are to continue on this theme."

"My darling, I have high hopes that not every scene in our future will be experienced with such life-threatening adventures."

"Perhaps not quite so life-threatening, but it has whetted my appetite for more tombs."

"Heaven help us all." Frederick's grin held much more enjoyment than any real concern, which meant he may very well offer her another Egyptian trip in the future. "But I am glad Timothy and Georgia can return to England for the trial," Frederick added, standing from the table. "We'll be able to provide support for them when we return from Venice."

"We're still going?" Grace turned to him as he offered her his hand. "I thought perhaps the events of the past few weeks might have altered our plans."

"Not at all." Frederick turned to Elliott. "I believe we have it all worked out, don't we Elliott?"

"Sir?"

Grace studied Frederick's face, but her husband merely winked at her. . .and her bottom lip dropped. He rarely winked at her. She burst into a giggle. A sudden awareness that perhaps her presence provided some healing in his heart from all the stifling hurts of his past smoothed over a tiny ache of still seeing the scars from the tomb fight.

Winked? It really pleased her much more than a wink probably should, but she just couldn't help it.

"This morning I received word from the authorities, and after some consultation with Lord Kerth, Lady Amelia has been released to his care to serve under house arrest for a time given by the local authorities in Derbyshire."

Elliott looked from Frederick to Grace and back again. "I'm happy for her, sir."

Her husband braided his hands behind his back, a smile on his lips. What on earth was he doing?

"The police wouldn't allow her to be transported without a trustworthy companion to ensure her safety and arrival." He nodded. "So I recommended you."

Elliott stared in silence a full five seconds. "Me?"

"I can think of no one more trustworthy, and I believe you and Lady Amelia may have certain decisions to discuss."

"I. . .I can't, sir. She's, well, a lady, and I'm—"

"A good man," Frederick finished, and Grace beamed at him with such pride she wondered if he didn't feel her smile warming his face.

"But sir—"

"Elliott, in her young life, Lady Amelia has already had many things taken away from her. Would you also take away her choice to find a future with whomever she chooses?"

"But her grandfather—"

"Is so happy to have her alive I feel certain he only wants the best for her as well. And I have sent a very good report of you. Would you wish to prove me wrong?"

"Sir, I. . ." Elliott looked down at the ground, his breathing short and scattered. "I'll be needed for you and Lady Astley in Venice."

"I've taken care of myself before, Elliott. I feel I can do so again. And it's my utmost pleasure to take care of Lady Astley." Frederick's smile brimmed. "Besides, it's only for one month."

"And there are no tombs for us to excavate in Venice, Elliott," Grace added, watching the deepening red of Elliott's face. Oh how delightful. Her husband was an excellent matchmaker. She would have never guessed! Had he been reading Austen's *Emma*, perchance? "That should put your mind at ease as to Lord Astley's safety."

The poor valet looked back and forth between the two, apparently grappling for something to say.

"Jason Elliott." Frederick placed his palm on Elliott's shoulder. "I don't know if there's a future for you and Lady Amelia, but if anyone deserves the opportunity to try for a happy ending, it's you, my friend."

A burst of air exploded from Elliott's mouth, half laugh, half shock, perhaps? "I don't know what to say, sir. Or do."

"You could start by packing your things." Frederick laughed. "Your boat leaves after breakfast tomorrow."

"What?" Elliott nearly dropped the tray in his hands. "Tomorrow? But I. . .and you. . ."

"Will be fine." He put his arm around Grace and pulled her to his side. "We'll both be fine."

Elliott stood, frozen to the spot, so Grace gently removed the tray from his hands and placed it on their table. Without any hesitation, she leaned forward and hugged the dear man. "Mr. Elliott, go see if this is your happily ever after. I shall do my very best to keep your dear Lord Astley safe in your stead."

Elliott chuckled, shook his head, and chuckled again. "Thank you both." Then he sobered. "But I can't."

"What?" Frederick said.

"Why?" Grace followed. Surely he was interested enough, and she knew very well he was brave enough.

"I must finish my duties to your lord and ladyship." He bowed his head. "So I will need you to return the tray to me."

Frederick released a loud laugh and placed the tray in Mr.

Elliott's hands. "Now off with you, before I change my mind."

Elliott walked to the door, stopping in the doorway. "Whatever happens from all this, thank you. To both of you. For seeing me as much more than a servant, but a. . ."

"A friend, Elliott." Frederick finished, dipping his head as if giving his own little bow to the valet. It was one of the tenderest things Grace had ever seen between two men. Two friends.

"Yes." He nodded, drawing in a deep breath. "One of the best of my life."

With that he closed the door behind him. Grace stood in silence for a moment, taking in the realization of what Frederick had done, and then she turned and vaulted herself into his arms. "You are remarkable!" She kissed him. "What a romantic thing to do for your very dear friend."

His arms wrapped around her, holding her against him. "You doubt my romantic nature, Lady Astley?"

"Not at all. You are extremely romantic to me, my dear Lord Astley." She grinned up at him. "But to display that kind and sentimental side to Elliott in this way? Why, it's the dearest thing." She leaned back from him, but his palms had already begun to slide down her back in a most telltale direction. "Are you certain you can get along without him while we're in Italy?"

"It will be a little less convenient, but perhaps I could enlist your help on things such as buttons and ties?" He raised a brow, and she leaned in to kiss him, her fingers moving toward his collar. "I don't know if I have as much experience with buttoning them as unbuttoning them, but I'm happy to practice."

His lips claimed hers in a long and lingering kiss, and by the time she pulled back, her hair was already partially down. He was incredibly efficient when motivated. Another of his many talents.

"I've never heard of a woman inheriting a title, but you alluded to that fact with Amelia."

His hands came up to her neck to begin unfastening her shirtwaist. "There are a few titles which can pass to the females to ensure the bloodline. Lord Kerth's title holds the statute of passing to the female line for no more than two generations, so Amelia would be a countess in her own right."

She worked another one of his buttons loose, frowning at its stubbornness. "But she would need to have a male heir to maintain the bloodline and title?"

"Yes."

"What about us?"

He pulled back from giving such delightful attention to her earlobe. "Ours only passes to a male heir."

"Oh." Grace moved to the next button. "Well, I certainly hope we have at least one."

"I should like to even the odds in the family a little."

Grace grinned at the reference to his darling little daughter from a previous relationship, Lilibet.

"I think we should certainly try until we succeed."

"I am at your service, Lady Astley."

Her blouse dropped to the floor, leaving her standing in her corset cover and petticoat, a much cooler option than all the layers women had to wear in this place to be viewed as proper. "I'm glad to hear it, my lord."

"Speaking of service, I do believe you should have someone along to assist you in Italy."

"I think I can manage on my own."

"But lady's garments"—he waved toward her layers and the ones now on the floor—"are much more complex than men's, so I took the liberty of having papers drawn up to keep Zahra."

"Keep Zahra?" Grace's fingers stopped on the last button of his shirt. "Do you mean she's coming with us?"

"Yes." His dark eyes glistened with a hidden smile. "She's ours."

"Ours?" Grace sifted through all the possible meanings of *ours*, trying to work it out. "As in we get to raise her? In England?"

He nodded. "If she wishes to come with us."

"Oh Frederick!" She wrapped her arms around his neck. "That's wonderful. To bring her into a place with such love and opportunity?"

"We'll speak to her together in the morning and let her make the decision." He drew back. "She needs that freedom as much as Amelia, but Inspector Randolph intimated that it may take a while to finalize the paperworks, so Zahra may not join us in Italy at first."

"The very fact she's going to be ours at all is wonderful. We can give her a true home." She placed a long, slow kiss against his neck and leaned back to smile up at him. "So I don't mind waiting."

His gaze dropped to her neckline, one brow slowly curling upward. "Where did you get that necklace?"

"Oh." She reached up to feel the oval shape. "Well you see, Mr. Smallwood was kind enough to leave it in my care at first, and then when I offered it to Inspector Randolph, he told me I could keep it."

"Did he?"

She nodded. "As a souvenir and in gratitude for my gift back to the archaeologists."

"Gift?"

"Yes, my drawings of the inside of the tombs." She smiled. "They wanted to study the ones I'd sketched from our brief visit, and since the area isn't safe for further excavation any time in the future, they were grateful for my work."

"Well, I suppose they gathered enough of the artifacts from Mr. Smallwood's boat, though they have no idea where his earlier shipment has gone, and the old bean won't give up the truth either."

"Yet another mystery in the world," Grace said, pushing his

shirt from his shoulders and nuzzling up close to his skin. She breathed in the scent of soap at his neck. "I wonder if we'll ever have another adventure as daring as this one?"

"If you consider all we've been through since our first acquaintance, I wouldn't be surprised." He took her by the hand and led her through the adjoining doorway to their bedroom, carefully turning the lock as the door clicked into place. "An unexpected switch of brides."

"For which you are eternally grateful." Grace squeezed his hand as he raised the mosquito netting for her to slip inside.

"Without a doubt." He joined her, pulling her back against him. "A runaway car."

"Which landed in a river," she finished, placing a few kisses on his neck before burying her nose there. "Then, of course, a man-napping."

"Followed by attempted blackmail and murder." He drew back and caught her chin with his fingers, his lips tilted ever so kissably. "And let's not forget your rather daring rescue."

"I'm surprised you haven't had nightmares of a massive green umbrella attack."

He chuckled and kissed her right on her smile, lingering longer with each time they touched. "And then we found ourselves involved in a tomb robbery."

"And illegal antiquities operation."

"While also managing two murders," he added, his fingers slipping through her hair to tilt her head back, giving him full access to her neck.

"Or even more if you count the professor"—her breath caught at the warmth of his lips on her skin—"Omar, and a few others along the way."

"True." His word proved more growl than consonants and vowels.

"And then"—Grace leaned her head back against the headboard

and gripped Frederick's shoulders—"our dear Elliott falls in love with a thief who also happens to be an earl's long-lost granddaughter."

"Exactly." Frederick raised his gaze to hers, his lips ever so close to kissing hers. "At this point, my darling, I believe that anything is possible."

"Spoken like a true lover of fairytales." She smiled, tugging him against her. Lover? For certain. And the fairytale part was all happening in real life, with villains and dangers and joys all mixed together. For the most beautiful and memorable stories were only the best because people had to overcome obstacles or fight for truth or brave dangers to get to the happily ever after. Risks and tears and moments when all seemed lost abounded, but the very best stories left a smattering of hope braided into every hardship to ensure the readers the ending would be worth the difficulty.

Frederick kissed her cheek and the juncture between her ear and neck. She sighed. "You know what? I am certain about two things." His lips trailed down her neck, and her whole body warmed at the touch. "I am determined to improve my shooting skills."

He growled his disapproval but continued his very thorough appreciation of her neck. Her fingers found their way into his hair, encouraging him to continue, but he drew his head up and stared at her, his dark eyes, warm with want and love, one of her favorite features.

"And the second?"

She placed her palms against his cheeks, her gaze roaming over his face, treasuring every angle and scar, every hue and expression. The way his dark hair fell across his forehead and his lips tilted slightly enough for her to know exactly what was on his mind. A sudden sheen filled her vision, and she smoothed her thumbs across his cheekbones. "You are the very best sleuthing partner in the entire world, and I am incredibly happy to be yours."

He studied her, those eyes holding her attention and offering her such tender affection. "My Grace, I look forward to every adventure as long as you're with me," he whispered, before breaching the distance between them.

PEPPER BASHAM is an award-winning author who writes romance peppered with grace and humor. She is a native of the Blue Ridge Mountains where her family have lived for generations. She's the mom of five kids, speech-pathologist to about fifty more, lover of chocolate, jazz, and Jesus, and proud AlleyCat over at the award-winning *Writer's Alley* blog. Her debut historical romance novel, *The Thorn Bearer,* released in April 2015, and the second in February 2016. Her first contemporary romance debuted in April 2016.

You can connect with Pepper on her website at www.pepperdbasham.com, Facebook at https://www.facebook.com/pepperdbasham, or Twitter at https://twitter.com/pepperbasham

A FREDDIE & GRACE MYSTERY

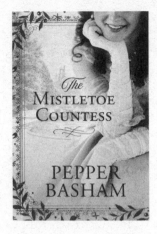

The Mistletoe Countess - Book 1

When a reticent earl must marry an American heiress to save his
fledgling estate, he never expects that a Christmas wedding to the
wrong sister will result in a series of events which lead to a murder
mystery, ghost hunt, and—the most frightening of all—the love
of a lifetime. But happily ever after may be shorter than the new-
lyweds plan when a thwarted widow has her sights set on the earl's
inheritance at any cost. Packed with history, romance, mystery,
and some good old-fashioned humor, *The Mistletoe Countess* offers
holiday cheer and so much more.

Paperback / 978-1-64352-986-8

OTHER BARBOUR BOOKS
BY PEPPER BASHAM

My Heart Belongs in the Blue Ridge - Laurel's Dream

The Heart of the Mountains

The Red Ribbon

Hope Between the Pages

JOIN US ONLINE!

Christian Fiction for Women

Christian Fiction for Women is your online home for the latest in Christian fiction.

Check us out online for:

- Giveaways
- Recipes
- Info about Upcoming Releases
- Book Trailers
- News and More!

Find Christian Fiction for Women at Your Favorite Social Media Site:

 Search "Christian Fiction for Women"

 @fictionforwomen